I0525210

Cirsova®

P. ALEXANDER, Ed.
Mark Thompson, Copy Ed.
Xavier L., Copy Ed.

Three Uncanny Novelettes of Terror and Suspense

Seven Strange and Thrilling Short Stories

Poetry + Essay

Winter Issue
2021

Vol.2, No 9
$15.00 per copy

For We Are Many

By PAUL LUCAS

Infinite universes are filled with myriad worlds of infinite possibilities—and infinite selves! One man hunts and is hunted across the multiverse, seeking absolution!

I arrived just in time to hear the beating and see the glass shower onto the dark street. Up above, the man's voice was loud and calm, with the occasional thud punctuating his remarks, but the woman, well, I've only heard farm animals squeal like that before. A distraction, I told myself, her screams are just a distraction.

The noise was coming from an apartment above a shuttered storefront. "Kelly's Conveniences." the sign said—not so convenient for the wailing woman. I tried to close my ears and listen only to my footsteps, and I almost succeeded. Then I heard one more cry, and I felt my feet turn without me willing it. I walked away from the storefront, back to the phone booth I'd noticed just a few doors down.

"Goddamn it, get a grip!" I said to myself. "You don't need this delay."

Still, I couldn't stop my hand picking up the handset. But what was the emergency number in this world? I shook my head and then punched in the obvious digits. Double zero? Nope. 911, 112? Neither of those gave a dial tone.

I continued to punch in digits, half at random, relying on intuition more than anything, until I was possessed by a sudden thought. My finger hovered over the keypad. I'd tried everything else obvious; it couldn't be *that* number, could it? The broken streetlights, the empty stores... This world was a sort of hell, anyway, the sort of place that worshipped evil... I placed my finger slowly on the number six, and pressed it. Once, twice, three times. It couldn't be... I heard the clicking and whirring on the line as I was connected. A few seconds later came the voice.

"Emergency operator, which service do you require?"

Jesus, the irony. The number of the beast as saviour. Well, it *was* a memorable number. I shook my head, knowing the operator couldn't see me with the telephone system they had here. I gave the details quickly, looking round to check the location and also to see if anyone was watching.

"And your name please, caller?"

I slammed the phone down and walked back across the street to take my place in one of the many doorways. It was dark out, the stores all closed, and a dry night apart from the glass that had showered down from the apartment, the scene of the crime. Fragments crunched underfoot as I passed below the window and into the shelter of a shop entrance further down.

I shook my head. Why the hell had I bothered to phone the cops? It could only delay me, and delay meant I might be caught. Not caught by the cops of this world. No, I had my own pursuer. Little fish are eaten by middling fish, which are preyed on by bigger fish. The thug upstairs was the little fish in this scenario, and I? I considered myself a not-quite-so-little fish at best. I looked around again, peering up and down the street from the safety of the doorway. Nobody was there. No sign of my own Nemesis, thank God. Not yet. Only the cops to worry about—that, and my stupid decision to phone them.

"Shit, I must be getting soft."

Well, too late now. Above me, Romeo continued to woo Juliet with his fists, as his voice got louder and wilder, and her wails died away to sobs.

"Five minutes, say, till the cops get here," I thought to myself and clenched my fists, "He's nearly finished with her, then I'll have him."

At that moment, I heard a vehicle coming down the street, off to the right. I jumped.

"The cops already? Crap!"

I reached in my coat for my beamer. I'd been hoping to catch Romeo on his own, out in the open where I controlled the encounter, but now I might never catch him. My luck held. I turned to see an open-topped automobile spewing fumes from the rear. Four young guys were sitting inside it, bouncing up and down in time to a horrible booming noise. They looked like savages: all tattooed faces and piercings in every bit of flesh.

I moved through the shadows along the street, from doorway to doorway, till I was well away from the apartment, and then looked back. The car came to a halt below the shattered window, and one guy, with a bald tattooed head, stood up in the back.

"Yo, Zed man, you coming to Scope's?" he shouted up at the window.

Somebody moved in the apartment and cast a shadow out of the window and onto the vehicle.

"Gimme an hour, bro," came the answer.

"Catch ya later," said Baldy, and then he turned forward and sat down.

The vehicle drove away down the street, the youths shouting and jumping up and down. The bald guy upended a bottle to his mouth, drained it, then threw the empty so it smashed on the ground a dozen yards away. Thankfully he didn't see me.

The vehicle had hardly gone around the corner when I heard doors banging, and Zed came out of his building. He was wearing a black leather jacket with 'Da Boyz' written in red across the back. He turned his collar up, pulled on a black woollen hat, and walked away. I looked up one last time at the apartment window, wondering if there was something I could do for his Juliet, but then followed him. I had my mission.

I took the Tracker from my belt, pointed it at Zed, and looked at the readout. Yes, it was still attuned to him. The circle in the centre of the display was mostly black. I couldn't see any white patches on the display, just a couple of gray dots in the darkness. Yes, the right man, evil little shit. I knew that I was doing the right thing, for this world and for myself; I'd atone for my own sins and save my soul.

In front of me, Zed strolled on, whistling a tuneless tune. He didn't care if anyone saw him, if anyone was following him. He didn't show any guilty conscience about what he'd done to the woman up in the apartment, no fear or anxiety. Bastard! Just then, I heard a noise from back down the street. It was nothing obvious, just a light clang. Nemesis—was it him?

I ducked into yet another doorway and leaned out. I couldn't see anybody, just shadows underneath the broken street lights. Still, my Nemesis never seemed to have a shadow of his own, he was cunning and damned near invisible with it, so I glanced back over my shoulder and slid my hand inside my coat for my beamer. If it was him, maybe I could fry him before he saw me. But no, it was just a cat walking on top of some garbage containers down the street. Another scrawny cat jumped onto the boxes and spat at its rival. They arched their backs and hissed. I breathed out and looked back to my prey. Zed was gone.

"Damn!"

I ran to where I'd last seen him, by an alley cutting between two apartment blocks. It was the only place he could have gone. I fixed the Tracker to my belt and then picked my way over the garbage on the street and down the alley to the far end. I made sure to reach inside my coat for the beamer, though, just to be safe. A good thing, too. He was waiting for me.

I fired—I'd done this so many times I didn't even have to think—but he was quick, and ducked under the blast. He jinked towards me, a knife in his hand, so I ducked, then weaved to one side and kicked at him. He dodged in towards me and thrust his knife at my belly, missing by millimetres. Years of practice, thank God, helped me keep my balance, and I brought the beamer's snout 'round as I fired again. The blast caught him on the hand, and the sleeve of his jacket burst into flames. He fell back over a trashcan, yelped, and waved his hand about his head. I couldn't tell whether the smell was from his flesh or his coat.

"Time's up, Zed," I said as I approached him.

He was lying on his back, knife gone, tearing off his coat. I pointed the beamer at him, and he stared at it. The coat, inside out now, hung from halfway up his forearm. He tried to point at me, but the coat just flapped about on his arm, slapping into the ground.

"What's up," he said, "why you shooting at me? Tell Johnny I'll pay him…"

I stepped forward so I was under the street light.

"Johnny didn't send me. Guess who did."

Zed looked from the beamer to me, and his eyes opened wide. He opened his mouth to speak, but nothing came out. He pushed himself back along the ground. A bottle rattled away from under him.

"Recognise me?" I asked.

He stammered something incoherent, so I stepped closer again. He retreated.

"It's time to be punished for your sins," I

said and stepped closer yet one more time. He found his voice.

"You, you wouldn't shoot a defenceless man, bro?"

He looked around. The street was long and empty. He turned his face back up to me.

"Whatever you want, you got it, bro!" he shouted. "Anything."

I was surprised to hear him pleading like this. It had been a long while since I'd heard any of my victims plead. He looked pathetic.

"Nothing, I want nothing," I said. "Nothing you can give, anyway."

He looked at me.

"Suzie, that's why you're here, isn't it? She's yours. Take her."

"What?" I said. For a moment, I was confused as to what he was talking about, then remembered the woman I'd called Juliet. I thought for a moment.

"If you were to leave her alone…"

He nodded his head madly.

"Sure, man, sure. Anything."

For the first time in a long while I wondered, was I doing the right thing? Was he willing to change? I looked down at the Tracker. The display was black, with the same few blobs of not-black swirling in its centre. Were the blobs getting paler? Was there any light at all in his soul? It was hard to tell in the dark street, but, yes, it looked like there was one dimmer patch on the display, not so much white as dishwater gray, and it was getting cleaner by the second. Maybe he *did* deserve a chance. I looked back down at him, scrabbling amongst the dirt.

"Go on," I said, making my mind up. "Run. Before I think better of it."

I gestured with the beamer. Zed looked back at me, then scrambled to his feet and ran away with the coat flapping around his arm. He got forty, fifty paces before he made his last mistake. As he got near to a burnt-out car, he turned round, laughed, and gave me the finger.

"Up yours, dumbass!"

I didn't need to look at the Tracker; there was no redemption for this fool. I knew its display would be black, not one point of light in it. I sighed once, then raised the beamer. Zed saw this, and his stupid smile disappeared. He dodged from side to side, but I've chased nimbler quarry than him. The flapping coat caught between his legs just as I fired, maximum setting. The blast threw him past the car and bounced him across the road. His head thudded as it hit the asphalt.

I strolled past the rubbish and cars to the body. Don't believe anyone if they tell you that the dead look peaceful. A leg and arm were twisted underneath him, while his coat was splayed out along the ground. The sleeve was still pulled down over the wrist, the coat inside out. A hole gaped in his back, reaching inwards and on towards his chest, but there was no blood anywhere; the heat had sealed the wounds. I knew that the cops of this world would scratch their heads when I'd gone.

I grabbed his collar and turned him over. That was just my little ritual, to make it a bit more personal. He looked older than he should have, but that was hardly surprising, given what he'd just been through. His lips were pulled back—that happens to lot of them, some final instinct, maybe—showing yellow teeth, and his open left eye stared up at me.

"Not looking so good, there, my old friend," I said.

I unlatched my Transmitter from where it rested on my belt and prepared to phase out, heading to the next universe, my next target. I pressed the button and glanced down. The last thing I saw, as the world turned gray about me, was my own dead face staring up at me. Another one of my duplicates dead. Another job well done.

When did all this start, when did my life change? I often wondered about this and did so again as I left the grubby world of star-crossed lovers and a dead man lying in the trash. The transition between Universes doesn't have to take any time, but this was my only rest, the only place where I had a little peace, and I needed the time, the breathing space, to think and plan.

I lifted the Tracker and checked its controls. It reminded me of the priest, its original owner. Did my new life start when I met him up in the mountains, him and his robes and technology, and his theology, poisoning me with his ideas? Like a scorpion, he couldn't help but sting me even as I carried him to safety.

"Goddamn you, I hope you rot in Hell!" I said to myself.

I hung the Tracker on my belt again as Unspace flickered around me. No, my new life began well before I met the priest; it all started with the great experiment. It wasn't so much exciting or boring, but dangerous—heretical. That old cliché, there are some things man was not meant to know... Well, sometimes I wonder whether we were punished for our hubris, thinking we could stand on His heights and see all the possible Universes spread out before us and so read the mind of God. In the grayness between the Universes, I thought back down those branching lines of probability to the zero point, back in the lab; back to that great bifurcation in my life, when one tiny sliver of metal fell in the wrong place and knocked me onto my bloody path.

I was sitting at my desk in the control room, waiting for our great experiment to start—the first controlled breach between one universe and another. Well, at least the first known breach from our universe, anyway. Who knew, at the time, how many openings had been made between other universes? Trillions and trillions, no doubt.

All I did was monitor the data and power flows between the control room and the transmission chamber. I had no real duties to speak of, not since my fall from grace. The rest of the team were in the transmission chamber itself, leaving just me and the boss, Director Johannsen, in the control room. She was at the wall between the control room and the transmission chamber and was fiddling with dials and tape-readers while I was at the far end. I did have computer and video screens in front of me, but for now I'd turned these off. I didn't want to see what was going on in the chamber until I had to; it hurt too much, seeing what I could have been doing but for a quirk of fate, a moment of indiscretion.

To relax, I switched on some music, Beethoven's 12th, my favourite, composed while he was in the cells in the last days of his life. I imagined him with his quill in hand, dipping the sharpened end into the ink, while the walls dripped and rats scurried under his feet. Such dedication, turning out his greatest work in such surroundings. Well, if he could work in those circumstances...

Unfortunately, Johannsen disturbed my reverie when she waddled up to me, waving a clipboard idly around. The surveillance camera up in the nearest corner of the room swivelled to keep us both in its field of vision. I turned the music up a notch. If the Ministry of Theology wanted to keep an eye on us, there wasn't much I could do about it, but I wasn't going to make it easy for them.

Johannsen put the clipboard down on my desk, but I just yawned and scratched at the scabs on the backs of my hands. She stared at the blood that flowed from the exposed wounds.

"How are you doing, Zak?" she said.

"Fine," I said and turned the volume up another notch. She ignored this hint.

"I see the cuts are healing."

"The injuries, you mean?" I countered.

At least she had the decency to look down at that.

"Look, I'm sorry about what happened to you, and I hope you realise that I did everything I could to get you out..."

"Yes, yes, no need to feel guilty," I replied, "I'm fine now. It's not often I get to see the inside of a Penitence Cell. Thanks for putting me in there in the first place."

"Don't be unfair, Zak, it wasn't me who put you there. You know that I have to report anything that's brought to my attention..."

At this her gaze flicked up towards the camera.

"...and your behaviour, well, it was..."

"Sacrilegious? Blasphemous?"

"Let's say theologically incorrect, shall we?"

"So, it's a sin to question established science now is it, not just the Scriptures? What happened to freedom of speech, the whole idea of scientific enquiry as a means of understanding God's plan, eh?"

"Things have changed lately, Zak, and you know it." She shrugged and rubbed her right temple. "Look, let's just go over the last few procedures, shall we..."

"Yes, yes, I know what I'm doing," I said, "I did help design half of the equipment! Christ, I know full well what the system's capable of and what needs doing."

She pursed her lips, but let my mild blasphemy pass, then held the clipboard up between us and reeled off a whole string of instructions. While she droned on, I fiddled with Beethoven's tone controls and occasionally mumbled something to keep her happy. As she came to the end of her list, I couldn't help but needle her again.

"Well, do you think we might find a better world?" I asked. "I've done the preliminary studies on finding a world like ours in that other universe. How about one with choirs of angels and sweet Jesus come to Earth again?"

"No." She continued to annotate her pad. "According to the computer, it should be an empty universe, as we wanted. If you'd managed to keep yourself out of trouble, you might have been on the policy committee and known all these details."

"But we could look for a world like that if we wanted," I said, "Where Jesus can take us straight to Heaven. See, if I just enter these parameters..." I reached across the controls.

"Stop that!" Johannsen said, but I ignored her.

"Thinking about it, quantum theory says that for every little thing we do, a billion, billion alternate Universes are spawned—let's say there's one universe where I turn the volume up," my hand hovered over the volume control, "another universe where I turn the volume down," I withdrew my hand, "and yet another universe where I do nothing at all."

"I don't get your point," said Johannsen.

"Well, how many universes are there where that angry crowd at Golgotha didn't chant the name 'Barabas' as he hung on his cross, but that of our Saviour? A world where our Lord Jesus Christ was brought down from his cross, He survived to bring his Word to the whole world himself? We only have to find one of those worlds to find salvation..."

"That's blasphemous!" Johannsen slapped her pad down on my hand.

I lifted my hand to my mouth and sucked at the newly re-opened wounds. Johannsen stepped back and reached up around her neck to fondle her crucifix.

"I'm sorry about that, Zak. That was uncalled for."

"That's okay. I probably deserved it."

"I know you don't like it, Zak, but we're not just scientists at the Institute, we're theologians. We've got to think of the morality of what we're doing. We're investigating the Many Worlds theory, not using it as a shortcut to salvation. We've got to live with the words of Jesus given to us here, in this universe, not go chasing for salvation in another universe."

"Well, don't expect me to believe in the morality of what we're doing, not after what I saw happening in the cells."

Johannsen shook her head.

"We all have to make our own decisions, Zak, not hope that somebody in another Universe will fix things for us. Take Jesus into your heart before it's too late. You need him more than any of us do. You might not believe that you have a soul, but I do. I'm offering you salvation."

"I'd rather you offered me a beer."

Johannsen turned her back to the camera and leant in close. With both hands, she took hold of the crucifix that hung around her neck. She lifted it over her head and pressed it into my hand.

"Zak, you know that Jesus loves you and, Heaven help me, so must I. But the Ministry, they don't!"

She looked me in the eye for a moment then turned and walked across the room till she was standing by the main exit. Through the window in the door, outside in the corridor, I could see the regulation white collar and black shirt of the site's Corrective Theologian, Father Donnelly. Donnelly peered in through the door and smiled at me, no friendship in his face. Without thinking, I hid my hands in my sleeves. He waved slowly at me, then moved away and out of sight. I shuddered as I thought about the previous times we'd met, and the wounds on the backs of my hands itched.

"That's right, not a sparrow falls but the Ministry of Theology knows about it," I thought. "Well, I'll get even with you someday, you piece of crap."

While Johannsen busied herself at the dials and machines, I tossed the crucifix onto the desk. Jesus's head bounced across the keyboard, and he cartwheeled out of sight. I turned back to the controls in front of me and willed my heart to stop pounding. After a couple of minutes of this, and Beethoven playing in the background, I was feeling calmer.

Finally, it was time to run the great experiment. Johannsen ran her hands through her hair, hung the clipboard on a hook behind the door, and headed into the transmission chamber. Before she shut the door behind her, she turned back to me.

"You know, Zak, I've just realised something. The world doesn't run how you want it, and so you rage against it. It's not that you don't believe in God, Zak, it's just that you're disappointed in Him. Every atheist is."

I didn't know how to answer her final statement, and she didn't give me the time. The door clunked shut behind her, so I turned back to the controls and switched on the video screen. The first thing I heard was Johannsen saying "...and congratulations to everyone who made it here to what could very well be any scientist's Promised Land." The team all laughed.

So here it was, years of work, all dependent on what happened over the next ten minutes, and here I was, sitting outside, never to enter.

"Quiet everyone, please, let's start the test run," Johannsen's voice interrupted the music on my speakers.

"Pre-ignition sequence. Ten minutes till contact."

She looked up at the camera as she spoke. She didn't blink, though she wiped her forehead with a tissue. She looked like she could really see me through the lenses and cables. The hairs on my neck stood up. After a couple of moments, she looked away, and so I went back to work. I checked the calibration and fiddled with the data-monitors as the machines warmed up. The power monitor turned red momentarily, then dropped back to normal. A glitch, nothing important.

"Five minutes till contact, one-minute duration," said Johannsen. "Prepare seals, and let's move out all non-essential personnel from the transmission chamber."

Inside the chamber, my cubicle-mate Angelo was pottering about. I smiled at him, even though he'd never see me through the walls and surveillance systems. He was the only one who'd come to see me in my Penitence Cell, the only one who'd dared show friendship to a blaspheming unbeliever. And the rest called themselves Christians? He was the only one who deserved that description, the only one who gave the name any meaning.

Angelo walked to the metal cage bolted to the floor in the centre of the room to check the Transmitter. The Transmitter, the source of our experiment, was a small box held in place inside the cage. Even though Angelo couldn't see out of the lab, he gave a grin and a thumbs-up into the camera, which I returned to the screen, and he walked back to the door. His hand was on the handle when there was a fizzing from the middle of the chamber. A black dot appeared, expanding quickly into a dark hole with fuzzy edges that hovered just outside of the transmission cage. It swirled black and gray, a couple of feet above the ground. The bars of the cage rattled, though the Transmitter itself remained steady.

"Huh, what the devil..."

Johannsen jumped back and knocked over the water tank. Then I couldn't see anything except white objects that fluttered about the room, and I realised that a wind was blowing documents and loose papers around the transmission chamber. Through the fluttering, I saw Angelo holding onto the door—he couldn't push it open against the pressure—with several other people rolling along the floor. I could just about hear muffled shouts, which went dead as the air spiralled into the vortex. Then the furniture started to slide. I reached across my desk and punched the emergency shut-off button; nothing happened. I punched it again and again, but on my screen the fluttering continued and objects fell into that unholy gap.

As Johannsen had said, we'd tapped into an empty universe, but now the breach was uncontrolled, before we'd put in place any of our safeguards. I sat in the control booth and watched as Director Johannsen and all her staff were blown in by the pressure difference as our universe met the new one. Johannsen was the first to go, pulled towards the deep-black hole floating in the room. She twisted in the air, bounced from the Transmitter's cage and then disappeared feet first. She was silent as she went. Angelo was the last to go; his fingernails scraped along on the floor, and I saw his mouth screaming, "Help me, oh God, help me," then he too was gone. I sat in my chair, watching all this through the television screen, and couldn't move.

The door to the control room rattled briefly after Angelo had gone, then the power shut off automatically. The room quietened, and the hole in the transmission chamber shrank and faded. One minute—that's how long the experiment was programmed to last, and that's exactly how long it did last; just long enough to get all of our preliminary measurements, just long enough to kill my colleagues, my friend, and my boss. I slumped back into my seat and stared into the empty laboratory. The desks, chairs, the people, everything, all gone.

I sat shaking for a long time. Red lights flashed in my eyes, and bells rang in my ears. I couldn't stop myself from panting and whimpering. Eventually, I calmed down enough to realise that outside the control room, the emergency klaxons were sounding, and the red emergency lights were flashing through the window in the door.

"Oh crap!"

I wiped my nose and eyes on my sleeve, and then I checked the instruments. There was nothing out of the ordinary now—all of the dials were at zero, the needles still. What had gone wrong? Why had the Transmitter activated itself when it did? Most importantly, why wouldn't it turn off?

I looked to the side of the display to the emergency shut-off button. I pressed it a few times, but it hardly moved, so I bent closer and poked with a finger around it. Something was jammed in there, stopping it from going all the way down. I unbent a paperclip and scratched away with it behind and underneath the button, until it caught on something. I pulled the paperclip back out, and attached to it was a sliver of metal hooked about a few broken links of chain. Jesus's tiny body on his crucifix was shorn of his head. Johannsen's last gift to me before her death, the gift I'd casually discarded, had jammed in the emergency shut off, and killed her.

"Oh God, no!" I put my head in my hands.

I sat like that for I don't know how long. My head was filled with a hole as large as that which had sucked in my friends, as empty as that other universe. For those few minutes, my mind barely existed. Finally, I was pulled from this nothingness when someone banged on the door to the control room and rattled the handle. I recognised Father Donnelly's voice.

"Open up, Zak! Let me in!"

I lifted my head and saw him peering in through the window. He beckoned me, so I rested my hands on my desk, pushed myself upright, and stumbled across to him. He smiled, then frowned as I grabbed the fire extinguisher and propped it up under the door handle.

"Zak, what are you doing?!"

I shook my head and turned away. I was alone, possibly for the rest of my life. I'd operated the controls—that's how the Ministry of Theology would see it—and my differences with Johannsen were on record. I'd never be able to prove my innocence in front of the Penitence Tribunal, so there was only one thing I could do. I went through to the transmission chamber and looked about.

There on the floor, scratch marks. I reached into Angelo's cupboard and pulled out his box of micro-tools and components. Good: as well as the calibration instruments for the Transmitter, it held the hand-held beamer that he'd used for major repairs. I'd probably need that. Inside the desk drawers, I found other small items: a penknife, a roll of string, and so on, things that might prove useful... elsewhere. I stuffed all of these in my pockets. Now across to the centre of the room. There on the table, a smear of blood. I unlocked the cage and pulled the Transmitter from its housing. I pressed the button to put it into 'Display' mode and checked its status. It was working fine; I couldn't see what had gone wrong, so I'd just have to take the chance that it wouldn't happen again. I did some work in my head, pulling up memories of coordinates and trajectories from papers that Angelo and I had written, data that Johannsen had thereafter refused to use as being blasphemous, but which now might save me.

"So, if our universe is zero point zero to infinite places..." I mumbled.

After a few moments, I had something halfway plausible worked out, and quickly re-set the parameters in the Transmitter, then waited while it did the final calculations.

"Open up, Zak, or there'll be trouble!"

As I looked back, an axe-head burst through the window of the control room door, and glass showered about the room. Father Donnelly's hand reached through, pushed the extinguisher away and then fumbled for the lock. I pressed a button on the Transmitter, and I was gone from my home-world forever.

My half-remembered data worked out adequately. No, it worked out perfectly. Suffice to say that after a disorienting whirl across the possibilities, I was safe, in my own quasi-paradise, one with no humans, no higher life forms, just a rich landscape and creatures that had no fear of man.

I spent the next six months in a wilderness. It was unspoilt and beautiful. I could see the stars at night, and there was no roar of traffic. There were no people to bump into or to avoid, no work, no money or finances to worry about. Most importantly, there were no Justice Officers at every corner. I didn't miss the tri-v and its propaganda, nor did I want anything from my home-world. I was at peace, for a while at least. I didn't have to think about the experiment, about Angelo... No, that could wait till another time. I enjoyed the solitude. But this peace, this ignorance, couldn't last forever.

The day was warm, and I was lying by a stream, a brace of fish gasping by my side. My arm was dangling in the water, my hand ready to hook out another fat fish, when I heard a very faint noise behind me, somewhere in the trees. It wasn't natural. I crawled under a spiny bush with my fish and looked out in time to see a man's feet go past. A few hundred yards further along the stream, he stopped. I peeped out and could see his back as he turned this way and that. He had a gun of some kind in one hand and another object in the other; I couldn't see what it was, but apparently it wasn't working. He rattled it, then strapped it to his belt and walked on, out of the glade. I knew who it had to be—Donnelly! Him and the Ministry of Theology, they wouldn't let me go free, even across the barrier and into another universe. Damn them!

So I left.

Several months later, I found myself on a world, this time populated by humans who had a comfortable level of technology.

They were still well behind that of my homeworld, though. I took a job as a repairman, hiding my knowledge and skills in case the Ministry tracked me down again, and I moved in with a woman I met. I can't remember her name now: Mary, perhaps, or Miriam? It was so long ago. We lived in a two-room wooden cabin on the outskirts of a small rural town. One night she had to leave—I didn't like to be on my own—but her mother was ill.

"Are you all right, Zak? It's only for a week," she said just before she left. She was standing in the open doorway with the sunset behind her. The light cast her face in shadow, and now all I can remember is the silhouette of her hair.

"Fine, I'll be fine. Just come back quick."

I opened a drawer in the dresser next to me and pulled out a wooden horse.

"Here, this is for your brother," I walked towards her. "I carved it myself last night, while you were asleep."

She smiled, took the horse with one hand, and placed her other hand gently on my cheek.

"I'll be back soon."

Then the door was closed behind her, and I was in the cabin on my own.

That night I stoked the fire extra-large and lay awake thinking of what had happened to my colleagues, to my friend Angelo, to Johannsen even. We'd all signed waiver forms when we joined the Institute, so we knew what the risks were. The other staff were believers, anyway, so they'd had nothing to fear about dying. Hell, they'd probably be glad to die early and meet the good Lord. As long as they didn't kill themselves deliberately, they'd find themselves in Heaven. And they did go to an afterlife of sorts, even one that an unbeliever like me could believe in, an afterlife justified by the Transmitter itself.

All that time, while Angelo and the rest were dying, the computer embedded in the Transmitter's circuits had still been working, taking measurements from the other Universe and carrying out its operations. I'd taken this data and, by hand, had worked out what had happened to Angelo and the rest, what would happen given the presence of human flesh in the new universe. It seemed that by their deaths, my colleagues had seeded a new universe, just like a piece of grit in an oyster leads to the creation of a pearl. There'll be atoms and stars and galaxies and possibly even life over there now, or at some time in the infinite future. Johannsen never thought she'd become God—and Jesus too, giving her life that another Universe might live. No Holy Spirit for that Universe, though.

However, I'd never believed in the Holy Spirit, or the afterlife, and during that night, the dream came back to me. Into the black hole slid Angelo and Johannsen, but then a light started to shine from within it. Father Donnelly's arms appeared from the hole; he grasped the sides and pulled himself out. He reached back in for the axe, turned to face me, and walked forwards. I screamed... and that's when I woke up. By the side of the bed, the Transmitter was beeping. I reached across to light the candle, then fumbled for the Transmitter.

FOR WE ARE MANY

"Damn it!" I said, "That bloody Donnelly, he's found me again!"

According to the readout on the Transmitter, a portal between the Universes had opened briefly, somewhere up in the mountains, a portal I hadn't activated myself. Well, the Ministry's motto was "The wheels of God grind slow, but they grind exceedingly fine," and I wondered how much time I had.

The night was cold as I followed the traces shown by the Transmitter up into the hills and through the forests. I passed above the tree line, up to where the air was cold and the wind refused to blow round me. I stumbled over rocks and under hanging boulders, using the Transmitter to guide me to the source of the anomaly. I hadn't dared to bring a lantern in case I was spotted by Donnelly and any helpers he had, but the moon was full, thankfully. I shivered as icy blasts came down from the snow-laden slopes. Even my furs couldn't keep the frost out.

Eventually, I crested a ridge and saw the twinkle of lights in a valley below. There they were, a party of men in grey robes far below, setting up a load of equipment and half a dozen tents. A couple of men patrolled the edge of the campsite, rifles slung over their shoulders, while the rest constructed something that looked like a cage. A few words drifted up to me. I caught the words 'capture' and 'fugitive.'

Corrective Theologians!

"Shit!" I muttered as I blew on my fingers.

I knew then that the Ministry of Theology had sent not just one man after me, but a team of hunters. Was there a way to distract them? Maybe by travelling away from this world so that they'd follow me, then doubling back? I shook my head. Too risky. Maybe they'd leave someone back here to wait. And I didn't want to leave this world, not now, not when I was happy. I had Miriam, or whatever her name was, to come back to.

I circled above, keeping behind snowbanks. One man directly below me was instructing them. He looked familiar: Donnelly? It had to be. I recognized that arrogant nod of the head, the dismissive gestures to his underlings. So, what now, I wondered. Could I persuade him to leave me alone, or would I have to do something more active? I looked at the rocks around me. They say cut off the snake's head, and the body dies; well, there was Donnelly, standing at the bottom of some scree, all that loose rock waiting for a nudge. None of his men were nearby, so there was no danger to them. Could I do it, could I injure, even kill him, to save myself?

I stayed like that for a few minutes, thinking about what to do, when some clouds cut across the moon. I looked up in time to see the wisps at the edge of one cloud streaming against the sky, with the light of the moon shining from behind the cloud. I'd never realized until then that a cloud, something you normally take for granted, could be so beautiful. That was when I decided that Donnelly would never take me away from this world, never ruin my new life, no matter what I had to do.

I only needed a few minutes to pry up a boulder and angle it towards the scree. I peeked over. Fine, Donnelly's men were still some way from him. I didn't want to hurt them; he was my target. I heaved my boulder down the cliff, and within seconds the scree was slipping down the slope. The boulders were no longer inanimate, they were alive, jumping this way and that, spreading panic across the hillside, until finally all their companions were rushing in a great tide downwards and outwards across the side of the mountain—a tide, and not the little stream I had intended.

Donnelly looked up in time to see the onrushing stones, and then he disappeared beneath them. I didn't get a chance to see the look of terror on his face; it was still so dark below. The rest of the stones burst into the campsite, knocking over the cage and rushing on to the tents.

"No!" I shouted and jumped up. "No!"

I watched as the avalanche crushed the tents and the Ministry men or sent their bodies spinning down the mountainside. Some of them shouted, of that I'm sure, but I couldn't hear anything over the great roar of the avalanche. That didn't last long, though. Suddenly, quicker than I could ever have realized, there was nothing but dust blowing about the now-ruined campsite and the rattle of a tardy stone or rock joining its companions. The mountainside was quiet and peaceful once more. I looked down at the ruins below me until eventually I felt the wind on me again, and had to move from my exposed place.

I came down the safe way, now and then disturbing a stone under my foot, but I made it to the bottom safely. After a long time picking my way down, I made it to the campsite. None of the bodies moved—those that I could see, anyway. Most of them were hidden under rocks with only an arm or leg sticking out. Things didn't look so familiar close up. The robes were only superficially like those of Corrective Theologians, and what I'd taken to be guns were large crucifixes carried over their shoulders.

As I got closer, I could see the smashed equipment and tents. A torn Bible lay on the floor. The cage that they'd prepared for me was now only a mess of jagged metal. On its side was a cross, and inside something that looked too familiar to me. There were no manacles in the cage, just a large version of my Transmitter, one big enough to move a dozen men and their supplies. I picked up a battered Bible that lay near it and opened it to the dedication page. "In Honour of His Holiness Pope Sixtus VIII, this new translation was commissioned in the year of Our Lord 1893, by Order of Our Glorious King James IX..."

Who the hell was Sixtus the Eighth? King James the Ninth? I threw the Bible to the ground as I realised the truth. I'd killed a group of innocent men, holy men, not from my universe, but from another. They'd been exploring the multiple universes in their adoration of God, and I'd killed them. I collapsed in the dust amongst the debris and cried, not just from grief, but for forgiveness.

After I cried myself dry, I wandered

about and realised my stomach was empty. The exertion, not just the physical of climbing the mountain, but the mental, had drained me, so I looked for some food among the belongings of the dead men. As I walked about the rubble, eating bread I'd found in one of their packs, I heard a moan from down the slope. One of them was alive!

After five minutes of picking my way down the slope, I found a man lying with his legs under a small boulder. I pushed this off and held my water bottle to his mouth. He was delirious and kept repeating, "Your Grace, have you forsaken me?" That's what it sounded like, though his voice was weak and his words not clearly formed. Perhaps I misunderstood him.

I went back upslope and formed a stretcher as best as I could from the remains of the equipment, then tied the survivor to it and dragged him down the slope. He moaned every time the lower end bounced from a rock, but I couldn't stop. The darkest part of the night was coming on, and he would have died if I'd left him while I went for help. I didn't realize, though, that by saving him, I would condemn myself.

Eventually, I got him into my cabin. I made him comfortable, then collapsed by the fireplace and fell asleep. I dreamt of angels flying through clouds, then falling to earth as their wings were plucked off by a giant. I woke once to stoke the fire, then fell into blackness myself.

A few days later, the priest, Father Sanchez, had recovered enough to talk and eat. I'd just brought him a bowl of soup. That was all he could stomach at the moment. His eyes were red, but the shaking had stopped.

"I'm sorry about your colleagues, Father," I said, "But there was nothing I could do for them. Your arrival must have shaken something loose further up the mountain. By the time I got there..."

I'd told him about the deaths during one of his lucid periods a day or so previously. This time, his face turned gray, and he held his beads to his lips while he prayed. I didn't like to see him looking stressed, so I tried to distract him.

"So, you're from the Copernican Order," I said "What were you doing up there?"

"Walking among the universes, spreading the word of God, where appropriate, and investigating the wonders of his Universe. And what are you doing here?"

Somehow, he knew that I was a wanderer as well; I'd not been able to hide that from him. Perhaps the way I'd talked to him when I was dragging him down from the mountain, or while he was recuperating, that showed my ignorance of the world we were in?

"I'm resting. Maybe I'll get married, stay here, I don't know. I can't go home; I do know that. The experiment we were running, well, it went wrong, and I was... stranded here. I don't even know if I could find my way home if I wanted."

He just looked at me, straight through me. Then he laid his hand gently on my arm.

"Tell me about it, Zak."

I waited a moment, wondering what to

tell him, then told him a shortened version of what happened with our great experiment and how it went wrong. He listened until I finished, and even waited while I whimpered and held back the sobs. It was only when he was sure I'd finished that he opened his mouth.

"You're lost," he said. "Physically and spiritually."

I shifted in my chair and stared through the window and across the fields. He continued.

"You blame yourself for what happened, but why? God doesn't blame you. Why don't you let go of your bitterness and embrace the Holy Spirit?"

"Because God doesn't exist," I shouted at him, then realized what I was doing and tried to calm myself. "Or if He does exist, then He's split across trillions of universes as well. No other God but me, that's what each of those trillion Gods say in their own universes, eh? You travel across the Universes, you've seen different worlds. Use your head and follow that concept to its conclusion. One God in each of those uncountable Universes."

He shook his head.

"No, you're wrong. To those of us with faith, there is no other god but God, not even an avatar of God, even across the infinite universes. One God over *all* the universes, the Alpha and Omega of every world, not just this one or that one. And this is a sign of His benevolence towards his children, that He spreads His love across more universes than could be counted if we lived infinitely."

"I don't believe that. There is no God, in any universe. I saw that when Johannsen and the rest were sucked into the emptiness."

"Ah, you're wrong yet again. In my world, there is no divide between science and religion. Our greatest minds, our whole culture, worship God by investigating his creations, and the greatest of those creations is the human soul."

The excitement of talking about his religion was too much for him, and he started to lose his breath. He leant over and half-coughed silent wheezes into his sleeve. I handed him a glass of prune juice and waited for him to recover.

"Thank you, that's better." He looked about for a second and blinked in confusion.

"The human soul," I reminded him.

"Yes, that's right, the greatest creation of God. I can describe the theories to you. Show you the experimental results, if you give me the time. Proof of His existence and the existence of an undying part of His love within all of us! We all have it, me, you, and our duplicates across the universes."

"A big problem with Heaven, then," I said. "It must have filled up eons ago with all of those souls from all of those universes. Same problem for Hell, as well."

"Ah, no! Not true, not true. That's a sign of His benevolence. You must have thought about freewill and determinism—every intelligent person has. You know that you behave the way you do partly because of the circumstances of your life. Your family, your school, your society, all these make you into the person you are. But is that right? What if you are good only because you live in a good society, and in a wicked society of sloth and greed you would become evil?"

"Well, I'd say it's because we're just insignificant little bugs, plodding along our well-worn paths, with no way to see the other paths that we might take."

The priest laughed at me here. I jumped at the noise, a dry whinnying. He shook his head.

"You've travelled across the universes; you know they exist. You're the scientist, so think it through. There are empty universes as you've described before, yes. But in all the rest, there is always humanity. That's all that God allows: the complete absence of life, nothingness, or the existence of man. And in those universes with man, with life, why does God allow so many to exist? Why so many trillions upon trillions of Universes, so similar, but leading to such extremes? To resolve the conflict between freewill and determinism, that's why!"

"In this one Universe, you might be a saint because your parents taught you the Scriptures, in that Universe over there, you are Satan incarnate because your society rewards greed. But on a few worlds, here and there, your avatar does the right thing, not because he is compelled, or moving along a well-worn path, but because he knows it is the right thing to do. Against all his teachings, against all the wicked influences of his environment, he has found his way to God."

He stared heavenward as he continued.

"So, you see, God has created the multiple universes so that each of us and our duplicates can live out our lives in every circumstance, to see whether good will win in all circumstances. And each avatar does not have its own soul. They share a soul, across all the universes in which they exist. All the different versions of you, Zak, don't have individual souls, but one spread amongst all of you! It is God's way of testing you with every temptation. Your soul is only judged once all of your avatars in every universe have passed on, and all of the contributions to the soul are gathered and weighted. So, if you are good only because that is easy, you will not reach Heaven. If you are only good when surrounded by goodness, what does that mean for the 'you' in another universe? Those other selves will be tempted to evil in other universes, and thence you, the summation of all those other yous, will fall into the fires of Hell."

He was sitting upright in his chair as he spoke. His face was flushed now, and his eyes were wide, as were his nostrils. He breathed heavily—panting. I shifted in my seat as I remembered those animated sermons I'd been forced to endure as a child: fire and brimstone and the screams of the damned as they writhed in the flames forever.

"I want evidence before I can believe that," I said. "You said you had proof."

"My equipment," he replied. "You'll find the proof there."

Then he collapsed back into his chair, and his eyes glazed over.

"Okay. You take it easy while I get it," I said.

I left him to recover for a few minutes while I went through to the front room in the cabin. The equipment that I'd collected was scattered where I'd been inspecting it. As I gathered up the bits and pieces, I thought about the priest's words. I was the scientist; I was amenable to proof. If he had it, I'd believe him—not that I really thought that he would.

I went back through to the bedroom and opened the bag for him.

"Here, this is all I could find."

I spread the pieces out in front of him: a notebook, some bits of electronic equipment, a crucifix. He picked them up and tossed them aside after a quick glance, but kept hold of a crucifix. He hugged it close.

"I also found this."

I handed him a black unit, about as big as my palm, and let him caress it. He smiled.

"This is the Tracker," he said, "The greatest invention of my world. Not nearly so great as the soul, but as near as we will ever get to perfection while remaining mortal."

He stroked the Tracker and smiled at me, then continued.

"It's a tool for following a person across the universes, or finding his duplicates. Would you believe that this is possible? It's another sign of God's grace. It can be tuned in to a unique pattern—the soul—and thenceforth can follow that person's progress across the universes. You can use it to monitor a person's portion of his group soul, filtering out those avatars across other universes."

I snorted. "Rubbish."

"Oh no, look here. Look at the display on the front."

He pointed to a circle split into a black half and a white half to show the good and bad. Within each area was a tiny blob of the other color to show the seed of one ever-present in the other. It looked a little like the Yin-Yang symbol that I'd only seen in history books about the Dead Orient. Sanchez continued.

"We're missionaries, and we try to convince people to change their ways. We tell them just what result their actions, and attitudes, can have to their chances of reaching Heaven. Sometimes we're chased away as heretics or demons, but sometimes we win over one person. It's worth it."

"What if people don't want saving?" I said. "Have you thought about that? Maybe we don't really want to be saved by sanctimonious do-gooders?"

He looked into my eyes and fingered his crucifix.

"Everybody needs saving. Everybody needs to embrace Jesus."

He held his crucifix towards me.

"I don't!" I jumped up and turned away from him. He sighed.

"If you didn't want to be saved, why rescue me? Why bring me the Tracker?"

"I, I don't know. It seemed the right thing to do."

"Well, do as you promised, my son, and listen to reason. As a scientist."

I returned to my seat and wiped my hands on my trouser legs. He opened his notebook and switched on the Tracker.

"Here, I'll take you through the mathematics..." he started, and so began a long lecture.

I listened while he described the theory and mathematics of the Tracker. He had to explain his terms sometimes, but we had enough in common that I could understand the theory. As the afternoon continued and the sun sank towards the horizon, he nearly had me convinced—of the science behind it. He even explained how all universes with life in them had originally branched from the one true universe without any previous branches—that single-track universe in which Jesus had lived and died for our sins. The branching into the multiverse had only started at the point that He had ascended to His Father's side. Sanchez treated me to a long disquisition on this. I was not enough of a theologian to pick any flaws in it, and he eventually went back to the mathematics of the Many Worlds Theory and his tracking device. At last, he looked up with a humble smile of pride on his face.

"So, my son, do you believe the Tracker works?"

"Well, the science, that's compelling." I paused. "It fits in with Johannsen's theories, and I believed her." Sweat dripped from my forehead and fell to the ground as I hunched over in my chair.

"So, if the science is compelling, how about the soul? Do you believe it exists?"

"Maybe."

"And if the soul exists, then what does that say about God?"

I stopped rocking. I couldn't help but think about Johannsen flying across the room, her broken crucifix pressed into my palm, a boulder cracking open the head of the leader of Sanchez's explorers. It wasn't my fault. None of it was my fault; I'd done what I had to in the circumstances. I jumped up and paced about. The air had become hot with the afternoon sun, and I flapped the front of my shirt to cool myself.

Sanchez closed his notebook, the notebook which contained the theories. I looked at him.

"That's all theories; I want the reality. Does it work?" I said. "The Tracker, does it really work? I need proof."

I turned and pointed at him.

"What about your soul," I said, "Your group-soul. Show me, what is it, good or evil?"

He blinked, then blinked again.

"I've never used it on myself before, that's the greatest temptation of all—knowing whether one is destined for Heaven or Hell, instead of relying on one's faith. To use the device on yourself, well, that's to pre-empt God's knowledge and prerogatives."

"So why bother inventing it? And you use it on other people. Hypocrite!"

I snatched the Tracker from him.

"And what about me," I cried, "what about me? I want to know—has my life, everything I've done, been worthwhile, or has it been futile?"

"No," he cried, "No! The settings..."

He grabbed at the Tracker, but he was old and weak. I stood up to get away, but he'd managed to take hold of my legs, so I had to push him off. He fell to the floor and hit his head against the woodwork of the porch as I activated the Tracker and pointed it at myself. It buzzed, and the display turned gray, a gray verging on the black. One speck of white stood out against the darkness. My soul, the soul that I shared with all my other duplicates, was nearly as black as sin.

"Oh God, no, God help me, no!" I cried out.

I could hear the blood pounding in my ears and the old priest moaning on the floor. The sun reeled across the sky as I stumbled away, across the grass to the fence at the end of the field, where I threw up. I knew now that I couldn't stay in this world while my soul, the soul I shared with my duplicates, was so ugly, so devoid of light. One tiny point of light stood out in the blackness; that's what the display showed for my soul. I was the only good version of me across uncountable spaces. Father Sanchez was right about the universes, about God and the human soul. My other selves, the other components of me, were sending me to Hell, unless I could stop them.

"Oh God, no," I cried, "I can't face it, that darkness."

I wiped the vomit from my face and looked at the Tracker. It could help me; my salvation provided by that which also showed me my damnation. I had to save my soul; I had to stop my evil selves, even, I realised, if the only sure way was to stop them permanently.

While I slouched against the fence, trying to think what to do next, I heard the sound of a Transmitter. But it couldn't be mine, as I had mine with me. I turned to look into the sun and saw a man appear against the glow. I couldn't see his face, but I knew who he had to be: Donnelly, or one of his colleagues, finally come to get me. My Nemesis. I saw then that I'd never have any peace. He raised his hand and pointed something at me. He was so close that I had time to jump on him and push him to ground. Before he could recover, I was over the fence and into the woods. A mile further on, I activated my Transmitter, which I never left out of reach, and left this world, my temporary home. I didn't care about the priest and let Sanchez lie in his own blood on the floor; his agony was nothing compared to mine.

And so started my mission. I travelled as I had done before I'd reached my rural home with Mary, or Miriam, but now I was directed. I had my solution; I had my prey to hunt, if I was to go to Heaven.

I tuned the Tracker to the strongest of my alternates' signals, the version of me with the most sin, and phased through the Universes, until I was standing in a rural landscape, the sun going down again. What sort of man would he be? A rapist? A murderer? A genocidal dictator? I followed the display of the Tracker as it led me along dirt tracks and across fields until I was eventually standing outside a barn. I walked round it to make sure, holding the Tracker in front of me. Yes, he was definitely in there. I pushed the door open and peeked in.

The sunlight came through a hole high in the far wall and lit up a crane, the sort that was used for lifting bales of hay in and out of the barn. An animal snorted in one of the stalls, and some hay drifted down from the upper level, but I couldn't see my duplicate anywhere. I went quietly in and looked about. Then I realised that it was the sunlight blinding me, and there was somebody here, in the shadow below the shining light. He had his back to me, with his arms wrapped around something that dangled from the crane. The thing on the crane whimpered.

I crept towards him, my beamer ready. My duplicate grunted and moaned, writhed and said something I couldn't understand. Then he went quiet, and his back stiffened. He reached across to a sack of corn near him, and his hand came up with a sickle. He turned his face to me. His mouth, the sickle, the whole front of his body, were covered with blood. He sniggered, put one blood-soaked finger into his mouth, and licked it clean.

"Want to join in the fun?" he said.

I looked past him at what was hanging from the crane and almost retched. I swallowed deeply, steadied myself, and stepped forward.

After that first one, every death came easier.

On and on I went, scything down my evil brothers, my corrupt twins. But no matter what I did, the black area on the Tracker's display stayed black, and the white seed never grew. I couldn't understand this until I started applying my knowledge. With each micro-second that passed, a million, million more universes were created, and with each universe there was potentially another evil version of myself. Of course, there would be other, virtuous, copies of myself, travelling from one universe to the next, but if there were slightly more evil versions of me to start with, then they would multiply faster than the good versions. I would have to work extra hard to catch up.

I can't remember how long I travelled like this—after all, I didn't have time to think about trivia—but it must have been many years. I always stayed ahead of Donnelly, who I now solely called Nemesis, and could usually complete my mission. Sometimes Donnelly, my Nemesis, came too close, and I had to abandon that world for another. Finally, Nemesis made a fatal mistake, and I was free of him.

I was hiding among the dumpsters out in back of an office block, waiting and watching for my duplicate on this world. I'd worked out his routine and knew this was the best place to catch him. After some time, I saw my duplicate come through the fire exit with one of the office juniors. The poor boy was crying as my duplicate ran his hands across the boy's body. My duplicate just laughed.

"If you don't want a job, you only have to say."

The boy whimpered and bowed his head.

I'd seen enough. I stood, ready to head across the alley, when I heard the soft 'thwup' of a Transmitter, and I whirled round. Nemesis had appeared behind the dumpster, but had tripped and fallen to the ground. While he scrabbled about with his back to me, reaching for the gun which had fallen out of his hand, I approached with my beamer. I looked round. Good, the dumpster was hiding us. Nemesis raised his gun hand and cried out as he turned towards me.

"No, no more deaths..."

I fired a glancing blow at his face, and he fell face down, spread-eagled to the ground. He wriggled in a pool of blood, with foam on his lips. The side of his face that was showing was half-melted and stuck to the road surface. I walked over and picked up his gun, which was loaded with darts. It looked like something that zoo-keepers would use to pacify the bigger animals. Maybe he was going to tranquillise and torture me before killing me?

"God," I thought, "he's the devil himself if he's followed me for so long, if he's so desperate to stop me. What sort of people are the Ministry of Theology recruiting now?"

He moaned and whined.

"Leave us...leave us alone...damn...to hell."

I looked down at him and pondered.

"Someone like him with the power to travel from one world to the next... Donnelly and his crew. Jesus, I hate to think what evil they could achieve."

I took off his belt and went through his pockets. A water bottle. A Tracker something like mine. Lastly, The Millennial Bible. I recognised the Mosaic and Kristos Testaments, of course, but I'd never come across the Humanist Testament on any of the worlds I'd visited. What was Donnelly, or his crony, doing with this? Was it a memento of one of the universes my Nemesis had tracked me through? I threw it down next to him then leant closer to hear his dying whispers.

"Repent, repent..."

"Realised your own evil nature, have you?" I muttered as his last breath died away.

I reached down to turn him over, to look into his soulless eyes, but couldn't make my hand move those final few inches. I was sweating. Anyone who tried to stop me in my mission had to be the ultimate evil. Did I want to face that, did I want to stare into the face of evil? I wasn't strong enough yet, so instead, I picked up his Tracker, then smashed it to the ground.

I moved out from behind the dumpster, but my duplicate and his pathetic prey were gone, scared off by the noises no doubt. By habit, I glanced at my Tracker, and the blackness was still there, spreading across the display, but what a change! The spot of white was larger—significantly larger. It swirled and pulsated in the middle of the display. I laughed! I howled and laughed, and then howled again.

Nemesis was gone from my life at last! He'd chased me for so long I thought I'd never escape, that I'd never have the freedom to pursue my mission with the vigour it deserved. Now my mission was suddenly becoming successful after what seemed a lifetime of futility. By destroying my Nemesis, somehow I'd helped, in a small way, to redeem myself. Sometimes I had thought that I was wrong, that Father Sanchez was wrong, that there was really no God and no shared soul. In my blackest depressions, I'd even wondered if the men I was killing weren't as evil as I thought, just misguided, but now... But now I felt uplifted, with a spiritual fire burning in my stomach. This was a sign that my mission was virtuous: God was on my side.

I was in danger of attracting too much attention, so I decided to leave, this world quickly. I turned back to the office building, then paused.

"You lucky man. How can I take you down after this? Looks like it's God's will."

I shook my head then activated the Transmitter and phased out.

I worked with renewed energy for the next hundred worlds. The display didn't change for the better—no more light shining in the blackness and drawing me towards Heaven. In fact, the darkness and evil slowly encroached on my hard-earned virtue. I couldn't understand why, if my mission was so virtuous. The light was going out for my soul yet again.

And then Nemesis returned.

This time, he was better prepared. He didn't approach me but fired his darts from the darkness of a hover park. The darts missed and hit a column next to me. I raced across the pools of light, and cornered him. As he babbled away, I fired at him once, twice, and then a third time in the head to make sure.

I prodded his body with my toe, but his brains were fried inside his head. No movement. This time he was wearing a golden robe and tall, thin hat. He had been wearing a golden mask on his face, but now it was mostly melted to the inside of his face. He had a holy book in a backpack, at least I presume it was holy from the gold leaf lettering on the cover. I didn't bother to read it.

I sat away from the body and rested my head in my hands while I thought. I could feel the shadows of the hover park come closer, their coldness gripping me. Donnelly's recruits were getting stranger and stranger. A Humanist Testament? A man wearing a golden mask? Had Donnelly or his superiors started working with foreign powers, or some interdimensional organisation? I couldn't decide. It wasn't worth thinking about, so I gave up trying. I picked up the dead man's Tracker and threw it across the park. I heard it smash in the distance, then a squeal of brakes. I looked down at my Tracker and saw yet again that the white spot was larger, a tiny piece was growing. Thank God, salvation was a little bit closer again. I lifted my head and continued with my mission.

I travelled across thousands of worlds, and Nemesis chased me in his many guises: Christian, Buddhist, Hindu and others, and I destroyed him each time. Sometimes he came at me with tranq-guns or nets, sometimes he tried to take me bare-handed. I didn't dare let him get too close, lest the devil fool me with his words, so one time I threw a fragmentation grenade at him. That worked pretty well, so I kept a handful of them with me wherever I went after that, until I ran out. If ever he did manage to get in close, I shot him in the face. The gorgon Medusa turned virtuous men to stone; I didn't want Nemesis to do the same for me with his evil features.

So, as I travelled, I found over and over again that I couldn't keep up, that the blackness threatened to destroy that little goodness in myself. But then... then Nemesis appeared again and threw himself at me, and when I'd destroyed him, the goodness came back. He didn't realise it, but each time Nemesis sacrificed himself so readily, like a twisted Jesus, my soul was regenerated. The display blossomed with white, and the blackness was forced back. Time after time. Ironically, I knew that without Nemesis, without the chance to remove his evil from the multiverse, I might never get close to God. I was certain of that, until the day he caught me, and I sprawled before him.

I was in the intra-universal space, just after I'd finished the job on my alternate self in that grim city, and hopefully saving Juliet from Romeo, that poor girl Suzie from my duplicate Zed. I thought about the bald guy shouting up to the window, and those evil bastards covered in gang tattoos.

As the grayness flickered about me, I was thinking of what I'd done, how I came to be where I was. How many worlds had I been in, how many of my alternates had I killed? Five thousand, ten thousand? I couldn't remember. Why hadn't that last one, Zed, taken the chance for redemption when it

was offered to him? I shook my head, even though there was no one in the empty space with me.

I was still working through my memory when I noticed a whining, the first sound I'd ever heard in the limbo. It was coming from the Transmitter. It screeched louder and started to glow red and then burnt out in my hand. It was so hot I had to drop it. The space about me shifted from gray to red and then to black. Something was pulling at me, here in the gap between the worlds. What the hell was happening?

I stumbled and instinctively grabbed for something, but my head hit the ground. I looked up at what I'd fallen on and nearly screamed; I was holding tight to my own dead body, the body with the tight grin and the bloodshot eye—Zed. I flinched, rolled to the side and pushed myself to my knees. It was only then that I heard somebody moving beside me. A man was standing over me. Nemesis had caught up with me, and for the first time I was helpless before him.

"Get up!"

The voice was loud and harsh.

"Get up, you piece of crap."

I rolled to the side, rising to a sitting position, and shot at Nemesis with my beamer. The shaft of light hit him but ricocheted, sending out a halo of light too bright to see through. I could only just make out a human form in the middle of the white glow.

"Come on, die!" I shouted.

I kept the beamer on full, but the figure strode through the heat. Just before the beamer ran out of energy—hell, it did need time to re-charge now and then—Nemesis booted me in the chest, then grabbed me by the collar. He dragged me to my feet, only to fling me back to the ground, away from Zed's body and face down in a pool of rain. He put his knee in my back and pushed my nose further into the water. I convulsed, mostly reflex, but whoever was holding me only pushed harder. He ripped my beamer from me, then let me go. I rolled onto my side and lay there gasping.

I thought I'd banged my head at first as I could see double images around me, flickering in and out. Zed's body was near me, surrounded by a haze, though the bags and dirt on the street were clear. The haze wavered, and I saw the body move within it. Zed rolled over and crawled away, though in another way, his body also remained exactly where it was. Zed stood up, and I could see that he had only a superficial wound in the chest, though again in a way I can't describe, his body also stayed exactly where it was. My duplicate Zed stood up with his arm held to his chest, and he was also dead on the ground, and he was crawling away on hands and knees, all at once.

Then something appeared in front of my face, a pair of hands, insubstantial but definitely there. I looked down and saw they were attached to wraith-like arms which came out of my shoulders. Then more hands appeared in front of my face, reaching towards me from my own body. Arms demerged from each other and spread apart until there were so many that they were just fronds waving before me. I screamed...

...until I was interrupted.

"No, you're not in Hell, not the real one, anyway. You're in my hell, you waste of space."

I didn't look up, and not just because I didn't dare. I was sweating and shaking and couldn't even think or listen. I lay on the ground, surrounded by a mist of body parts.

"Look at me!"

I whimpered. A pair of feet moved towards me in big hard boots, probably steel-toed. One booted me in the gut, and at the same time the haze around my body dissipated. I could see clearly again.

"So, you thought you had all the technology, the best Tracker and Transmitter, eh?"

He pulled his Transmitter from off his belt and waved it in my face. I still didn't look up at him though.

"See this? It's better than yours. Allows us to straddle the Universes, not just stand in them, and we can see the results of all our choices, at once, here and now. You're alone in limbo with your judge, Zak."

His after-images mimicked his movements, and some of them even strode closer to me. Fortunately, none touched me.

"If you don't get up, I'll kick your face in and shoot your foot off. Get up."

I rolled over and pulled myself to my knees, but kept my head down before Nemesis for a few seconds. He was wearing some sort of armour, red and black it was. There was a long blade, a sword almost, strapped to one side of his waist, his Tracker and my beamer on the other. He slapped me, but not hard enough to really hurt. I looked up.

He had no face. On his head was a helm of light, hiding his face from me. A glow surrounded his body, so bright I couldn't see the dark streets beyond him, and I had to shield my eyes with a hand. Nemesis looked down at me.

"So, you're the one. I thought you'd be tougher than this, the way you killed...my brothers...who were hunting you. Still, they were soft, wouldn't take you down properly. Tranquilliser darts, nets, bare hands—Jesus, they should have used an elephant gun on you."

He turned away from me and took a couple of paces, and the haze returned. A blurry after-image of him remained where he'd been, as if several similar pictures of him had been projected onto the same screen. A trail of other after-images flitted between his many different positions. I was still shivering, but I accepted the strangeness this time. Nemesis, the solid one, turned round and unsheathed the sword from his belt.

"Time's up, Zak," he said.

"What's happening?" I whimpered, "Why are you doing this to me? Did God send you..."

"God didn't send me. Well, not directly. Take a guess."

I shook my head. Nemesis continued,

"It's time for you to face up to your sins, Zak."

I stammered and spluttered and finally found my voice.

"But I'm helpless! You wouldn't kill a helpless man, would you?!"

Nemesis didn't answer, he just strode closer, his right hand around the hilt of his knife-sword, his left hand supporting the tip.

"Tell me what to do," I shouted. "Anything, I'll do it!"

He rested the blade of his sword on my left shoulder so that the edge rested cold against the side of my neck.

"Do you mean that, Zak? There is something I want from you, but do you really mean you'll do anything?"

I nodded.

"Okay," he said and moved the sword away, "Just listen to me, and I might let you live."

I nodded again.

"You want to know what's going on? You and your mad hunt, that's what's going on. Killing your doubles, your avatars. Do you know what you're doing? Do you really?"

Nemesis and his images stepped back away from me, all of them. I was confronted by a hundred ghosts and their mad parent, all staring and raving at me from a dozen paces away.

"They're evil," I replied, "I've got to kill them, to save my soul."

"Even if killing is wrong?"

I nodded. "I don't like it, but I have to. Better that one of us suffers now than all of us suffer when we're dead!"

"So, you're Jesus, are you?" he shouted. "Taking the sins of your duplicates onto yourself like He took the sins of the world onto Himself? You really are bloody stupid! They're not evil. You are, you prick."

"No, no, I see it in the Tracker. My soul, my shared soul, was turning dark. And you're evil, for trying to stop me."

Nemesis and his images approached me again. Most of them merged back into the real Nemesis.

"Tell me," he said, "When you killed that latest avatar of yours in this world, did you think about the people left behind?"

I shook my head.

"You can't change what the other Zak had done, but did you try to fix anything that he'd broken?"

I shook my head again.

"How do you think his actions affected other people's souls? Did you think about helping to repair other people's souls rather than your own?"

Yet again I shook my head.

"Selfish prick!" he shouted. "So, nobody else matters but you, the actions of you and your avatars don't affect anyone else, is that right?"

"Well, I didn't think..."

"That's right, you didn't think. And if you don't help others, what does that do to your own soul, your shared soul?"

"I don't know, you're confusing me!" I lowered my head and rested my face in my hands as Nemesis paced up and down in front of me, occasionally pointing his sword at me as if to remind me that he could cut me down at any second.

"So, putting aside your selfishness as regards other people, let's look at how you've used the Tracker. You've used it to hunt your doubles, you've checked your shared soul and their contribution to your soul, I expect. Did you ever check just your own contribution?"

"Well, that one time with the priest, I checked our shared soul."

"But was the Tracker set to read your shared soul, across all universes, or was it really set for just your own part and nobody else's? When you got that reading, the reading that set you on this mad killing spree, did you even think to check the settings on your Tracker?"

"Well, no, I just sort of assumed..."

I paused as I thought about what he'd said. Father Sanchez had been in the middle of showing me the Tracker when I'd snatched it from him, and my memory was blurry about what had happened. When I'd used it, was the Tracker set to display the goodness and evil for the group soul, or was it set for the immediate soul, my portion of the soul? When I pointed it at myself and got the reading of such wickedness, what was it attuned to? Was it my duplicates who were evil, or was it just me?

"Can I stand?" I asked, and Nemesis nodded.

I rose unsteadily to my feet and felt for my Tracker. I took it from my belt and held it in front of me, ready to test it on myself again. My thumb strayed to the control stud, wavered over it. All I had to do was press it.

"Do you really need to check?" said Nemesis. "Do you need confirmation of what you already know to be true?"

That's when I knew that he was right; I knew what Father Sanchez had been telling me. Why did I need a Tracker to see whether I was good or evil, whether I was destined for Heaven or Hell? I could use my conscience rather than a tool of science as my guide. I dropped the Tracker to the floor. I was evil. Not my other selves, not my shared soul, me. I was evil. And I'd left hundreds, thousands, of innocents behind me, victims of my collateral damage.

And the men I'd been killing, well, maybe they weren't innocents, but who's to say whether they were evil? With each murder, I'd moved further away from the light. I thought again of everything that had happened to me, right back to the moment I threw Johannsen's crucifix across the desk, casually throwing away what was meant to be my salvation.

"Oh Christ," I cried, "I was guilty all along, right from the start."

"And you've known it since then, haven't you, hidden deep inside that diseased mind of yours?" said Nemesis.

I nodded. I had known, but had never admitted to myself, and so I'd fled from world to world, all the while carrying the source of my problems with me. All those irrational decisions, those stupid actions...fear and guilt had driven me from the start.

I didn't know what to do. I couldn't even move, and could hardly even think. The enormity of my crimes, the sins I carried...a tear dripped down my cheek.

"God forgive me," I whispered.

We both stayed that way for several minutes. Nemesis lowered the tip of his sword to the ground and rested his hands on the hilt as he waited. The glow from his armour faded. Eventually, I wiped my hand across my nose and eyes.

"But, but I must have been doing some- thing right, sometimes. My soul did become cleaner, more pure, when all of those other Nemeses died," I started, but this Nemesis interrupted.

"When they sacrificed themselves, you mean."

"Yes. The Tracker display went white— whiter, at least—whenever a Nemesis died. Immediately afterwards. Sacrifices, you said? So, if my soul became less evil because of the *sacrifices* of the other Nemeses, that means they must have been..."

"You know who I am, Zak," he said, "You always have. Every time you've looked at one of our dead avatars, you've known who I am."

I nodded. He sheathed the sword and reached up to his helmet. He fumbled with some catches for a few seconds before finally lifting the helmet up and off his head. Standing there with the helmet under one arm and his face burnt a dull red from the effects of my beamer, he looked like shit.

He was me, of course. The eyes were redder than mine, and the lines deeper, but he was me.

"If you'd looked at the faces of all those other Nemeses," he said, "the other ones who'd chased you, you'd have seen your own face looking back at you much earlier, Zak. Donnelly gave up a long time ago. The better versions of you, of us, didn't."

I stared back at him. His hair was gray and thin, and his face was dirty.

"And with every sacrifice, Zak," he continued, "our soul was redeemed, not much, but enough to show on the Tracker."

"But, the other Nemeses," I said, "the

ones I killed, if they were good men, but they couldn't catch me, what about you? Why could you catch me?"

"I was you, but worse. I didn't let anything stop me from my mission—bystanders, families, anything—until my own Nemesis caught up with me. He was kinder than me, captured me, and showed me the truth. But my hands are covered in as much blood as yours; more, even."

I could see tears form in the corners of his eyes as he spoke. He may have been evil once, but he'd repented, I could see that.

"So here I am," he said, "a mass-murderer, trying to stop you from doing the same thing. But I still hear the cries in my head. I can't do anything about that. I can, at least, stop killing."

He threw the beamer down on the floor near his feet and then rubbed the side of his face with one hand. He looked tired, now, rather than threatening, as tired as I felt. I knew what he felt. I knew the same guilt and felt the same moral sickness. At one time, he'd been everything I was, only more so: obsessed and hateful. Now, he was just sad. And I? I had a feeling of strange growth inside myself as well as the pain.

"I couldn't kill you," he continued, "because Jesus told me... told us all, not to. Love your enemy as yourself, he said. He never said that the greatest enemy was your own self."

I nodded, and at his words I felt something move inside me, a freeing in my chest and a churning in my mind. My soul felt lighter somehow, and my conscience eased. I stared at Nemesis, my mind working.

"My sins have been too great," he continued, "and I can't bear to live anymore. But suicide is as great a sin. I have no escape."

He turned away from me. He didn't leave any after-images behind him this time. All of his avatars must have done the same. All of my avatars must have done the same thing as well. I knew what I had to do. I got out my Tracker and looked at its display, the one showing the group soul. Mostly black, with a small blob of gray in the middle; all those times in the past when Nemesis had sacrificed himself, when I'd martyred a good man, a white seed would spread in the centre. I knew what *this* good man wanted me to do to help the white seed to re-appear and grow. I knew what he needed me to do to remove his guilt and pain. He couldn't kill himself, but could I do it for him, if he was really part of me?

I reached over and picked up the beamer. I twisted the dial to its widest setting, the one that would destroy anything, flesh, bone, metal even. I realised as I handled the beamer that the feeling in my head was still there, as if something was reaching out, putting roots down and sending out shoots.

"Give me your Tracker," I said. "Everything."

He nodded, handed over his Tracker, Transmitter and started to rip off his suit. The instruments were very similar to mine but with a few additional controls. I worked out which one held us between universes and turned it off. The real world—well, one of the many real worlds—phased in around us as the phantom limbs and body parts phased out of existence.

And just like that, we were standing in the street where I'd left Zed's body. It was a dozen yards away, but it was no longer alone. Four guys stood around it; well beyond them, their vehicle sat with its engine running. The car boom-boom-boomed at us, that noise that I suppose they called music on this world. Zed's posse, or whatever you call them, had caught up with him, but not at the bar they'd arranged. The guy with the bald, tattooed head was on his knees, holding Zed's body. He poked a finger in Zed's back.

"Shit, man, look at that hole!"

I buckled Nemesis' armour on and lifted the helmet into place. I activated the force-shield, and the world around me faded as the glow obscured my vision, but I could still see well enough what was happening. The youths were approaching us now, holding knives out in front of them.

"Gonna cut you up!"

"Gonna eat your brains, man!"

"Fuck you, in your trick or treat outfit!"

"Be silent!" I shouted as I swung the beamer round and fired at their car.

The upholstery burst into flames, the tyres melted, and the boom-boom-boom became a squawk. Finally, the metal body of the car shone red, then white; it buckled and dripped molten blobs. Within a few dozen seconds it was a slag-heap. The youths stared at the car, then back at me.

"Kneel!" I shouted.

They knelt. I turned my head to look at Nemesis, who was behind me, hidden from the youths.

"Be quick," he said and lowered his eyes, ready for the final blast.

I put my hand on his shoulder and shook my head. I looked at the youths who were still kneeling in front of me. Their faces were pale and their limbs shaking.

"You are evil men," I said to them, "and Zed was the most evil, and that is why he died."

I pointed the beamer at Zed's body, and their eyes turned to follow my motion. I fired, and the corpse burst into flames. His flesh crackled and spat as it quickly burnt to ashes. Soon, there was nothing but a gray smear on the road to show where Zed had been. The youths huddled together.

"But there shall be no more killing! Instead of death, I bring life. Your friend was dead, but is alive..."

I grasped Nemesis and thrust him in front of me. The youths gasped as they saw their friend resurrected. Baldy started to shake, and tears rolled down his cheeks.

"Alive again to put right all of his wrongs. Alive again to atone for his sins."

I nodded to Nemesis. He stumbled forward and approached the youths.

"And you will help him!" I roared, pointing my sword at each of them in turn.

Baldy dropped his knife and crossed himself.

"Holy Mary, Mother of God!" he croaked. The other guys were crying and shivering next to him. Meanwhile, the seedling that I'd started to feel growing in my mind—the seedling planted long ago by my friends Angelo, Johannsen, and many, many others—pushed upwards, sprouting leaves and petals as it did so. Finally, it stood before me, a blood-red rose, and it was beautiful. I grasped it by its thorny stem, took it into my heart and stepped forward into my new life. The weight of my sins lifted from me as they transferred to His stronger shoulders.

"Open your hearts to Jesus," I cried, "and do good with your lives!"

The youths bobbed their heads up and down. Nemesis put his hand on the bald guy's shoulder and turned to face me. I lifted my hand in farewell, as did he. I activated the Transmitter to phase out, and the last thing I saw was my own face, smiling and serene, looking back at me.

Paul is far too mundane to have anything exciting to put in a bio. This is his third story to be published in Cirsova.
T: @realpaullucas
W: paullucaswriter.wordpress.com
A: https://tinyurl.com/paullucasamazon

The Wreck of the Cassada

By JIM BREYFOGLE

The Mongoose and Meerkat have been hired to lay claim to the salvage of a wrecked ship... and will be partnered with none other than the Hand of Bursa!

Twenty-two months after the fall of Alness.

The heat brought out the smell of everything: the fruit in the market stands, the offal in the gutters, the vomit and stale ale about the tavern entrance. Mangos covered his eyes and winced, his head pounding. He didn't mind missing the best produce by sleeping through the morning, but he wished he could miss the worst by sleeping through the afternoon, too.

The enormous lady who sold vegetables sat against the wall of the building behind her, as far under her canvas tarp as she could get, and still the sun roasted her protruding belly. Sweat beaded on her face, and instead of greeting Mangos with a cheery voice, she watched him as she did the flies buzzing about her stall.

Mangos walked past, trying to marshal his hung-over brain into telling him why he came down to the Alomar market. He hoped it wasn't for the overripe fruit, spotted and oozing in the sun, or the meats, three shades too brown and covered in flies.

He gagged in front of the fish stall, his stomach protesting the stench. Worse, he remembered he had come to get fish. A fellow drinker had told him a cure for hangovers that required raw fish.

The fish hung heads down, eyes glassy, mouths open. Try as he might, Mangos couldn't step closer. Instead of curing his misery, the mere thought of eating one of these things compounded it.

"Fish?" said the seller, a man almost as glassy-eyed as the goods he sold.

Mangos looked them over—none appeared better than any other. Even the small shark hung limply, looking like something found on the shore instead of freshly caught.

"I think I prefer my fish fresher," Mangos said.

"Grab your weapons," said a voice. "You'll need them."

Mangos spun around, drawing his sword as he turned, searching for the threat. A man, older, dark hair with grey at his temples, obviously fit, armed with a sword on his hip, stood regarding him with an amused expression.

"He didn't mean now," Kat said as she walked up behind the man. She carried a pack over each shoulder, pulled one off and tossed it to Mangos.

It landed at his feet.

"What?" he said.

"Job," said Kat. "The *Cassada* went up on the rocks last night, and we're to help." She nodded at the pack. "Just in case you get wet."

Mangos didn't put his sword away. Something about this man seemed familiar, a little threatening. "Have I tried to kill you before?"

The man laughed, low, companionable. "Is that what you call it? I wasn't sure."

Kat snorted. "Don't bait him," she told the man. "He's not at his best."

"He'll need to be," the man said.

Mangos lowered his sword but kept it extended, a low guard. "What job? Who are you?"

"I'll tell you as we walk." The man turned toward the docks, clearly expecting them to follow.

"What job?" Mangos mouthed to Kat. She just smiled and started after the man, leaving Mangos to curse and catch up.

"How much do you know of ship's salvage?" the man asked over his shoulder.

"Some," said Kat.

"Nothing," said Mangos. Each step jarred his head, making it pound worse. Buildings crowded the streets, holding in the heat, making Mangos feel there was too little air to breathe. The taverns, normally raucous even in the afternoon, exuded quiet. Nowhere, it seemed, was immune. "Why hire us if we know nothing?" he asked.

"I've seen you work," the man said. "I think you can do this. You're better than most of the local talent."

"Fair enough," said Mangos, perfectly happy to believe the exalted status assigned him. "But you say you've seen us..." He trailed off, trying to remember where he might have met this man of good manners and unconscious menace.

"Terzol," the man supplied.

"The Hand of Bursa!" The memory burst through Mangos's headache, and he could almost smell the jungle from his first meeting with the Hand. "So the Bursa wants something off the ship?"

"The Bursa wants *everything* off the ship," the Hand said. "The *Cassada* carried bales of silk, fine tableware, raw silver, even a consignment of silvecite. Wreckers might take off small articles, but to salvage it properly you need to use cranes and barges to lift the bulk goods. The wreck is too close to the harbor to do that illegally."

"Who owns an abandoned ship?" Kat asked.

"Alomar naval law says the original owner does unless the Naval Court assigns it to someone else."

Mangos shook his head, trying to sort this out. Either you could take it legally or take it illegally. Clearly, he didn't know enough about maritime law. "Why does the Bursa care if it's legal or not?"

"There is a delicate separation that must be maintained," the Hand replied. "Certain types of activities should not be publicly acknowledged. It's bad manners."

Mangos snorted.

"Appearances matter in Alomar," the Hand said. "It is not what you do, but how it appears."

"So it needs to be legal," Kat said. "But

CIRSOVA

the Bursa wouldn't hire us if it were as simple as going to the court and bribing a judge."

The Hand let out a sharp bark of laughter. "No, he wouldn't. To be granted ownership you need the keel plate."

"Keel plate?" Mangos asked.

"A metal disc attached to the keel when it's first laid in the shipyard," the Hand said. "You show it to the judge to prove possession of the wreck."

"We're not sailors," Mangos said. "Why us?"

"Fighting. There are plenty of scum from the wharfs who will take anything they can carry, but the real danger is the crews working for a banker or merchant prince. Especially Bardor," he added. "If anybody tries anything clever, it's likely to be Bardor."

Kat turned her head slowly, her face unreadable. "The banker?"

"Yes, he's a nasty bastard, but clever," the Hand said. "Always finds a way to do something you don't expect."

Kat nodded, her green eyes veiled, expression thoughtful. "So we go get the keel plate and bring it back?"

"Why not wait for somebody else to get the keel plate and take it from them when they bring it back?" Mangos asked.

"Two reasons," said the Hand. "The plate is much harder to catch in someone's hand than it is on the keel. Secondly, prior to the Naval Court bestowing ownership you must swear before a Priest of Gelean that you checked to ensure the wreck was abandoned."

"Ah," Mangos said. The Priests of Gelean

could always tell when a person lied. "What if the ship isn't abandoned?"

"Then you make it abandoned," the Hand said.

They approached the port, long stone quays jutting out, ships tied along them. Heat shimmered on the dark stones paving the quays. The water rose and fell lazily, as if doing so only because it must. A few sailors moved about, but mostly it was quiet; it was too hot in the inner harbor for strenuous work.

"Can you swim?" the Hand asked Mangos.

"Not out to where the wreck is," Mangos said, shading his eyes and searching the port. "I don't see it."

"It's beyond the lighthouse. We'll be rowed out. Can you swim?"

"I don't like to," Mangos admitted.

The Hand turned his gaze to Kat. "Yes," she said.

"Good. You'll be the one to get the keel plate." He led them out one of the long piers to a skiff tied amongst the merchant ships. Two men waited, a bulky pack next to them. When they saw the Hand, one climbed down into the skiff and the other handed him the pack.

"Climb in," the Hand instructed.

"What of the pay?" Mangos asked. Once aboard the skiff, they wouldn't be in a strong bargaining position.

"When dealing with the Bursa," the Hand said, "you take anything he will pay."

"No," said Kat, "that, we won't do." She jumped off the quay, landing lightly in the

36

skiff. "But it might be useful to have him indebted to us."

Mangos frowned, "Your word it will be fair?"

The Hand seemed amused. "My word."

Mangos looked to Kat. "Can we trust him?"

"One of the few in Alomar. He's a professional. We should be more concerned with the wreckers."

The sun was already halfway down the sky as the rowers pulled away from the quay. Ahead of them, the Outer Point lighthouse stood at the end of a spit of land that formed the north end of the harbor. The spit had fallen, Mangos knew, so that in times of high tide and storms the sea broke over it. But the builders of the lighthouse had left nothing to chance. Massive blocks of granite formed the base of the lighthouse. More blocks formed the house, a square building, tall and strong, with a round lantern room at the top.

Mangos turned back to look on Alomar, sweltering in the heat. Haze filled the streets, smoke and fumes of everyday living, turned golden by the lowering sun. On High Hill, the Prince's palace rose above the haze, but the rest of the city seemed ghostly, half-obscured, as though it would vanish if the wind dispersed the sunlit fumes.

"You don't see that when you're in the city," Kat remarked.

"Competition," said the Hand, ignoring Kat's comment. He pointed ahead of them, and Mangos turned to look. Another skiff cruised from behind the lighthouse. It car-

ried six men, and the man in the bow spotted them. The oarsmen pulled faster. "They're a lot closer than we are."

Kat sat in the stern, the weak breeze lifting her hair. She pushed it back. "Only part of this job is a race. You have to survive the rest."

"I'd rather fight on something more solid than this skiff," said the Hand. "The tide is high and ebbing. We can take a shortcut."

The oarsmen steered them to starboard, and they rode the tide over the old lighthouse road, saving the trip around the lighthouse itself. The waves were higher outside the harbor and a stiffer breeze cooled them.

The Hand stood up to get a clear view of their destination. Dozens of rocks stuck from the sea, some small islands, some no larger than the boat in which they rode. All rose from the ocean as vertical fingers of stone. One could step off them into thirty fathoms of water.

The Hand balanced in the bow, tense, watching the other boat like a hawk. The oarsmen grunted, driving them forward so the waves slapped the hull with each stroke. Kat sat, hands on the gunwale, watching the sea that ignored them all.

The sea, Mangos thought, following her gaze. *What about it holds her fascination?*

A crate rose and fell with the waves, a gull riding on top. Some distance away floated a barrel, half-submerged. There were smaller things: boxes, clothing, and bits of wood that bobbed in and out of sight amongst the crests and troughs of the waves.

"Shark," Kat said.

It took Mangos a second to spot the giant fish. It cruised below the surface, a vague threat. "That's why I don't like to swim," he said.

The Hand said something to the oarsmen. They turned toward the bow to look and, when they turned back, adjusted their strokes to move more toward starboard.

The other boat turned sharply and quickly closed the distance between them. Mangos drew his sword and rose. He swayed a bit.

The man standing in the bow of the other boat brandished a harpoon. "Don't think to steal our spoils!" He drew back his arm and threw. The harpoon flew true, passing between Mangos's legs and thudding into the side of the skiff.

The prow of the other skiff struck their own, throwing Mangos and the Hand down. Two men leapt into their boat; two more clambered past their oarsmen to follow.

Kat appeared over Mangos, blocking the swing from a man with a double-edged billhook. As Mangos climbed to his feet, another man leapt into the boat, heeling it over and throwing him back down. The others fell, leaving only the man who leapt and Kat standing.

Again, Mangos gathered his feet beneath him and rose. One of the attackers grabbed Mangos's ankle and pulled. It wasn't enough to pull him down, but he shifted his weight, causing the boat to rock enough to topple him once more.

"These men are used to this kind of fighting," said Kat. She somehow managed to avoid the billhook, but she was too close to use her sword.

The man fell on Mangos, and he could not tell what else happened. The man's sweaty, unshaven face filled his vision. A flash of sun on steel and Mangos barely caught the hand driving a knife toward his head.

The boat rocked, and water sloshed over the gunwale.

Mangos flexed his muscles, forcing the knife away. The man grabbed his throat—not a good grip, but enough to make breathing difficult.

The boat rocked again, and more water rushed over the side, filling the bottom before the boat settled upright. The water soaked Mangos as he struggled to free himself.

Mangos pushed, forcing the man away. He tore the man's hand from his neck and rolled. Water splashed, and the boat pitched as they struggled. Now, Mangos was on top, twisting his attacker's arm behind his back and forcing his face into the water filling the bottom of the boat.

"You're going to drown him in ten inches of water," said the Hand.

Mangos didn't look up. He pushed the man's face down harder. "Is that a problem?"

"Not for me." There was the sound of water splashing, and the Hand said, "Don't bail until Mangos is done with the water." The splashing stopped.

After the man stopped struggling, Mangos looked around. The two oarsmen leaned on their oars. The Hand stood in the prow over two more bodies.

A couple dozen feet away, Kat stood in the center of the other boat twirling a sounding line. Two dead men floated in the water that half-filled the boat. A third man leaned against the stern, eyes wide, clutching his side. The dark stubble of his beard stood out on his pale face.

Kat let go of the line, and the lead weight dropped neatly into their boat. The weight caught on the gunwale, and Kat drew the two boats together.

"Dump the bodies into the other boat," the Hand said.

"We can dump them overboard," Mangos said.

"That'll excite the sharks," the Hand replied. "Kat doesn't want that when she dives for the keel plate."

"Makes sense."

After putting all the bodies in the other boat, Mangos pushed it away. It rode low with five dead men and one dying.

"That was just one group," said the Hand. "There are others."

The wreck lay on the seaward side of a rock island. Only the masts angling toward them and the starboard rail were visible above the salt-encrusted stone.

As they came around the island, Mangos could see the *Cassada* was caught near the bow, thrown up by high seas or caught when the tide was higher, and the stern sloped down until the decks disappeared underwater. It was a large ship, easily over one hundred fifty feet, but Mangos couldn't tell how much more.

They could see much of the hull, even some of the keel near the bow, and Mangos thought this might be very easy. Then he noticed the skiffs pulled up on the rock. "More competition."

The Hand laughed. "There is half a million worth of goods here. You still think we'll be the only ones after it? The first thing is to make sure nobody is on deck to interfere with diving for the keel plate."

"I have a feeling," Mangos said, "a few people are about to abandon it."

Mangos, Kat, and the Hand climbed onto the island in the shadow of the bow. One of the oarsmen tied the skiff while the other tossed the Hand's pack out on the rock. Then they both settled down, apparently to wait.

"Aren't they going to join us?" Mangos asked.

"They've been paid to row, not to fight," said the Hand. "The three of us will look over the ship, then Kat will get the keel plate while you and I go through the lower decks to make sure she's deserted."

The ship canted toward the island. Bales, crates, and other goods lay jumbled against the port rail. They climbed up the slope of the deck until they could hold on to the starboard rail and look down the length of the ship. Men shouted below decks, the continuing struggle to ensure the ship was abandoned.

A voice called, drawing Mangos's attention before he could truly survey the ship, "This be your only warning. The *Cassada* be ours. Leave whilst you can."

Mangos noticed a man standing with one foot on the bulkhead of the deckhouse and the other on the deck. "The men below decks disagree."

"Fools they be. Whether you be a fool, I'll be able to say in a minute," the man answered. He held a large three-hooked gaff in one hand and an oversized scimitar in the other.

"Not fools—," the Hand said.

"Beware in the rigging," Kat said, quietly so only Mangos and the Hand could hear. A man lay on the sloping mast, out beyond the deck of the ship but close enough that he could join any fight.

"—but here to claim the ship nonetheless," the Hand finished, giving a small nod to show he had heard Kat.

"Fools you be, and death to follow," said the man. He seemed to recognize the Hand. "Didn't expect you to come in person, Hand."

"Do I know you?"

"Reckon not. I took over from Lannel."

"Bardor's men," the Hand murmured so Mangos could hear. He lifted his voice to the man on the deckhouse, "Too hot in the city."

"You'll be cold soon," the man said.

"You've given us a warning," said the Hand. "It would be a discourtesy if we didn't give you the same—an opportunity to leave alive."

The man on the deckhouse laughed. "There be five of us here, and another half-dozen below. Another be coming for the keel plate." As he spoke, the man on the mast gave them a jaunty wave.

Five? Mangos only counted four. Kat gave a cry of surprise. Mangos looked be-

hind to see a fifth man slide off Kat's blade and tumble down the sloped deck, leaving a trail of blood until he came to rest against the rail with the other debris. Blood ran down Kat's leg.

"I deserved that," she said through gritted teeth. "Should have checked the bow."

"You're lucky you're dead," Mangos growled at the man who had wounded her. "You okay?"

Kat nodded.

The Hand reached behind his head, casually, as though to scratch an itch. And everybody exploded into motion. The Hand whipped a flat knife at the men below him. Kat leapt up on the starboard rail and ran along it. Mangos let gravity help him run toward the men at the port rail, one of whom clutched the Hand's knife in his shoulder.

Mangos barreled into the wounded man, knocking him over. The second man swung a belaying pin. Mangos instinctively dodged, but when the man swung again he caught the pin in one hand. He jerked the man closer, then drove him back with a blow to his head. The man let go of the pin as he collapsed.

A shadow made Mangos look up, and he saw Kat dueling, driving her opponent up the sloped mast toward the cross trees. He did not watch long: instead he reached down to pick up a crate. He strained to lift it above his head.

"No, mate, you don't be wanting—" The scavenger raised his arm as he spoke. Mangos half-flung, half-dropped the crate, ending the man's sentence.

Mangos went over to the man the Hand had wounded. It seemed a little cold-hearted to kill him, helpless as he was.

Before either could act, a man landed on the wounded scavenger with a chorus of broken bones. Kat smiled down from the mast. "He didn't have good balance."

"Is scavenging always this deadly?" Mangos asked.

"The *Cassada* has a very valuable cargo," said the Hand from where he crouched on the deckhouse. "The fighting didn't start when we arrived, and we're not the first to kill. Let's go after the keel plate before Bardor's other man arrives."

A drop of blood sparkled as it fell from Kat's leg. Its movement caught Mangos's attention as it fell past him to splash at his feet.

It was a shallow cut, but it bled copiously. Kat quickly bound it, tying it tightly and testing it. It didn't seem to bother her.

"You're going to have to get the keel plate."

Mangos looked around. The Hand was looking at him. "Me? Kat's going to get it."

"I can get it," said Kat. "This wound is—oh." She cut herself off.

The Hand nodded. "Sharks."

Mangos frowned. Kat couldn't go into the water while bleeding. He would have to do it. "My price for this job just went up," he muttered.

"If the Bursa gets ownership of the *Cassada*, he'll be *more* than fair," the Hand said. "But we need that keel plate." He looked around, scanning the waves. "Before

Bardor does something clever."

They gathered below the bow. Mangos pulled off his boots while the Hand opened the pack that still lay on the rocks. He pulled out a flaccid bladder with a long tube coming out of one end. Next, he took out a small bellows. He inserted the bellows into the tube and inflated the bladder. It was larger than Mangos expected. Then the Hand put a small clip on the tube and detached the bellows.

"The bladder floats; you put the tube in your mouth and use it to breathe," the Hand said as he pulled the last thing from his bag. "It won't last long before the air becomes stale, but it'll give you several minutes. Work quickly, and it should be more than enough."

The Hand gave Mangos a small object. "What is this?" Mangos asked.

They were two small pieces of glass, each set in a tiny cup of greasy leather. A small strap held them together, while a long string connected the opposite edges. Mangos turned them over in his hands, noting a small cylinder inside the leather, giving it rigidity, but cushioned by the leather on the open end.

"Underwater glasses," said the Hand. "Put them on, and you can see underwater."

"Clever," said Mangos. The water looked dark. He would be working in the shadow of the wreck. "I hope they help."

"Just grab the keel and work your way down until you find the keel plate," Kat said. She stood on the side of the hull, looking down along the ship toward the underwater stern. "You should have enough breathing tube to get down that far." She paused, clearly thinking. "Unless it's all the way down near the rudder."

"I—," Mangos didn't continue. He didn't like it, but he could do it. Just swim down, find the plate, and use his knife to pry it from the hull. What could go wrong?

A couple minutes later, Mangos lowered himself into the water. He shivered and could feel goosebumps rise all over his body. A wave broke on the rock, splashing his face, and he tasted salt. He pulled down the glasses, wiggling them so the supple leather formed a seal around his eyes. He took a deep breath and put the tube in his mouth, took off the clip, and ducked underwater.

The world changed, turning black and grey. Sounds seemed deeper, fuzzy, and muted. *Better hurry,* he thought, *before I run out of air and it's too dark to see.*

As he started to swim, something caught his eye. Two glowing dots approached, evenly spaced, moving as one, as eyes would move. *What is that?* he wondered. They were large, as big as his head, and headed toward the ship. As they neared, he saw small glowing bubbles rising up behind them. He felt a momentary panic, not knowing what kind of creature this could be.

As it drew nearer, he saw a face inside of the eyes, a man, peering out, illuminated by the light. Now, he could make out two long, skeletal-looking arms ending in claws sprouting from a dark outline that grew clearer as it approached. Runes pulsed, barely visible, around the portals, near

where the arms attached, and along the top edge, revealing a ship much the size and shape of a coffin.

The ship coasted to a stop, and the small bubbles ceased. The man piloting it moved from portal to portal, obviously getting his bearings.

An undersea magic boat! Mangos thought. *It's after the keel plate.*

Mangos kicked toward the hull. His movement must have drawn the pilot's attention, for he looked surprised. The bubbles started again, and the boat started forward.

Mangos tried to outswim it, but a claw closed on his ankle. He kicked hard, making the undersea boat rock, but he couldn't break free. The pilot grinned as he worked controls.

The second claw extended, reached for Mangos's head, and snapped closed as Mangos jerked back. The claw reached again, missed high, and closed.

Mangos's lungs hitched, trying to draw air that wouldn't come through the tube. He reached up and grabbed the claw, felt it clamped on his air tube. The claw was too blunt to cut, but it pinched the tube closed so he could not breathe.

He started to thrash, instinctively trying to break free. He felt the claw on his foot, chafing, tearing at him, and the sharp sting of salt in an open wound, but he could not escape. His lungs started to burn.

The pilot drew in the claws, bringing Mangos closer. He smiled, clearly enjoying Mangos's struggles and wanting to see them better.

Mangos struck, smashing his fist against one of the portals. The water slowed him, dampened his blow, but he struck again and again. He gave up trying to free himself but began pounding on the glass with both fists. Water began to trickle down the inside of the glass.

A look of horror crossed the pilot's face. He moved frantically, and the claws both released and pushed, but just then, Mangos broke the seal of the portal completely. The runes flared and vanished as the glass blew inward on a rush of water. Great bubbles of air forced their way out, and the undersea boat began to sink. A burst of glowing bubbles rose from the back. Still it sank. The bubbles stopped, the inside light vanished, and the undersea boat disappeared into the depths.

Mangos floated, drawing huge breaths. In spite of the numbing cold and the burning sting in his ankle, Mangos felt happy, almost light-headed.

A shadow passed over him. He looked up.

Shark! A big one, drawn by the blood from his ankle. Mangos needed to find the keel plate quickly.

He kicked and reached to grab the hull as the shark circled at the edge of his vision, drifting downward until it was at his same level. He grabbed the keel with both hands and ran them along it, pulling himself along as he searched for the keel plate. Barnacles flayed his skin, but he didn't stop.

Deeper he edged, and it grew darker. He hoped the plate wasn't completely covered in barnacles, or he might not feel it. The shark passed, languidly, and Mangos felt the water stir from its passage.

There! The smooth edges of a circle, the ridges of a design, and a rough-edged barnacle slid under his touch. He ran his fingers around it once then pushed his knife under it. He twisted the knife.

The keel plate *may* have moved, he couldn't tell. He twisted harder.

A quick glance told him the shark was moving faster, more aggressively. He knew it smelled his blood. He twisted again and felt the edge of the keel plate rise. The shark swam away, dropping slightly, and he hoped it might leave, but it turned back and rushed toward him, rolling over as it approached.

Mangos drew up his legs just in time, but the shark brushed against him, jarring him. The knife handle slipped from his hand. *Gods of Eastwarn!* he thought as he grabbed for, and missed, the sinking knife.

He could not see the shark, but he knew it must be near. He stuck his fingers under the keel plate, placed his feet against the hull, strained. The shark tore out of the darkness toward him along the hull, rolling to bring its open mouth to him.

The keel plate came away, and he pushed away from the hull. The shark rushed past, barely missing his feet. He kicked, stroked, and thrashed his way to the surface. He spat out the breathing tube and sucked in fresh air as he tried to climb the curve of the *Cassada's* hull.

He slipped off, thrashed his way toward the bow where he could climb onto the island. "Shark!" he called. "Shark!"

"Hurry, then, lad," shouted one of the

rowers, climbing into one of the skiffs and reaching toward him.

Somebody appeared over the curve of the hull: Kat, staring down. He ignored her, swimming as best he could, so slowly, toward safety.

"HURRY, LAD!" the rower shouted. Mangos's heart pounded. "HERE IT COMES AGAIN!"

Kat ran down the hull, a harpoon in one hand. He lost sight of her in his own splashes, but then he saw her foreshortened feet, and she struck the water beside him. Miraculously she stood, half out of the water, now moving forward, and she plunged the harpoon down. She then, somehow, leapt and grabbed the gunwale of the skiff and pulled herself in.

Mangos swam the last few strokes to the skiff. The rowers each grabbed a wrist and pulled him aboard. He set the keel plate on one of the seats and shook his head as he tried to catch his breath. "I hate swimming," he said.

"It's not so bad," Kat said.

"You *like* this?" he asked her.

"As long as it's the shark swimming away with a harpoon in its back and not me." She laughed, wiping her wet hair from her face. "You may want to choose your playmates more carefully."

Mangos laughed, which turned into a cough. "Where's the Hand?"

"Finishing abandoning the ship. I thought I'd check on you. The men below decks had mostly killed each other already."

Mangos nodded his gratitude. "Good thing. What if others come?"

Kat shrugged. "We don't care, as long as we can swear it was abandoned when we last saw it."

Mangos picked up the keel plate and ran his fingers over the inscription: *Cassada eijn Dex lentern.* He translated it, "The Gods give *Cassada* safe journeys." That hadn't happened.

He set it back down, looked out over the sea, and realized his hangover was gone completely. Maybe there was something to that fish cure after all.

Jim Breyfogle is the author of Tales of the Mongoose & Meerkat. Volume one, Pursuit Without Asking, is available on Amazon and other fine purveyors of books, out now through Cirsova Publishing. Audiobook out now! Mongoose and Meerkat's adventures continue in the next issue with The Flying Mongoose! His new novel, The Paths of Cormanor, is out now from Cirsova Publishing!

Wychyrst Tower

By MATTHEW PUNGITORE

A strange find on a Caribbean expedition haunts the atavistic Dulf Abbandonato...
Why would the family name of an old New England friend appear in the West Indies!?

From the audio files of Dulf Abbandonato

AD 2015—a damnable year—that be the very year when foolishly had I, whilst drunk on thrilling, starry-eyed seeking of knowledge, of adventure, then taken me first trembling step downwards into the one-way lane of rock-hard, fast-sobering reality. I'd spent too much of that strange year trudging through the wildest pits brooding within the Caribbean, the West Indies, and much of miraculous Hispaniola, all while in the company of a suspect party led by the enigmatic and stone-faced Dr. Ildefonso Arias Álvarez.

First, for clarity, you should know me name: Dulf Abbandonato. I'm a reputable, successful man, and I am currently of thirty and four years of age as I'm recording this. I've been a well-regarded teacher and writer of architecture and history for twelve years. Never ever have I written anything like this before, have never before told such secrets, such horrors, like those I'm about to reveal here in this dictation. With the sublime nature of this unbelievable material in mind, I'll be keeping this testimony very informal and friendly. May me professional work and past writings be a signal to me honesty and

good esteem; but I'll warn ye, many have called me a modern buccaneer, somewhat anachronistic and a wee bit of a kook.

A second note: I'd like to assume I've not been touched by any mental detriments; however, on occasion, the grip on sanity feels numb. At times, doubt in me own mental stability enlarges like the lump in me throat or a weighty pressure in me chest.

For a long time, I'd never felt truly understood or welcome, always been feeling an emptiness where friendship, intimacy, and honesty should've been. Neither me successes nor the bond of family had calmed me aching heart. Me family and kinsfolk had always been a cankered knot of secrets and despondency, showing little warmth and offering few smiles. We'd always say to one another, mostly in half-jest, we were followed by bad luck, working much too hard for everything and never able to enjoy our riches in peace—troubles of finance, in-fighting, and maladies of the brain following in our shadows.

I started really fearing for me sanity after I began traveling with Dr. Ildefonso Arias Álvarez and his mercenary crew in 2015 to study new rock formations. Truly unprecedented amalgams of mysterious stone and unrecognizable metals, seemingly melted out the natural terrain, as if they'd always been there or had been slowly developing unseen, layer-by-layer, for hundreds of years. How'd no one seen these before now? Who put them here? What were they made of? These questions cemented to me every thought.

It was after reading about these discoveries by several scientists that I'd reached out to Álvarez, whom I'd met years before one time in Cape Cod, and after a brief conversation, he'd agreed to me joining him and his team.

Aye, that reasty crew, that threadbare gang of his—Dr. Álvarez's—truly made of a wanton lot they were; forsooth, don't know meself where in tarnation he'd found them or why he'd chosen them, for they were a brawly bunch, always fighting and stealing and whooping in dingy dives. I'd seen them draw blades on one another many a time, seen them shoot dead several townsfolk who'd offended them with an "evil look o' them wack eyes" too. Alackaday, it helped me none to know these Fomorian-seeming, promiscuous criminals would be protecting us and carrying our equipment; howbeit, the doctor didn't seem to mind at all, didn't seem to have any trouble commanding them, and never did he offer no heed to me urging for the removal of these "men." Dealing with them was a source of high dread for me the whole trip. Just me luck!

On a torrid noontide in the Dominican Republic, we entered a sweltering jungle; 'twas an exotic scene of tropical pine trees amidst lurching palms, where the weblike, swollen roots of overgrown mahoganies wrung the rainforest floor. Calabashes jumbled with nopals, and an unaccountable understory thrived with abnormal shape and curious susurration. As we ascended, gigantic branches shot higher into a mist-obscured wildness surmounted by lofty, heaving mountains of grim grandeur, all of which threw me into a state of ecstasy and awe. Staggering over a dizzying steep, fearing the vertiginous drop, I beheld with wonder a terrifying manifestation of eternity carried by boundless mountains and the all-seeing greenness tempting me to rush into the endless unknown, putting a superb tremor of dread in me heart. Angry wind threatened to push me over the edge, so I escaped into a lush forest, though I feared being lost. This buggy, poisonous forest and its uneasy hills tried to bury me, swallow me; nevertheless, I'd become intoxicated with the vastness of the mighty mass and the sight of those infinite-seeming mountains, which were visible through holes in the canopy and yawning openings between the trees. A bosom of paradise! An imposing cage lifting me into celestial exultation yet squeezing me as I plunged through! The towering landscape gave no care to me tiny existence; yet it connected me, for a sublime instant, to exalted perpetuity in nature and forsaken oblivion, a glimpse at extreme forces greater than all things of this universe. For comprehension of me fervor, of this unsettling euphoria, I agonized to no avail: me presence—the presence of all human existence—deemed insignificant against such unfathomable greatness here.

Merciful Virgin! I soon encountered a clutter of stone monstrosities, silent, motionless, exuding out of large rocks as if they'd come from a long-forgotten, netherworldly source of torment and frenzy. Repellent sculptures of orgiastic nausea!

None had ever heard or seen things like this. No one had ever reported these. This must've been a ribald joke, I first thought—or, perhaps, part of a lost monument that had regrettably risen up by a divine-fated earthquake.

Ample scrutiny ushered me on to something else, something of a far worse intimation; I began to suspect anon what'd happened here must've been nothing short of awesome, exhilarating all psychic faculties of the morbid and irrational within me. A dark imagining gripped me mind: I thought of giant beings carrying the boulders out of sinister, underwater caverns, and then silently, with metaphysical force, they carried them here for some sacred meaning.

The boulders and their sculptures were covered with seaweed and many, many barnacles. So terribly cracked and holey were the stonelike beasts, their resemblance was like that of pockmarked skeletal carcasses of alien design. A rankling chimerism had been imprinted into these huge and contorted beasties, vaguely anthropoid colossi whose attributes might be described as part-dragonfish, part-earwig.

Ratlike pests had tunneled into the greasy statues, feasting on the lichen, piddocks, and rotting fish deep inside the stony cavities. Even when we got there, those plump, furry multitudes were chewing through the rock. All agreed they be no ordinary rats, these thrawn rodents, these voracious menaces. Capturing some became dangerous when they began spitting mephitic venom. This riled the mercenaries to shooting and killing many of them, which damaged the statues. The bullet-holes in the carvings bled a sludgy, bilious liquid pouring out, their rocky veins also producing a red, seeping fluid.

The boulders, which from their surfaces protruded mutilated appendage-effigies, must've been dragged up here from out the water of Davy Jones—but how? Did titans swim up and drag these monuments here, as I'd imagined?

Did I dare remain? Wirra! By Jove, stupid me, right then I shoulda sailed hence on me own. But stayed in that steamy, green demesne, I did, with the doctor and his crew, and for two bat-plagued months were we studying, experimenting, and note-taking. Yet—for all our research, skills, and tests, we understood nothing of what we found. Nothing of the resulting data.

Mystery and suspicion haunted us; a threatening air of fright and secrecy sat upon our shoulders. We all felt it, me and the crew and our leader the doctor; we all looked at one another as if silently saying "this don't feel none right," because we'd never speak the words aloud, lest the everlistening voodoo-brujas and hell-phantasms should be offended and curse us. The way townsfolk and even travelers would look at us—always with this foreboding sense of our doom—was enough to shudder me down to the marrow. If only I'd been forewarned of the baneful future ahead.

One day, during the final week of our expedition, we'd caught word of spooked villagers begging townspeople for help with a problem concerning hushed matters and secret omens: something about an Edenic dwelling, a "primeval paradise," or so we figured from all the whispered rumors and folk-translations. There just weren't many who wanted to talk to us or tell us the truth. We were being kept out from something, unless, that is, we could offer the right motivation, the right coin of the realm: money, lots.

Our money got us a few guides that led us on a night-journey across several secluded locations: forlorn beaches, sorrow-laden mangroves, and deserted ridges—places where loneliness itself cried with the retching, stifling wind. An eerie sameness, a dark relation to these locations, encased me in fear—fear I'd never leave these lands. I'd be abandoned. Every step o' the way, while I couldn't stop me own melancholy growing in these places, there were heart-hammering moments I felt targeted as if by a malicious presence in the pitch-black. When I brought up such sensations of this and how I'd seen red fangs behind us, no one knew what I was talking about. Perhaps it was only me; maybe they were too afraid to say.

While passing a ring of megalithic columns, the guides warned us not to look at it. Of course, I was always gonna, like rebellious instinct, so me eyes set on those scintillating earth-giants of sylph-charmed silver mesmerism; I considered the idea we might've entered a forbidden land, some-how crossed a threshold into a place the eyes of most would only see when closed or dead.

The profane shadows of those rocky pillars jumped out into the moonlight and danced around the great ring. As the dancing quickened, there was a moment I felt numb. Hardly can I remember what it was like, but I know I started toward the dancing, guttural darkness until someone pulled me away. It was like waking up screaming out of the worst nightmare. One of our crewmen began a wicked giggling, dancing too, and he moved towards the giant, shaitan-borne shadows.

The guides yelled for us to pull the man away, and it took all our combined muscle to do so. We asked our guides, but they refused to talk about it. At that time, I couldn't understand what just happened. I'd become dazed; me brain barely focused. All sensations were shadowy. As we hurried away from that spot, I kept looking back, wondering what it all meant. The dancing shadows were gone, and night hid those stony columns of white.

I wanted to forget it all; so, still moving with the group, I says to meself, "Blasted heat! It just bein' the heat. Don't go bloody off 'n' losin' it now."

I sheepishly looked up at the doctor and seen he'd heard me. He was looking back over his shoulder at me. Then, he gave a sidelong look down at me and laid his broad hand on me shoulder so he could grip it. With an austere nod, he'd successfully encouraged me and inspired a wee bit of bravery for me spirit.

Our guides brought us before the grim mouth of a huge cave, right on the witching hour, and it was only then they told us of a cult making human sacrifices here to exalt a "heavenly garden." From what the guides were saying, the cult couldn't have been more than a small, ragtag cabal of psychopaths and extremists. Its members believed this cave was where their "god" slept among the primordial soup from which all life had started.

Allegedly, angels had been seen and photographed floating above the pinnacle of the cave. Plenty of black-and-white photos of these "angels" were shown to us, some just looking like odd light-formations and others showed something else: a glowing-white, plated gauntlet, one with wings and sharp-ridged lames, pointing down from thunderclouds.

I'd been ruminating for so much time on the photos, the others had already walked in the cave without me. They found a grisly chasm anguishing from a fetid gut loaded with flyblown clumps of human corpses rising from deep down at the bottom. I hurried in at the sound of echoing fear. I leaned over to see into the dead-filled chasm, placing one foot on the moldering edge.

What I would then see was something no civilized man should ever witness, a scene so egregious it continues to creep over me red-tired eyes while I'm in bed trying to sleep— as if me dreams could ever be safe from it— and keeps me mad-awake until dawn. Even now, I find it all too difficult, trembling as I am, to write the words. It's just—there were so many young faces down there, re-

duced to thin slices of flesh. So many heads looked up at me, all flayed, the skin and hair peeled back over their bloody skulls. The most ugly, deformed crabs I'd ever seen moved between the limbs. Other things there be, much too unsavory, down there in the midst of the gut-churning ghoulishness. Black, thorny hands and feet moved in the Stygian darkness, clinging to the chasm walls. Were there truly things living down there? What could it have been?

The frenzied screams and vomiting from the crew only amplified me own terror as I recoiled from that hellscape. Those with more anger than fear started yelling and shooting at something down there. I ran to the doctor and found he'd just pulled down a strange oak-wood chest from a skeleton-guarded alcove, and the chest had a shocking engraving on it: "Wychyrst."

I'd known that name well: Wychyrst. I was reminded of me friend Valamir Wychyrst and his family. Why would his surname show up here?

No time to reflect—we were being ambushed.

A strident and ringing yawping, as thrumming and rhythmic as a raiding war cry, flew ghostly into the night, filling the cave with its haunting echoes. I'd been saved from a bullet to me own heart by Álvarez's cannonball-solid fist crushing through the now-splintered jaw of a robed figure behind me; I'd felt a bracing rush of wind across me face as the doctor threw that mighty punch. The doctor's team was firing back at unseen assailants, enemy gunfire coming at us from somewhere out in the darkness afar. Cloaked tatterdemalions, zombie-seeming brutes in moth-eaten rags, had come for blood as they swarmed in. Our guides had been throat-cut, and they were now dying and gasping, bleeding all over the sandy floor.

Standing back-to-back, Álvarez and I repelled howling waves of hooded gunmen and dagger-slashing, cackling hags with all the thick bullets our revolvers could dispense. I was roaring with every trigger-pull.

'Twas Hades itself a-callin', but Old Nick be damned!

Our ferocious, brawny doctor, stomping his fallen enemies, dropped his firearms and unleashed his gleaming axes. Towering very tall and strong, Álvarez looked daggers at the rawboned, half-naked primitives trying to kill us. His shirt was now torn to ribbons from the work of guns and cuts. Blood and beady sweat shimmered on his exposed masculine form. Ceaselessly, he chopped off arms and fingers, spraying rotten blood into the smoky moonbeams glistening along the animalistic lines of his ripped, bronzy pecs.

Utterly tense was our combat, and so barbarous it forced me into resorting to unsheathing me ancestral falchion and wielding it in me left hand while firing the revolver with me right. I'd block with me black blade, or just keep unwelcome curs away, while me gun was still blasting those incoming adversaries, whose faces were covered by gaunt, demoniacal masks.

A masterful stroke of me sword successfully bisected the mask of one of these lunatics, revealing the face of this attacker— 'twas a starved waif, just a scuddy woman,

must've been not older than twenty-five. Her maniac eyes had the marks of hallucinogens and vulgar toxicants—I'd seen this kind of look before on junkies linked to hoodoo packs, druidic clans, and urban gangs. The strange signs on her body expressed her involvement with something uniquely esoteric and bizarre. On her right thigh, a tattoo depicting a hand reaching out of a cave; under her lower lip, a gold crescent mark; and on her arms and shoulders, painful-looking scars twisted into convolute labyrinths folding around one another.

This woman was the only one we could capture.

It was almost impossible to say how many we killed, because all the bodies were gone—all of them. The crew, the guides, our enemies—spirited. Nary a trace. Álvarez and I had been the only survivors, and all we had now was the woman and the Wychyrst chest.

I couldn't go on like this. I'd had enough, really. We spoke with law enforcement and handed the woman to them. I told them everything, everything I could think of in me state of mind. Álvarez had some shady connections here, and he'd handed more money to the authorities so they wouldn't give us any trouble about anything we were doing. When the doctor and I returned to our camp, we'd found it in flames. That meant more time dealing with authorities, who really just seemed like they didn't want to help or couldn't do much. I can't express how extremely livid I'd become. I didn't even want to deal with any hospitals here.

I'd take me wounds as they were and just keep going.

In the spring of 2016, I was helping me parents in Massachusetts and surprised to be loving time with them. I was happy to be back in the United States of America, and I wanted to start writing several books on architecture and folklore of New England.

Me research took me out of Back Bay as I traveled southward, down to the ol' dreaming, misty bay of Hingham, where pinkish clouds did peek across soothing water, rejuvenating me spirit. Floating with the plashing and soughing of this enthralling bay came a numinous, gloriole-mantled emanation, a smoldering ambience harking back the eld eidolons still present here. The violet horizon lifted a miraculous silveriness to the greenish azure over the venerable town of Hingham.

On returning to Boston, I received an eloquent yet startling letter from Álvarez. It said the chest we'd found in the Dominican Republic contained majolica, delft, other earthenware pieces, and a box. In the box— a stone tablet and a gris-gris—the stone tablet being eighteenth century AD; the gris-gris a clay mystery.

I almost burned the letter without reading more. I didn't need this. What could I've done in another life to make this happen? In fear-fueled curiosity, I held the paper with clammy, white hands. I had to read.

His letter mentioned markings in Vulgar Latin, odd runes, and Early Modern English inscribed on the tablet. What could be translated said something like:

"O lords in night and dawn, we adore you! Immortal our souls are with you among the void and fire in the heavens. Vapor, rock, and flesh are in us. Your servant Gotthilf Wychyrst, who conjures the star-sailed ones and abyss-climbing messengers of outer worlds, shall allow not trespass nor misdoing against you."

When I called me old friend Valamir Wychyrst about this, he sounded happy to hear from me, yet troubled and anguished as well. He'd just lost his gran'dad Romualdo, and he'd invited some friends to stay with him to help cheer the air: Adolfo, Adolfo's wife Clothilda, and Clothilda's friend Ealhswitha Segreti. Valamir even said I could stay with them for the fall and winter if I brought the tablet with me.

He also mentioned he recently replaced one of his cooks and that some of his friends had been feeling sick. I was confused as to why he was telling me all this, but I was delighted to see he wanted to help edit me manuscripts, even give me some help on getting answers about this tablet. Of course, he wanted to buy it, so that meant me paying the doctor and waiting for it to arrive.

While long-trusted at-home nurses were aiding me parents, I traveled in hope of seeing Valamir and his parents, Odovacar Wychyrst and his wife Osyth. I arrived with the tablet at the gloomy, time-decayed Wychyrst mansion at the ending of fall. Their very private home was in an old place deep in an isolated, dark woods north of Plymouth. How was their thorn-shrouded dilapidation still standing? It was almost ruins. And to where had everyone else gone?

The first I encountered at the mansion was Ealhswitha, a heavenly damsel of soul-stirring beauty with porcelain-white skin and rosy cheeks. Her long, golden hair had a natural warmth of red. A diaphanous gown of white was snugly tight-fitting against the narrow waist and womanly hips of her slender, lissome body and feminine physique. Those white gloves and that cape she wore gave her an air of sophistication and high-bred class. She slinked out the fog to greet me, freezing me for an instant with awe and splendor.

We talked for hours, her and I, as we dallied around the foggy estate. What an experience! She was nineteen and came from a wealthy family who, like mine, had deep roots in England, the Netherlands, Ireland, Scotland, and Italy. We were amazed at how similar we were to each other. Like me own family, hers also held a respect to the past, to tradition, and to mystic superstitions of the ancestors. She clung to me arm all the time. Listening happily was she as I told her about me work and me recent adventure in the Caribbean.

When I asked more about her family, she stopped and shuddered. A mysterious mien seized upon her. She stared up at something behind me, and—I promise you—the look she made put me cold: a look as if she'd recognized an unforgiving haunter. I looked behind me, now seeing we'd come far away from the mansion. We were standing in the shadow of a gargoyle-begirt Gothic tower.

I turned—Ealhswitha had disappeared.

Upon returning to the mansion, I asked the maid, Fyokla, if she'd seen anyone.

She warned me, "Those who're smart would've left this accursed mansion."

I tried to get some clarity, but she wouldn't say. The maid did bring up how Ealhswitha'd become oft-visited by a dark angel escorted by the dead. After I asked her about that, Fyokla insinuated Ealhswitha was a doomed virgin who'd turned unwell from ill-dreaming—something about a warning, a prophecy that death would come from the Wychyrst tower. Serafino, a manservant, didn't like us talking.

The maid hurried into the shadows, and I left to recheck me belongings.

I couldn't find the tablet! It was missing!

After I'd been unable to find anyone, I walked into the mansion kitchen and discovered only a female cook. When she turned around, I'd instantly recognized her face! It was the woman who had tried to kill me in the Dominican Republic! The hellcat with the gold crescent under her lower lip!

I tried to capture her, but ran off she done, into the shadows of the servant-hallway. I followed but bumped into Serafino. I described the evil woman to him and told him who she really be. He said 'twas Rohese, the family's newest cook. We chased after Rohese together but lost her.

However, what we did find was a grisly mess—Adolfo's and Clothilda's corpses mutilated in a secret alcove behind a trick wall in the cellar. Serafino pulled out some shooting iron and rushed an attempt on me life! I drew me own pistols and filled his head heavy with lead before the dirty scoundrel could blink! But 'twere not the end o' that rat! Nay! What happened was pure madness—tell you what! Not so sure meself it was really happening, but tell it as I remember, I must.

Fyokla came in screaming with a great, big rifle. Before she could pull the trigger, I'd blasted her skull clean off. Out of bullets, I tried to run. Then, something grabbed me! The corpses of those two servants hadn't given up the fight! Me sword finished them, and their bodies transformed into piles of plates and nails!

Calling for help was useless—none of the telephones or electronics were working, and the phone in me hand tried to bite me ear! It became a fat, black spider—big as me head—hissing, wailing evilly. I smacked it away and crushed it under me boot.

With great surprise, I found a flashlight that worked well enough, then headed out through the fog. When I arrived at the tower, I kicked down a locked wooden door and infiltrated. I screamed for Ealhswitha to hear me!

A fog of glowing-white wraiths flew before me, and terror pulled at me every sense. I jumped back and put the weapon between them and me. Their unholy forms burned at me sanity so harshly I closed me eyes.

Amid the shrieking, I heard one say, "All who are Abbandonato have been cursed by us for many years, for you took our lives!"

I cried out, "Nay! 'Twas not I!"

"Centuries ago, your forefathers spilled our living blood as an offering to Gotthilf Wychyrst! For that, he wrought Tartarean power to enchant that sword you carry now! Do you know what it is to be his slave forever? Our only pleasure is the curse we wrought upon you and your family! We've haunted your souls and the dreams of those doomed to love you! We've been causing you all misfortune!"

I opened me eyes and yelled, "I done no offense!" I sailed at the ghosts; with them, I made vehement battle. Dodging their icy breath, I hollered, "Blameless, I be!" Stabbing and smiting the hellish foes, I shouted, "Me blade o' thine ire takes ye to thine end!"

The shades faded into the walls. The gargoyles now became animate and hungered for me death. Their daggers sailed through the darkness to reach me. I took many a wound but never surrendered. The heavy strikes and swings of me sword vanquished the hideous guardians swarming me.

"Gotthilf do come," came the voice of a spectre. "He transforms everything. He brings the world closer to that other side. He'll awaken his most high deity. His servants celebrate all across the globe! You'll be here with us forever, Dulf Abbandonato!"

Their words dragged me heart into the inferno, but I continued on, searching inside, lost in the labyrinth within the tower, an endless-seeming labyrinth eliciting woebegone phantasmata clung to the shadowy realms at the corners of me vision. Winding corridors, wounded by neglect and vandalized by abandonment and loneliness, loudened all me own misery and delirium. Every broken archway or crumbling statue here was another lament of me very own melancholy, me dissatisfaction. This unending maze of pitfalls, trapdoors, and dead ends was increasingly more and more slimy and convoluted as I ventured deeper in, as unfathomable as the pandemonium and hopelessness growing in me mind.

All thoughts were springing up from a side of me which wanted to hand over me soul, to give up this virtuous search, and go mad with self-annihilation. An unknown and uncanny bane of depravity and desolation was frothing and looming upon me. I trusted none of me panic-torn thoughts. Me heart clashed against sudden waves of self-loathing and abandon. Gone haywire from angst, I felt a dreadful malignancy taking form from the very blackest corners of me brain.

A bristly spider fell upon me neck and stung with horrid torment. I crushed it in me hand, but its venom burned. Bedeviled by half-paralyzing pain and hysteric with agony was I, now a marionette to an excruciating tarantism.

I began running aimlessly until me legs stopped, me limbs uncontrollable. An oppressive force mastered me body; I was forced into dancing and screaming and laughing wild. As I was in the grip of lunacy, so was the labyrinth—its walls and floors metamorphosed into bloody, pulsating inhuman flesh.

Sheer terror and frenzy cut away at me sanity. The insides of the tower changed and shifted, all halls moving. Through mangled passageways of blood and bone, I danced, screaming loud. Against me wishes, me hands dropped the light and sword, and me feet danced me toward the edge of a wide pit! I could do nothing to stop jumping down into the oubliette and falling far down into total darkness! But something caught me! A holy presence, a knightly hand, brought me to safety and pointed the way, revealing with glittering illumination a gilt door out from the blackness! I was free from the morbid tarantella, me flesh healed, and now I was in command of me bones and senses. And the glinting door did then open with a thunderous sound of valor, bringing forth merciful spirits who proclaimed themselves to be me long-dead ancestors! They bestowed to me a lamp and returned me ancestral falchion.

They were gone so fast, and I could say not a word to them, but before they dissipated, one of them shrouded ghosts imparted a message, "Because of your valiancy, the angels have restored your mind and body. They've allowed us to tell you this and only this: you now have a chance to free us, to free all our family forevermore from the curse that condemns us to perdition in the hereafter!"

When the ghosts were gone, me gut somehow knew Ealhswitha needed saving from the horrors and dangers of this vile mess. Another message from the ancestors. I wasn't leaving without her.

I ran through the gold door and avoided being crushed by giant masses of fat, skin, and muscles swallowing the existing rooms while new rooms of raw viscera took odious shape. I fled indescribable forms emerged from integument creeping between floor and ceiling.

I was racing lost in the labyrinth when I saw Rohese, that Caribbean she-devil, turn a corner, and she called me name. She was different, changing—a revolting kind of molting. Tentacles emerged outta the walls and wrapped around me throat, legs, and arms! That quean lengthened herself taller—an ugly spectacle. I swung me rage-enhanced arms and stabbed the skin-wall, hot blood spraying. Me left hand grabbed a tentacle, and I pulled on it; I dragged the blade up and sliced through the ones holding me sword arm. With the weapon free, I cut off the others and was unleashed, dripping evil blood.

Rohese had now finished her transformation into a freakish nightmare, a semi-arachnidan creature fouler than the deepest-thrown devils of hell, an awful lifeform whose hair-raising image torments me sleep.

This fata morgana grotesquerie wanted to drop a sticky net on me, but I threw the sword hard enough to pierce one of them eight black eyes. I evaded her pounding fins and hammering legs as she slammed the net down with incredible speed and repetition.

A thick tentacle jerked up from her mammoth, hairy head! This limb ended with a different head, a human one with a human face—Rohese's! She tauntingly called me name, but it was an infernal rasping imp-heaved outta Orcus more than it was a voice.

"Dulf, dear. Dulf, darling, lad," croaked the spiderish ogress.

I gripped the sword and pulled it across her belly, splitting her dead open. Her tentacle-head disjoined the main head and slithered into the witchy hands of shadow, too fast for me to catch.

No time for that, I grabbed me light and hastened to the next room, where I quickly found Ealhswitha in chains, crying. We were in a stone crypt—even here, a veil of purity and goodness surrounded Ealhswitha; seeing her brought me back to a state of clarity and responsibility.

I cut her bonds, and she embraced me with a hug and passionate kisses. She said the Wychyrst family and their servants had suddenly gone insane and locked her here, said the family wanted to use a cursed tablet to raise up from death their true ancestor, an evil enchanter who cursed all his descendants to servitude and misery after his children killed him almost two hundred years ago.

"Where they be?" I asked but soon realized I didn't need to.

I followed a trail of blood over to the corpses of Valamir and his family beside the great sarcophagus of Gotthilf. Their blood joined and climbed up the rattling coffin of stone, and I recognized the tablet on top. I gave the light to Ealhswitha, told her to stay by the door. She wanted to leave, but I knew this had to be dealt with now, here, had to try before all bravery left. Victory would me sword taste, some revenge for the dead who suffered because of me ancestors and their trade with Gotthilf hundreds of years ago.

I tossed open the coffin; saw the putrescent, maggoty corpse of Gotthilf himself; and then plunged the sword through his shadow-guarded heart. Flapping tentacles and inhuman eyes grew out of the heart! The two eyes of his face melted, and demoniac black sludge poured from their sockets! His talons grabbed me throat! I was resisting and trying to keep the sword in him.

"I am Gotthilf Wychyrst!" he bellowed with an otherworldly voice that swept out of some unspeakable Gehenna. "A true vassal of the most-ancients cannot die! I've only been sleeping for nearly two hundred years, and I had lived for two hundred years before that! My children hated my power, so they destroyed me, but only my body! I cursed them and all my descendants and theirs; I have been haunting them and manipulating them with madness and nightmares. They do my work! Valamir and the others thought they could buy my mercy, my love, with their sacrifices! Never! When I return, this planet will be returned to the antediluvian ones and the highest that ruled before them!"

Once free of his gnarled claws, I left the sword in Gotthilf's preternatural heart and grabbed Ealhswitha's hand. We ran out of the tower together while it was collapsing. And by Jove we made it out by the skin of our teeth!

The fog rolled away, as did the Wychyrst family, their tower, and their mansion. Nothing of their servants or belongings or even bodies. Where they all went, no one can say.

We spoke with police and investigators about everything, but no one believed us. Some tried to help, but nothing could be done. The whole incident was left as an abandoned mystery, a secret thrown into darkness. The Wychyrst family had been forgotten. Vanished.

Ealhswitha's dreams of a dark angel never again returned. Me parents started getting better, healthier by the month. In 2020, Ealhswitha and I married. There be nights we'll ask each other what really did happen at the Wychyrst tower, and there'll be moments the past seems foggy or unreal. Mostly, what we'd experienced involving the Wychyrst family all feels as if it had been a terrible nightmare we'd been walking in and out of for far too long.

I'm a-holdin' fast to me loves, me family. I make me prayers before bed, especially so at dead o' the night when eerie wind cometh rattlin' on storm-shaken windows as if 'twere whisperin' for me: "Dulf, dear. Dulf, darling, lad."

Prithee—let not ol' Wychyrst tower, and whatever unearthly fiends doth remain in its bowels, rear from out that fog of alien non-realities.

Matthew Pungitore graduated with a Bachelor of Science in English from Fitchburg State University. He writes articles for the DMR Books blog. He volunteers with the Hingham Historical Society. Matthew is the author of The Report of Mr. Charles Aalmers and Other Stories. You may email him at: matthewpungitore_writer@outlook.com.

She Saw It Creeping Up the Stairs

By MARK PELLEGRINI

Lisa and her mother have moved in with her grandmother! Grandmother is wheelchair-bound, and Mom is in the other room... So who is walking around upstairs?!

After her grandmother's stroke, Lisa began to feel a peculiar sense of unease that refused to lift. It wasn't due to concern for her grandmother's health; she was confined to a wheelchair but otherwise stable. No, the fear that tingled her extremities and bedewed her eyeballs wasn't the kind she could point a finger at. It was pervasive, it was oppressive, and it was all around her. The nearest thing to a source that she could lay the blame on was the house—her grandmother's house—but she knew even *that* wasn't quite right.

When her grandmother had fallen ill, Lisa and her mother had been given no choice but to move in and care for her. Her mother had surrendered a good job, and they'd been forced to bid farewell to their cozy little apartment, but neither of them felt any resentment toward the family matriarch for the predicament. Lisa loved her grandmother and never once questioned the choice to upend everything for her sake. The girls in her new 4th grade class weren't very mean, which made the transition infinitely more tolerable, although they didn't

seem to want to talk to her, either. Summer was around the corner, so it didn't matter very much, anyway.

At first, the possibilities of living in a suburban house had seemed quite promising, but when the realities of their new arrangement had solidified, Lisa realized it was, at best, a lateral move. She and her mother now lived on the first floor of the modest dwelling, most of which was underground and only invited sunlight in through the sliding glass backdoors. Her grandmother had the top floor, the entrance to which was on ground-level, and neither Lisa nor her mother ventured up there unless it was in answer to her grandmother's electronic push-button ringer. It was cozy living, as cozy as their old apartment, only now there was that oppressive, inexplicable sense of dread to put up with. So perhaps it wasn't such a lateral move after all.

And in regards to venturing upstairs only when summoned, the practice had nothing to do with Lisa's feelings toward her grandmother. It wasn't that she didn't want to help her; she liked boiling kettles for tea and climbing onto the countertops to retrieve cups from dizzyingly high cabinets. And it wasn't that she didn't enjoy spending time with her; she treasured their hours spent at the kitchen table, going over catalogs and marveling at the pretty things she never knew existed. No, it had nothing to do with her grandmother. The atmosphere was simply so much *thicker* upstairs. The floorboards whined loudly on their own in empty rooms, the air was fuzzy with an ocean of tiny floating specs, and there always seemed to be a growling, breathless hum inside her ears.

School was a respite from hairy oxygen and screaming wood, but as the unstructured half-days of early June ebbed away, it was clear to Lisa that she would soon have drastically fewer excursions away from home. And although the girls in class rarely talked to her, they frequently talked *about* her. Or, rather, they talked quite a bit about her house: an eavesdropped topic that made her feel like she was back home even when she was in the cafeteria. It seemed that her house bothered other people, too, although this was terribly discouraging common ground to share.

"Nobody makes it past that house," whispered one of the girls (Lisa thought her name might have been Sara) while scooting her chair in closer to the table. Sara whispered very loudly. They all did.

"I heard that six years ago, before any of us went here, there was a kid in Ms. Tanzler's class," a girl, possibly named Hannah, added. "He never came back from his paper route one morning. But they found his bike on the curb in front of that house."

"I heard that if you look in the bushes, you'll find piles of running shoes, like the kind joggers wear," said some blonde girl. "Because joggers can't make it past the house without something getting them."

"You ever notice that none of the houses on that cul-de-sac have pets?" Sara asked her rhetorical question. "It's because something keeps stealing the dogs and cats. I bet there are piles of collars in the bushes, too."

They hushed up when they noticed Lisa glance inquisitively at them for a fraction of a second. They didn't collectively giggle—as girls often do when they see the topic of their secret conversations looking at them— since the discussion was much too grave for giggling. Lisa internalized the magnitude of their words, digesting them all the way until the last day of school. She did not cheer with the rest of children when the bell rang and the teachers turned them loose. All she had to look forward to was two-and-a-half months sealed inside a house with walls that breathed down the back of her neck.

Lisa hadn't lasted a week in that round-the-clock environment before snapping and relaying all the gossip she'd heard to her mother, desperate for some sort of answers. Her mother provided and, in fact, seemed like she'd had a script prepared and memorized for that exact circumstance.

"People have been saying stuff like that for years, but none of it's true. It's all lies," her mother sighed as she stacked groceries in the freezer, which was stationed in the gloomiest, furthest corner of the subterranean first floor. "I lived in this house when I was a girl, and nothing got me, did it? And your grandmother's been living in this house since *she* was a girl, and she's lived a long, happy life. It's all just rumors," she added, closing the freezer door and extinguishing its frosty yellow light. "No one who has lived in this house, or visited this house, or jogged in front of this house has ever disappeared."

That was her mother's final word on the subject, Lisa could tell, but she had chosen her concluding word very poorly. "Disappeared." Lisa had heard that word used in countless contexts, but there was only one subject that she associated it with on instinct. According to her mother, her father had "disappeared."

Of course, Lisa had seen enough TV shows that she wasn't supposed to be watching to know what "disappeared" really meant. "Abandoned." "Walked out." "Left." He hadn't *actually* disappeared, which was the word her mother had used to describe his absence, but had simply decided, shortly after she'd been born, that he didn't want to be a part of her life. However, in the dramas on TV, the characters tended to sound angry when using the word "disappeared," like they were spitting it out because it tasted awful. Her mother hadn't sounded that way when she'd said it. Lisa recalled, only half-remembering that conversation exchanged half her lifetime ago, that her mother had sounded *sad* when she'd said it.

The best course of action was to play outside. Being *in sight* of the house wasn't near-

ly as bad as being *inside* of it, and she found the remainder of June expired semi-tolerably. If she'd had it her way, she'd play at the top of the street where the house couldn't see her, but her mother wasn't that relaxed in her duties. Her playtime was confined to the front, back, and side yards, where she hunted for shoes inside the bushes and shrubs, always in sight of the house that she knew was looking at her. The curtains rustled in old bedrooms that no one slept in, and the window glass made tapping noises when the air was still. Of course, this only ever happened when her back was turned, and wisely, she never looked back to match the house's gaze.

By July, things got worse. Her grandmother had begun to "lose her faculties," as her mother had worded it. She was getting weaker, sleepier, and spoke much less. She also pressed the button on the ringer less often, but that only worried Lisa even more. She didn't want her grandmother to die, and when hours and hours passed without the summoning ring, that was all she could think about.

The house had gotten noisier, too. The floorboards overhead creaked continuously, doing so at a pace that didn't match the rolling tread of her grandmother's wheelchair. No, it was distinctly the creaking crafted by feet; pressuring down upon the old wooden planks one heavy step at a time and navigating in straight lines across the ceiling. When this would happen, Lisa found the only solution was to crank the volume up on the TV shows she wasn't supposed to be watching, even though she knew she'd get in trouble if her mother heard the bad words. But her mother was always in her bedroom with the door closed, watching her own TV, and rarely came out anymore.

Eventually, the footsteps came downstairs, too. The staircase of the house was built in an L-shape; three steps up and there was a landing, then an immediate left turn and the rest of the steps ascended to the top floor. Lisa's bedroom was on one side of it, with the staircase separating her room from the living room on the other side. Being so staircase-adjacent, she could hear the steps creaking very loudly, very slowly, and very late at night. The creaks always came down first, then climbed back up, and never came down again.

"I didn't go upstairs last night," her mother informed her when she asked the obvious question. "It's just the house settling. It's normal for wood to creak when temperatures change at night," was her mother's follow-up remark, diffusing the situation before Lisa could become too visibly distressed.

But Lisa was already distressed beyond the remedy any words had to offer, and she began to feel desperately alone in the house, despite it seeming as though there were more people living there than were supposed to. And so one evening in mid-July when it was still purple out, Lisa heard the electric ringer go off, but she didn't do anything. She told herself that her mother would get it, but she knew that when her mother's bedroom door closed, it stayed that way until morning. The ringer went off

again, and she pretended not to hear it. She repeated this reaction until the purple had turned to black outside, and she heard the muffled voice of her mother call from beyond her bedroom door, ordering her to answer the ring.

Hastened by her mother's call, Lisa hurried up the first three steps of the staircase. Turning at the landing, she wasn't sure what would be looking down at her from the top of the steps, and her feet prepared to pivot and send her careening out the nearby backdoor. To her relief, she saw only the folding doors of the hall closet; a banal sight that lent her the courage to climb the rest of the stairs.

That courage had evaporated by the time she found her grandmother in the kitchen. She was parked at the table, lit beneath the dim orange glow of the overhead light. Her eyes were closed, and her chin was touching her collarbone. If she was breathing, it wasn't visible from the hallway. Lisa's heart began pumping ice water in a frigid circulation that made her fingers tremble. And, after inching her way across the linoleum floor, she used those trembling fingers to tap her grandmother on the shoulder.

"Grandma...? Are you awake...?" she asked in a timid voice that sounded like thunder amid the stuffy quiet.

"Hm? Oh, there you are," her grandmother said, first snorting the fog of sleep away and then fending the remainder of it off with a yawn. "Help me into bed, please."

Lisa smiled and nodded and felt her veins rapidly defrost. Her grandmother was okay.

Sleepy, but okay. While it would have crushed her if her grandmother had died, it would have *killed* her if it had been her fault. Pushing the wheelchair down the hallway, passing the open door of the staircase, she resolved never to ignore the ringer again. The worst scare she'd ever felt in her life had been her own doing.

Parking the wheelchair by the nightstand, Lisa turned down the bed and then helped her groggy grandmother rise from the chair and onto the mattress. She wasn't nearly strong enough to lift her grandmother, who did most of the work herself, but at the very least she could lift her plump, diabetes-ridden legs onto the bed. As she pushed the wheelchair into the corner, she heard the fading voice of her grandmother begin to mumble as sleep took its inevitable hold over her.

"*All these years, and I've never once looked it in the eyes,*" she said before trailing off into a blissful snore.

Lisa didn't understand what that meant, but as soon as she heard a linoleum tile in the kitchen begin to crinkle and creak, and then another, *and then another,* she realized that she didn't *want* to understand. She was down the hall and down the stairs in a flash, only this time, she closed the door at the top of the steps behind her.

The following afternoon, something happened. Something worse.

Lisa had played enough outside for one day. It was hot and it was humid, and she just needed a break. Being mostly underground, the downstairs was shady and cool; it would've been nice, if it weren't so scary.

But to curb those scares, Lisa resorted to her tried and true strategy of watching TV and zoning out. Camped out on the living room floor, she found herself engrossed in an hour of *Looney Tunes.* She was only nine years old, and there were still plenty of *Bugs Bunnies* and *Daffy Ducks* that she hadn't seen yet.

So Lisa never heard the door at the top of the stairs squeak as it opened. And she didn't hear the creaking of the staircase until whatever was coming down was halfway to the landing. When she finally *did* hear it, though, the ice water from yesterday returned to flood her veins, and her body went as rigid as a glacier.

There was a deeper, heavier noise as the mysterious weight came down upon the landing. Lisa's eyes, peeled clear and unblinking, were resolutely fixated on the television, although she wasn't really watching it. She'd focused on a tiny pixel near the bottom-right corner and was observing it change colors as the cartoon proceeded. There was a higher-pitched creak that sounded just a bit nearer. Now whatever-it-was had turned the corner at the landing and was descending the final three steps; the ones facing her back.

It could be mom, Lisa thought, but knew better than to say anything out loud. Because what if it wasn't? What if it was something else? Something that lived in the house? Something that had been watching her through bedroom windows, listening to her through closed doors, and breathing down the back of her goose-pimpled neck?

Whatever it might have been, it was

standing right there at the bottom of the stairs.

A minute passed. And then another. And then enough minutes passed for a commercial break to come and go. Lisa didn't budge. By the time the next *Foghorn Leghorn* started, she began to hear the creaking of the steps again. The sound moved away and then up, followed by the soft click of the upstairs door closing behind whatever had just passed through it.

She didn't shift or take her eyes off that one flickering pixel until she heard the glass door slide open and her mom come noisily in, making normal mom-noises. Hesitantly, Lisa turned and saw her mother setting her purse on a sideboard, fumbling with the paper bag full of her grandmother's prescriptions she'd just picked up at the pharmacy. Lisa blinked, which felt very good, and concluded two things in the time it took her parched eyeballs to moisten. First, it hadn't been her mother on the steps. Not now and never at night. Second, if whatever-it-was didn't see that *she* could see *it*, then it would leave her alone. Hopefully.

August soon arrived, but the month did not bring any hope with it. Lisa's grandmother had taken a turn for the worse and was rapidly declining, both physically and mentally. Before the month's calendar had made it to double-digits, facts had to be faced, and something had to be done. With a great sense of melancholy, Lisa's mother made arrangements with a nursing home, and a day later, her grandmother was escorted by some very friendly gentlemen to a place where she could "get better." Watching from the driveway as those gentlemen helped her grandmother into the back of a station wagon, Lisa observed that the wizened family matriarch did not seem to be aware of what was happening or even that she was going somewhere.

Lisa's observations were confirmed upon their visits to the nursing home, where her grandmother mostly stared at her hands and mumbled things in her mother's general direction. Her mother would nod, though that was the limit of the exchange. It seemed that Lisa's cheerless summer was getting gloomier with each new day.

Back at home, the door at the top of the stairs had been shut the morning her grandmother was taken away and it hadn't been opened again. The food in the kitchen refrigerator was left to rot, as neither Lisa nor her mother felt inclined to spend any amount of time on that empty floor alone, no matter how slight or how needed. The door was sealed and they lived exclusively in that shadowy, semi-subterranean bottom floor which still somehow felt less like a catacomb than what was above them.

The sealing of the door did not pacify Lisa's nerves. Because, be it daytime or nighttime, the busy hours or the small hours, she could still hear the steps overhead. Playing in the yard, or playing with her dolls, or even watching TV, nothing was distracting enough to pull her imagination in a direction away from those noises... and what might be making them. Her mother was spending more time in her bedroom with the door closed than ever before and seemed to be talking on the phone a lot. The conversations sounded upsetting, but Lisa never bothered trying to listen in for clarity amidst the muffled tones. She had troubles of her own to keep her occupied.

As August began to wind down, Lisa found herself not so much playing in the backyard, as pacing around its grassy slopes. It was more challenging than anticipated to stay within range of the house without actually looking at it. Playtime had lost its zest thanks to the chorus in the back of her head chanting, "Never look at any of the windows." And she knew the curtains in her grandmother's bedroom window were rustling. She couldn't see them, and she couldn't hear them, but some instinct deep inside told her that something was animating them and it wasn't the air conditioner.

"Hello there, Lisa," said a voice that was old but energetic. "Enjoying your summer?"

It was a momentary shock for Lisa, but her heart resumed its normal pace a beat later as she recognized the voice almost as soon as she'd heard it. It was their backyard neighbor, Mr. Sullivan, greeting her from the other side of the tall wooden fence that separated their yards. She had never seen Mr. Sullivan, as the fence was too tall for him to peek over the top, but she could tell from the cadence of his voice that he was an older man, a few years shy of her grandmother, and that he was generally very friendly. He must have been, as he was their only neighbor who didn't make it a point to avoid them. As to how Mr. Sullivan seemed to know she was in the yard when he couldn't see her, Lisa assumed he probably had a powerful hearing aid.

"Hi, Mr. Sullivan. Summer's been fine," Lisa answered, unable to coax even a glimmer of enthusiasm out of her vocal cords. "How are you?"

"Oh, I'm doing swell, just swell," said the voice of Mr. Sullivan. "But I hope your summer vacation has been more than just 'fine' so far! You won't have free time like this again until you're retired, like me. Then you'll be too old to enjoy it!"

"I know, I know. I'm having a great summer, really."

"Well, how's your grandma doing, then?"

"Grandma?" Lisa froze for a moment. She knew Mr. Sullivan was going to ask about her; it was a standard formality. But she hadn't quite finished preparing her words before the question presented itself. She did the best she could, anyway. "Grandma's gone. I mean, she had to go to a home. A nursing home. She got sick, but mom says she'll get better and come back in not too long from now."

"Oh my, that's terrible," said the voice of Mr. Sullivan. "What time this morning did they take her away?"

"This morning?" Lisa asked, uncertain of her concealed neighbor's assumption. "It wasn't this morning. It was a couple of weeks ago."

The voice of Mr. Sullivan did not vibrate through the cracks of the fence in immediate reply. Lisa stood quietly waiting for a response, but after a very long minute elapsed, she began to get nervous. Was he even there, anymore?

"Now, that… that just can't be," Mr.

Sullivan's voice finally whistled between the wooden planks. The suddenness of the belated sound gave Lisa a start, but it was his tone of incredulity that bothered her more.

"It's true. She went away two weeks ago. I'm sorry," Lisa rattled off, knowing better than to argue with an adult, but not entirely certain of what else to say.

"But, I've seen her," the voice of Mr. Sullivan replied, sounding even more distressed than Lisa. "I've seen her sitting at the kitchen window, where she always sits. I can see her from my kitchen window. She was there this morning."

Now it was Lisa's turn to be very quiet and very still. She felt dumbstruck; her mind wasn't trying to put the pieces of the puzzle together, it was simply suspended in a fog of confusion.

"Lisa? Are you still there?" asked the voice of Mr. Sullivan, who didn't have the patience to wait a full minute in silence for a response.

"Y-Yes, Mr. Sullivan. But," Lisa's brain began to defog, "it couldn't have been grandma. It must have been mom." Lisa knew that couldn't be true; just like her, her mother never went upstairs. No one had been upstairs since the door at the top of the steps had been shut. But still, it was the only explanation she could think of that didn't involve calling Mr. Sullivan blind or crazy.

"Well, I suppose," replied the voice of Mr. Sullivan, not sounding especially convinced. "I guess it was really just a figure. I'm so used to seeing your grandma at that window, I must have just glanced and assumed all this time. Well, give my best to your mom. I know this has to be hard on her. And tell your grandma I hope she comes home soon."

"I will. Bye," Lisa replied in a voice so low, she doubted even the powerful hearing aid of Mr. Sullivan could have picked it up.

She didn't hear the sound of rustling grass come drifting over the fence; perhaps Mr. Sullivan was just going to stand there all day. Lisa wasn't, and so she turned and marched back over the slopes of the yard. She didn't want to go back inside, but she felt even more nervous and exposed with the house looking down at her. Her eyes remained glued to her toes and sandals as she made that lethargic march toward the sliding glass doors. No matter what, she wasn't going to look up at the kitchen window. Whatever was watching her from up there, it wasn't her grandmother and it wasn't her mother. And she wasn't in a hurry to see what it was for herself.

Lisa *thought* about it for the rest of the afternoon, though. And she thought about it late into the night as she lay awake in bed with the covers pulled up over her face. The muffled sound of her mother having another heated phone call penetrated the drywall separating their bedrooms like molasses through a pasta strainer. She couldn't understand a word of the conversation, but the unhappy tones were distinct enough. Lisa wasn't interested in the goings-on of her mother, anyway. She had a much darker topic on her mind.

I wish it was grandma's ghost, Lisa

thought to herself. It wasn't that she wished her grandmother was dead—she loved and revered her far too much to ever contemplate such a thing—but she wished the presence in the house was her grandmother's ghost. Because then it would no longer be scary.

If her grandmother had died and she then heard floorboards creaking, or heard steps coming down the stairs, or glimpsed a shape in the kitchen window, she wouldn't have felt afraid. She'd have felt relieved. It would have meant that her grandmother was still there and that the presence stalking about had never been malevolent at all, but loving and sweet. Maybe they could even still have tea together and go back to looking over catalogs, like nothing had changed. Her grandmother would never hurt her, and neither would her grandmother's ghost.

But her grandmother *wasn't* a ghost. Her grandmother was still alive and still wasting away in a senseless haze at that nursing home three cities away. The thing in the house wasn't a ghost, either, Lisa suspected. She didn't know of anyone who had ever died in the house, at least assuming the stories she'd heard at school weren't true. The thing in the house was, at least in its own way, *alive*. And if it was alive, that meant it wasn't a ghost. That meant it was a *monster*. And monsters were so much *worse* than ghosts.

When the sun rose, Lisa was awake to greet it. She hadn't slept at all, though not for lack of fatigue. How could she sleep with a monster loose in the house? That would be crazy. Irresponsible. Stupid. And catching a

glimpse of her mother in the hallway as they took turns using the bathroom, it was clear that she hadn't gotten any sleep, either. There were bags under her eyes and wrinkles on her face that Lisa had never noticed before. No greetings were exchanged, and they both went about their dreary morning routines.

By lunchtime, neither of their dispositions had improved. For Lisa, it was due to the weariness from having been up all night and the refusal to risk taking a nap. But for her mother, she seemed to be dreading something else. There was an anxiousness to her, and for once, she was avoiding her bedroom, where the only telephone on the bottom floor of the house was located. A sense of secondhand anxiety washed over Lisa as she watched her mother's nerve-rattled behavior from the corner of her eye. From breakfast through lunchtime, her mother had done nothing but sit fidgeting on the couch, slurping down mugs of coffee that smelled funny. It wasn't normal coffee, not as Lisa recognized the aroma; it smelled less like a beverage and more like something found in a medicine cabinet. But clearly to Lisa, both of them were anticipating something unpleasant. However, while Lisa's dread was that something would happen eventually, her mother's expectancy was far more immediate. As the secondhand anxiety grew from seed to blossom, Lisa began to fear that her own fateful outcome was just around the corner, too.

The day continued in such fretful fashion until early evening when the phone finally rang. Lisa's mother set her mug on the coffee table, not even trying to find a coaster, and with hands that were jittering wildly out of control. A combination of nerves, caffeine, and whatever bad-smelling liquid had been added to the coffee had left the woman a trembling wreck, but still, she was on her way to the bedroom after hearing the first ring. Lisa waited until she heard the bedroom door close and then, having been aroused to suspicion for the first time all summer, followed on her tiptoes.

Before she'd even put her ear to the door, she could tell the conversation was a bad one; as bad as her mother had been dreading. The words weren't any easier to decipher than when she'd only been half-listening several rooms away, but she could tell that her mother was running the gamut of cry-talking. She was scream-crying in anger, whine-crying in protest, and whisper-crying in timid frustration. All the crying made it impossibly difficult to understand what was being said, though Lisa was able to pick out one word: "Mom." Her mother had been saying it a lot, and so the repetition gave her multiple opportunities to puzzle the syllable out.

Mom…? Lisa thought, depressing her ear from the door. Did that mean she was on the phone with her grandmother? Is that who her mother had been having stressful phone calls with all these weeks, at all hours of the day and night? It couldn't have been. They'd visited her grandmother the previous weekend, and she had hardly had the energy or awareness to maintain eye contact, let alone dial a phone and engage someone in an emotional debate. Lisa put her ear back against the door and listened on.

The intensity had ended, and her mother was still crying, but in the sniffling and gulping sort of way that meant the tears were spent and the tantrum was wrapping up. Her voice was very low and she sounded resigned to a state of agreeability born more from exhaustion than compromise. It reminded Lisa of how she used to feel when she was a few years younger, refused to eat her lima beans, and so her mother made her sit at the dinner table for hours until she, at last, choked them down. She still hated lima beans but accepted she had no choice but to consume them as told.

With the eavesdropping concluded, Lisa resumed her place in the living room, ignoring the sights and sounds of the television, and focusing her attentions primarily on the tiny green "on" light of the cable box. Her thoughts were elsewhere, desperately trying to put together what had upset her mother but doomed to failure for lack of tessellating pieces. An hour might have passed this way, or at least enough time for evening to transition into night.

That was when Lisa heard the bedroom door open and her mother came out. She had her shoes on and her purse slung over her shoulder. Her hair was messy, but a hasty attempt had been made to fix it. Likewise, some rudimentary layers of makeup had been applied, but more so to hide the puffiness of her post-sobbing visage than to impress anybody in the outside world. Lisa opened her mouth and began to speak, to ask her mother if everything was okay, but she was cut off before the first syllable could escape her throat.

"We have to go, honey," she said with a slight quiver in her voice that was struggling to steady itself. "We're going to go on an end-of-summer trip. We'll spend the night in a motel, but we'll find someplace fun, tomorrow."

"Sure!" Lisa responded as her face racked its muscle memory, struggling to recall how to smile. She didn't really care if they were actually going someplace "fun" tomorrow or not. They could be going to the dentist, for all she cared, but the promise of getting out of the house for even one night was enough to put a grin on her face.

"All right," her mother continued in a voice that was stable but not calm. "Get a suitcase out of the hall closet and pack your things. Enough clothes for a week. Be quick. We need to go!"

Lisa's smile became confused. A week? They'd be gone for a week? That made the corners of her mouth try to touch her earlobes. But the hall closet? There was only one hall closet in the house, and it was upstairs. Her smile died.

"Hurry up! We have to go before…" Her mother's frantic speed took a momentary breather as she searched for better words. "We have to go before the motels close. Now go on!"

Lisa was too young to know that motels never closed, so the explanation sounded convincing enough to get her moving. She wasn't thrilled about the prospect of setting foot upstairs, but she knew it was a chore she could complete in seconds. The hall closet was directly across from the top of the stairs. She could practically reach across the hall, open the closet, and pull out the suitcase without ever having to leave the top step. It would only take a second, and she could do it with her eyes closed. One second at the top of the stairs, and then they could leave the house for a week, maybe longer. It was worth the risk.

Leaping over the first three steps to the landing, Lisa ricocheted against the wall, reoriented herself, and rapidly ascended the stairs, two steps at a time. If she had to do this, she had to get it over with as quickly as possible. So with little heed to the caution and discretion she'd been applying for the past few months, she turned the knob and shoved the stairway door open with all her weight and momentum. It swiveled on its hinges at a dangerous speed, making a deafeningly loud crash as it impacted with the spring door stop set in the lower molding of the hallway. Had she ever flung a door open like that at any other time and in any other place, she would have been thoroughly grounded. But this was different. This was an evacuation. And that meant the rules were suspended, if only for a few seconds.

Lisa's resolve began to weaken, not from the sight of the dark hallway but from the stench of the musty air. Nothing had stirred that dusty, isolated level for weeks; or nothing human, anyway. Inhaling, she felt the tiny, itchy fibers cake the walls of her throat, and the air smelled so disgustingly stale, she couldn't help but feel like she'd just cracked open a long-forgotten crypt.

Perhaps she had.

Laying her eyes on the two shiny knobs of the hallway closet, Lisa was reminded of her task and the urgent haste with which she needed to complete it. Motivated anew, she proceeded with her original strategy, keeping her feet firmly planted on the top step and thrusting both arms outward toward the twin silver knobs. Grasping one in each hand, she spread the folding doors out to the left and to the right. They clattered violently along the metal rails and the consequences of such noisy methods began to dawn on Lisa. Surely, the thing upstairs had heard her. Surely, it was coming. But so long as she didn't look to the left or to the right, so long as she didn't see it and it didn't *see* her *seeing* it, then she should be fine. At least for the handful of seconds it would take her to yank the suitcase out of the closet.

But *what* suitcase? She scanned the interior of the closet again and again, but she wasn't finding any suitcases. There were coats on hangers, an old chrome-detailed vacuum cleaner, the leaf to the dining room table… but no suitcases. Could her mother have been wrong about where they were kept?

No, she just hadn't been looking hard enough. The curtain of hanging coats, some in plastic dry-cleaning bags, masked the far wall of the closet. The suitcase must have been back there. Lisa stretched her arms to their limit, but couldn't quite pinch the sleeves of the coats. If she was going to spread them apart and reveal the suitcase beyond, she would need to go *up* there. She

would need to go *in* there.

It would only take a second. Two steps forward, a swipe of both arms, a quick glance, and then back down the stairs, suitcase or no suitcase. *It would only take a second.*

Lisa took the two steps, shivering as her feet felt the filthy caress of the hallway carpet, and plunged her hands into the barricade of heavy winter coats that no one had worn since well before she'd been born. She began to part them, or she tried, but they were all packed in so tightly that she couldn't get the hangers to slide along the pole. Lisa shuffled her feet over the metal rail that marked the doorframe and entered the closet, the crinkling plastic of the dry-cleaning bags sticking to her arms and face like spider silk. She groped blindly through the sea of heavy wool until at last her fingers found the unyielding surface of the drywall, with nothing concealed between it and the coats. There were no suitcases in the hallway closet. She was certain of that, now.

Creeeaaak!

Lisa heard the sound over the crinkling plastic, the rustling coats, and the jangling hangers. It was such a distinct sound and one she'd been suffering all summer long. It was the sound of a step creaking; the bottom-most step of the staircase, just past the landing. It wasn't the tread of her mother, she could tell, as her mother ascended and descended the stairs quickly and lightly. No, this was a slow, gradual impression of weight upon the step, drawing out the whine of the carpeted board. She knew the moment she heard it exactly what was climbing the steps.

Creeeaaak!

Now it was on the second step. Lisa stayed motionless, her face buried in the musty-smelling coats. It was just like when she'd heard it coming down the stairs, or all the times when she knew it was watching her from the windows. If she just didn't look at it, if it didn't see her looking at it, it would pass her by.

Maybe. The strategy had worked in the past, but tonight felt different. The thing was coming up the stairs, but she'd never heard it come *down*. That meant it had been downstairs with her all day long, perhaps even longer. It had been watching her from around hallway corners and through the cracks of doors left slightly ajar. It had been waiting for her to do something stupid, like go upstairs all alone. And now it was coming up to get her.

Creeeaaak!

That was the third step. One more and it would be at the landing. One more and it could turn, look up, and see her trembling inside the open hallway closet. One more step and it would have her. It would only take a second.

And that was when Lisa panicked. Swatting the coats aside and tearing the thin plastic of the dry-cleaning bags from her face, she spun around in a crouching position and pressed her back as deep into the closet as she could fit. She could already see something—she wasn't sure what—begin to edge into view down the incline of the staircase. Flinging both arms out wide, she gripped the edges of the folding doors and pulled them noisily closed along the rail. She did so just in time.

Creeeaaak!

It was a deeper sound, the sound of something stepping heavily upon the wider platform of the landing. She couldn't get the closet doors to close completely flush, not from the inside, and so there was a slender crack between the edges where the two doors met. Lisa knew she shouldn't look; she knew she should just close her eyes and curl up tight and stay silent and motionless until everything was over. But she was too scared to turn her head away and much too scared to blink. Peeking through the crack in the closet doorway, she saw it creeping up the stairs.

At first, it appeared as though a shadow was being cast upon the landing, but it did not distort at the corner where the two walls met. It was *solid*. The thing was dark, and its complexion was fuzzy, almost misty, and if there was a texture to it or nuances beyond its awful silhouette, Lisa could not discern them at all. Its arms were like pairs of skinny polls and were so long that she could not see where they ended; their dangling lengths appearing to dissolve into the bristles of the carpet. Its legs were likewise pole-shaped, and they terminated at the carpet without any stabilizing shapes that might suggest feet. The thing almost looked like it was growing out of the staircase, but Lisa knew that couldn't be true, because it moved with heavy steps. Its appendages looked as though they were pasted onto the sides of its torso rather than set naturally into the joints of hips and shoulders. And the torso itself was a chunky thing, unwieldy and wide enough to span nearly the entire width of the staircase. There was nothing north of the torso, which made sense, because it was tall enough to brush the ceiling.

When it turned, it moved both ponderously and gracefully at the same time. The edges of its silhouette would fade, and new edges would grow from nothing until the thin air was blotted with the darkening shade. Then those edges would fade and new ones would manifest, repeating the pulsating effect until its bulk was facing the steps and it was looking up the stairs, directly at the closet door. It had no eyes, or at least it didn't have any that Lisa could see, but she could tell it was *looking* in her direction. It might even have been looking *at* her. So she held her breath and squeezed her knees tighter to quell their instinctive trembling.

It began ascending the steps, its own knees (if that's what they were) bending the poles of its legs (if that's what those were). Although they moved up the stairs, its legs never left the carpet, drifting up the steps until coming down with a terrible weight that made the wooden boards scream at length. The dark, eyeless, headless thing could step without ever leaving the ground. Lisa could see it accomplishing this act repeatedly, but she could not understand how it worked. Looking at it made her head hurt and her eyes lose focus.

It continued up the stairs in its weird, flowing way that made the steps scream so much she thought she could hear them splinter. Lisa had no idea what it would do when it got to the top of the stairs, and it was only a few steps away, now. All she wanted to do was cry, but she couldn't be sure if the thing had ears hidden somewhere within its dark confines, so she had to let her eyes and nostrils leak silently without any sobbing satisfaction.

She clutched her knees even tighter and nestled her chin deeper into her pulled-in thighs. If she began to shake, the dry-cleaning bags draped over her would rattle like tambourines, and then it would all be over. And if the thing was going to hear her, now was its best opportunity. A screen of dark, undulating fuzz curtained the crack in the closet door as the thing crested the top of the stairs and drifted its awkward bulk into the hallway. An inch-and-a-half of wood were all that separated her from it, and though she could see its body right there within poking distance, its flesh and skin looked no more distinct up close than at a distance.

The floorboards of the hallway began to creak, and in a minute's time the curtain concealing the crack in the door lifted, allowing the dim light from downstairs to rise and meet her teary eyeballs again. The creaks grew gradually more distant as it drifted down the hallway toward her grandmother's room. But even though it had passed her by, hadn't known she was there, Lisa refused to budge. It was still too close, and she didn't trust her wobbling knees to support her if she tried to make a break for it down the stairs. All she could think to do was keep still, keep quiet, and hope that it would retire to wherever it went when it was at rest.

The thing was restless, though. She could hear it moving through her grandmother's bedroom, then through the connecting bathroom, then back out into the hallway, then into the guest bedroom that had never been used in her lifetime, then back out into the hallway, then into the sewing room that hadn't been used since her grandmother's stroke, and then back out into the hallway again. It was moving through those rooms quickly, much more quickly than it had plodded up the steps, and its pace never seemed to fatigue. Lisa could tell that it was searching those rooms; that it was looking for something. It was looking for *her*.

The creaking of the boards grew louder. It was coming back. Lisa did not have to brace herself, as she was already curled up as tightly as she could be. The dark curtain passed by the crack without stopping, and then the creaking began to drift away. She listened as the thing made a circuit through the parlor, the dining room, and the kitchen. Then she held her breath again as it once more crossed the hallway, passing by the closet and resuming its search through the empty rooms. When it was done, it crossed the hallway again, searched the other end of the house, and then went back. It continued this loop without once stopping or tiring, and did so many laps that Lisa soon lost count of how many times the dark shape had passed by her hiding place.

She lost track of time, too, and as the minutes waned into what may have been hours (she couldn't tell), her ears began to search for a potential salvation. She listened for her mother, who had sent her upstairs to fetch the suitcase quite a while ago. Surely, her mother must have begun to wonder what was taking so long? Faintly, and scarcely audible over the perpetual whimper of the floorboards, Lisa detected the now-familiar sound of her mother crying. She was sobbing somewhere, maybe in her bedroom, and likely too lost in her own miseries to consider where her daughter might have gone.

This did not fill Lisa with reassurance. She needed her mother now more than ever, but all her lonely parent seemed to want to do was sit alone in her bedroom and cry. Lisa listened on anyway, silently begging for her mother to snap out of it and come save her. There was a break in the sobbing, followed by muffled words that carried the same resigned rhythm as those she'd heard while eavesdropping. Then there was the *click* of a telephone receiver hanging up, followed by more light sobbing. Eventually, even that trailed off into a silence that was interrupted only by the moaning of abused floorboards.

Lisa waited. It was all she could do. Her mother was done talking to whoever she was talking to, and she was done crying about whatever she was crying about. She should be coming up to get her any minute, and then everything would be all right.

Yes, everything *would* be all right. Lisa wasn't worried about the monster getting her mother. If anything, it was the *monster* who should be concerned about her mother getting *it*. She recalled many times when she was very small and thought she saw monsters in her bedroom at night. They were seeping out of the open closet door, or reaching out from under the bed, or standing vigil in the darkest corners where the nightlight couldn't reach. But every time she called for her mother and she fearlessly strode in without even turning on the lights, the monsters vanished and did not return for the rest of the night. Children feared the Boogeyman, but the Boogeyman feared mothers. Mothers could *always* beat the Boogeyman.

So Lisa waited some more, only now a glow of hope was beginning to thaw her frozen bloodstream. Her mother would have to come up looking for her soon, and when she did, the thing would go away. And then they'd leave the house and go on their trip and have fun and smile and laugh again. She just had to wait.

After a while, a longer while than she'd anticipated, Lisa heard the sound of floorboards creaking. Not the ones upstairs, still being assaulted by the pacing entity, but boards that were further away and supporting a much lighter weight. They were the boards of the first three steps leading up to the landing. Lisa smooshed her mouth harder into her thighs to keep the squeal of joy from escaping her lips. Her mother was coming, at last.

Lisa fought back the tears so that she could see without impediment, and to her delight, it was true. Her mother was standing on the landing, looking up the staircase and directly at the closet door. Giddiness

welled up in her, and she wanted to spring out the closet and rush down the steps into her mother's arms. Then they could hurry out of the house and leave it behind forever. Her mother was standing right there on the landing; she was so close. It was almost over.

Creeeaaak!

The sound of a moaning floorboard, as near as the sewing room, urged Lisa to favor discretion. The thing had *very* long arms and could grab her before she made it across the hallway, well before reaching her mother's arms. No, it was best to play it safe and wait until her mother came all the way up the stairs and scared the monster off with her presence. She'd been careful for this long. She could be careful just a little bit longer.

Her mother was beginning up the stairs, albeit very slowly, and Lisa felt her anxiousness draw closer to detonation levels. Why was her mother taking so long? Lisa suppressed her nerves, took a more sober look at her mother's face as it drew incrementally nearer, and the unsettling truth began to manifest: *she* was scared, too.

Lisa refused to lose faith, even in the presence of this disheartening reality. No, mothers beat the Boogeyman the same way rock beat scissors. Her mother would save her. Yes, her eyes were puffy and her wrinkles were deep and her fingers were trembling, but that didn't matter. She was practically at the top step. In just one more breath, she'd be in the hallway, and the thing would cringe away and then Lisa could finally come out and escape. Only half a breath, now.

And so Lisa watched, eager and at the ready, fully prepared for the do-or-die moment when her mother stepped into the hallway and she could come leaping out like a spring in a trap. She watched as her mother stopped at the top step, closed her puffy eyes, and groped blindly over the surface of the stairway door. She watched as her fingers found the knob and began to carefully pull the door shut. She saw—only for an instant—a fresh cascade of tears leak through her mother's tightly clenched eyelids just before the door shut and the hallway was plunged into absolute darkness.

She listened and heard her mother's footsteps rapidly descend the stairs, squeaking the boards on the way down. She listened and heard the backdoor slide open and then slide closed on its grimy rollers. She listened and heard the engine of their car rev up, followed by the sound of the car backing recklessly out of the driveway. She listened and heard the engine's rumble fade into the distance until not even a late-night echo remained to keep her company. And she listened until the only noises she could hear were the floorboards of the hallway rhythmically creaking louder and softer as the thing paced up and down in its tireless search.

It would be many more lonesome and terrifying minutes before Lisa began to grasp her situation. For a time, she remained huddled up, convinced that her mother would be returning soon, perhaps with the police or some other cavalry who would drive the monster away and save the day.

But as the small hours of the night proceeded one after the other with nothing but the creaking footsteps to count the passage of minutes, Lisa at last realized that her mother wasn't coming back. Even her mother was scared of the Boogeyman.

I have to get out, she thought, trying her best to uproot the despair that was planting itself in the soil of her heart. And if she was going to get out, she would have to do it herself. Lisa considered what she knew about the monster and what she knew about herself. She'd heard the monster moving for months, and now she'd even witnessed it. The thing was slow, even when motivated. And she knew how fast she could move, especially when motivated. She also knew just how far she had to go to get out: down the stairs and out the backdoor. She'd even have gravity on her side, boosting her momentum down and out. The path to escape was realistically quite short. She could make it. It would only take a second.

Lisa waited and listened. It was the same series of sounds she'd been hearing for hours, and she didn't expect them to be any different, but she had to be sure. She traced the path of the thing as it made its endless rounds and waited patiently for her chance; the chance she knew in hindsight that she should have taken when her mother was still home. The chance came and went as her nerve steeled and softened, but that was all right. The thing's path and pace never altered. The chance would come again. And again *and again*, if need be. Lisa let her adrenaline build steadily until the lid suppressing her eagerness finally burst. Her chance was coming back; she just needed the guts to take it.

At last, her chance looped back around to her, and now was the time to seize it. The creak of the boards, she could measure by ear, was as far away from the closet as it was going to get. The thing was at the far end of the hallway, either at the threshold or just inside her grandmother's bedroom. It wasn't a tremendous gap between them, but it was the most she was going to get. Digging her fingertips into the crack between the closet doors, she spread them open with a clatter so loud, it startled even her own hysterical heart.

Her movements were clumsier than intended. She hadn't realized how cramped her body had become during the hours spent in the same position, and so her joints moved stiffly, achingly. But she powered through all that, and no sooner had she spread the closet doors, both of her hands found the knob of the hallway door and gave it an immediate turn. She flung the door open with a violent crash, and the light from downstairs plowed into her eyes with an almost equivalent intensity. Her right foot went streaking through open space as it plummeted downward in search of the top step. Stiff and cramped as she was, Lisa had cleared the two major obstacles to escape in *less* than a second.

But then she *looked*.

She didn't mean to. It was intuitive. Mechanical. An instant before she evacuated the hallway, her curiosity demanded to know how much space was between her and the thing out to get her. And so her eyes, ever-so-briefly, darted to the left. And she saw it. And worse than that, *it* saw that *she* saw *it*.

And that's when its eyes opened; the eyes that her grandmother had mumbled about in a state of fatigued delirium. The eyes she'd said she'd never looked into. Lisa was looking into them now. She only did so for a time too short to measure, but that was all it took. The milky, swirling orbs embedded in the center of its dark, blocky torso sprang open. Their empty, blank voids caught her jittering pupils, and without hesitation, the thing moved toward her with a speed like spilt water across a kitchen table.

Its long, pole-like arms slid across the hallway carpet without ever disconnecting from the surface. The floorboards screamed in rapid succession, like a steamroller was careening overtop of them at racecar speed. In the instant it took Lisa's right foot to touch down on the top step, something that felt like a clamp made from a hundred icy caterpillars squeezed tightly onto her left ankle. She did not deviate from her path, but found herself descending the staircase even faster than she'd anticipated. She tripped and dove headfirst down the stairs in a series of whirling summersaults. She could feel the frosty, squirming grip ooze rapidly up her leg as she struck every step on the way down. Her neck was broken by the time she hit the landing.

But that wasn't what killed her.

By the time the sun came up and the morning joggers began their wheezing ritual, the police and the paramedics had just about finished cleaning up. Through a sopping wet face and with a panic-stricken tone, Lisa's mother explained to the authorities that she'd left in the middle of the night to run a quick errand at the convenience store. Her daughter had been soundly asleep and none the wiser when she'd crept out the door. While an investigation would still have to be followed through as a matter of procedure, the police were confident that it was all just a tragic accident.

At the same time, Lisa's grandmother was undergoing the checkout process at the nursing home. She'd made a full recovery, both physically and cognitively, and was ready to return home with a clean bill of health... much to the bafflement of the on-site physicians. As they watched her pack her things with a smile on her lips and a whistle through her teeth, they whispered to each other that she didn't just look "back to normal," but a whole ten years *younger*.

It would be a few minutes after the departure of the ambulance that Lisa's mother would receive a call from her own mother, telling her to pick her up and bring her home. Bidding a languid, heartbroken farewell to the police officer who'd interviewed her, she shuffled toward the backdoor to sit in the dark of her bedroom and await that inevitable phone call. Watching the poor woman drag herself around the back of the dark and lonely house, the officer couldn't help but note that despite her pink eyes and grieving visage, she was *very* pretty. In fact, she looked much too young to be the mother of a girl that had been even Lisa's tender age.

It was a callous thought and the officer felt immediately guilty for it. He recalled the terrified look on that poor little child's face, her head on backwards and her eyes still wide open, staring sightlessly toward the top of the staircase she'd fallen down. He tried to forget, but it was the kind of image that would haunt him until his temples went grey and dementia wiped his brain clean of all but basic bodily functions.

From the margins of his vision, he thought he glimpsed something. At that moment, he was willing to embrace any distraction, but something in the back of his mind told him to let this opportunity go. It might have been a curtain in the parlor window of the house rustle ever-so-slightly. Or it might have been nothing. The house was supposed to be empty—he and his partner had checked and confirmed that—and the young, pretty mother was by now only at the backdoor, if she'd even made it that far. It was probably nothing. But he didn't look, anyway.

That something in the back of his head didn't speak to him in words but communicated through a more primal urging. It rekindled a sensation he hadn't felt since he was very small—as small as that little girl he was trying to forget—when he slept with the covers over his head and his back to the closet door. It was that instinct that told him to never look the Boogeyman in the eyes.

Mark Pellegrini is a native of Bunnyman Country in Northern Virginia, though he currently lives just East of Boggy Creek Country in Central Arkansas. Mark is a prolific comic author, having written the war-action-rabbit **Black Hops: U.S.A.-*-G.I.**, *the tokusatsu send-up* **Kamen America**, *and the political parody* **Wall-Might**. *His horror-fantasy novel,* **They'll Get You** *is currently available on Amazon.*

Fail Early, Fail Well

By W.L. EMERY

Some projects are doomed to failure... Sometimes, it's better they fail sooner than later! It is Vinellius's job to ensure the worst of these projects fail just right!

Vinellius leaned back on his couch and read the transmission again. The Most High Chair of Transformix was offering a compensation package far above the current rate. In addition, there was a substantial bonus for early completion and shareholder options that would make any Klazonian offer up his mate and firstborn offspring in trade. Along with this, the proffered perquisites were deemed sinful in twenty-seven separate and distinct religions. The catch was that the current planetary simulation project had to be failed before it was allowed to begin. Time was of the essence... and Vinellius had heard it all before.

He'd begun his career in ecological science and management, then after three planetary revolutions and six meaningless assignments he'd switched to power generation and transmission grids, which seemed to suit him better. He was in the middle of his second project and was socializing with a few friends after the local work period. There were seven of them, all imbibing their favorite recreational judgment-impairing substances when Raheed-Ralell jokingly suggested that if someone had failed his current project before it started, the FreeGen corporation would have saved itself a forty-point crash in their stock price, sixty million stellar credits in bribes to planetary officials, and a black mark in the interstellar news.

"Why?" someone slurred.

"Because the power plant is a guaranteed failure, that's why."

"How so?" Vinellius asked.

"Solar energy succeeds, providing you have an adequate or better electrical energy storage system, and if the sun shines all the time, and if there's no atmospheric impairment between the solar collection device and the sun."

"We know all this. What's the problem here, because this is the first I'm hearing of the plant construction project failing?"

"The local bureaucracy opted to invest in high temp H_2O cells," Raheed paused to take a long pull at his substance delivery device, "meaning that the resultant power is stored as heat. Now we discover that the climate around the energy plant is below freezing at night. Every night."

"What?"

"That's right. When the sun falls below the horizon, the temperature falls below the freezing point of H_2O."

"Ah... excuse me, genius, but has it occurred to you that spraying some insulation around the cells might actually solve this seemingly major setback?" Slysius asked, speaking carefully so as to avoid biting his tongue. Raheed gave a short laugh.

"Yes, all-knowing one, someone did think of insulating the cells. In fact, the first being to make that suggestion was an excavator pilot during his refueling break. He was ignored. Instead of listening, upper-middle-lower management strongly suggested that the cells be buried underground, where the temperature is always constant. So they did that, which set everything back... a long time. But as a bonus, since the cells are buried, they won't be an eyesore to the inhabitants and won't disturb the mating habits of some local quadruped whose name escapes me, nor will they destroy the entire planet if they leak."

"Wait... if they leak? Leak what?" Allasis asked, trying to bring Raheed into focus.

"Water."

"Water?"

"Sh'right. Water. The water got contaminated by the radiation from the sun, and if it ever spilled, it would get all over everything and destroy the world," Raheed said carefully.

A short silence followed, then Allasis started to laugh. The rest of the group joined in.

"How do they know this?" Allasis gasped.

"Some elected governmental official said so, and a lot of people believed him," Raheed replied.

"Do they know about the temperature down there?" asked Slysius, desperately trying to concentrate.

"Maybe, maybe not. It's too late, now, unless they want to cut their losses and either build more cells on a superstructure of some sort or import Zy-Three cells in defiance of six or eight political groups who object to the whole business."

"I suppose someone could always poison the members of the political groups," Allasis offered.

"Yes! Use the contaminated water," Ithley suggested.

"Wouldn't work. You'd poison half the government along with them."

"And this is bad because?"

Vinellius stopped listening. If someone, a group of engineers and technicians, had successfully failed the project before it started, the local government would have saved itself a lot of credits. Millions, hundreds of millions, maybe even several billion.

The next day he invested in an option to sell FreeGen at its current price. Then he placed an advertisement for a journalist, no experience necessary. In three hours, he had nine newly licensed journalists who were eager to put some blood in the water. Working separately, they published investigative reports for the next fourteen planetary days. Elected officials named in the report went into denial mode, then started a finger-pointing and name-calling contest. When several highly placed governmental officials were arrested for bribery, fraud, and market manipulation, FreeGen stock dropped to a fraction of its former price.

Forty-two planetary work days later, Vinellius exercised his option to sell and transferred a significant number of galactic credits to P-Bank Three, a galactic financial system that had an unsurpassed reputation for privacy. He then bought one ticket off-world, luxury class. He cheerfully stiffed the journalists as he left.

The idea was slow to catch on, but a small corporation hired him and his team at a slightly discounted rate. The project, a subterranean transportation system that was projected to cost in excess of three hundred million stellar credits, had been created and designed by government officials. Neither the officials nor their staff had the slightest idea of just how this project might be accomplished and what the cost might do to the local economy. Unsurprisingly, the officeholders were a group of overpaid actors who attained their positions in government by winning a popularity contest. Vinellius did a brief study, then made his presentation to the local government and the commercial media. When he got to the part about the area being prone to earthquakes, the projected fatalities of people caught in the tunnel when it collapsed, and the cost of the subsequent civil suits against the government, the project was officially failed in a flurry of defamatory accusations, derogatory insults, and emphatic denials. A segment of the government tried to revive the project and was dismissed on grounds of malfeasance; one took refuge in his private workspace and had to be forcibly extricated by a security team. Vinellius collected his fee and received two more offers before he left the planet.

Failure was his business, and business was good.

Vinellius sent the Transformix proposal to his legal firm of choice and received an updated version that favored his company over the client, and which was impossible for a lay-being to decipher. The concerned parties and their official representatives argued for over an hour before a grudging acceptance on both sides was achieved, with the caveat that all parties concerned were equally displeased. Vinellius then booked his flight to Stannis Five, Orbital Station Two.

The flight was uneventful, and five standard galactic periods later, Vinellius stepped through the airlock and into OS2 along with several hundred other beings. He had no trouble finding his living quarters, where he stored his few personal belongings in the security locker. He then sent an auditory message to The Most High Chair of Transformix, a being he'd never met and whose name he knew. He was reclining on his couch, watching the holo-tube with the auditory set to silent when his comm-link signaled a connection request. He accepted the request, and a life-sized hologram appeared in the space six feet in front of him.

The woman was a Ch'chellian, and her feathers were standing up, indicating that she was in a state of stress and somewhat angry.

"You're Vinellius?" she asked.

"I am," he responded. "And you're The Most High Chair of Transformix?"

"I am, but my tenure in that office is in serious jeopardy."

"I understand. We should meet, then, in a secure, private location along with whatever trustworthy staff and political allies you choose," he replied, rising to his feet.

"I've reserved a rest and recreational facility for six hours at the end of the current work period. Will that be suitable?"

"If it suits you, it suits me. Send me the time and location numbers, and I'll be there."

"Sixteen hundred hours, standard galactic, at level seventy-three, subsection twenty-seven, unit eight-point-three."

"So be it."

Vinellius broke the connection, then waited. When nothing happened, he returned his attention to the holo-tube. A local company was offering xeno companion rentals for any and all purposes, including religious ceremonies.

He had no trouble finding the meeting place, but the sign over the entrance gave him cause to wonder if he shouldn't cancel the entire business. This section of the station was near the skin, and the department of maintenance hadn't bothered to cover up a plethora of welds and patches that held the atmosphere inside the station. Most of the area was either unused or designated as subsidized living quarters. A crudely lettered sign over the open doorway announced *Whalix's Recreational and Relaxation Area—We Are Xeno Friendly*. An electrified security grating blocked the doorway, behind which stood three Messtoovian security guards.

He walked up to the gate while the guards fingered their long-barreled slug throwers and twitched their tails nervously, their outsized ears flicking back and forth.

"I'm Vinellius. I'm here for a business meeting."

A small security mech rolled into view.

"Present standard galactic identification," it said in a well-modulated tone. Vinellius reached into his side pocket, and the three Messtoovians each took a step forward while simultaneously raising their long arms threateningly. In a gesture meant to outshine the other two, the lead Messtoovian took a second step which brought him too close to the electrified security grid, allowing the barrel of his slug thrower to ground out. The unfortunate guard made a peculiar howling noise as he performed a brief dance before falling over and breaking the connection. He lay on the floor, twitching and panting while the others laughed.

Vinellius ignored all three and showed his galactic identification to the mech. The grid folded up into the ceiling, and the two remaining Messtoovians stood aside to let him pass. The room was dark, illuminated only by vestigial lights along the floor. A lamp placed in the center of one table at the rear of the room was abruptly switched on. He had no trouble recognizing the large female Ch'chellian seated at the table with her back to the wall. He went over and seated himself across from her, saying nothing.

"You're punctual. Most beings would compliment you, but I don't care one way or the other."

He smiled thinly and remained silent. The silence stretched out with neither one speaking. After some minutes, she relaxed.

"I'm called Styxal. I'm still The Most High Chair of Transformix, although the gathering of the High Chairs, which is three days from now, may change all that."

"And the project you want me to fail is?"

"One orbit and a half ago, an independent explorer sent Transformix and three of our largest competitors an announcement. They claimed to have discovered a new life-supporting world that fell within the parameters of a class one planet, and a second planet in the same system that was class five. They offered the location up for sale to the highest bidder. The one little factoid that spoiled this discovery was indigenous intelligent life. Carbon-based life."

"I assume this lifeform is on the class one planet?"

"If it wasn't, you wouldn't be here. If we can establish friendly relations with the indigenous inhabitants and convince them that we are a peaceful, benevolent race, and we would never think of exterminating or enslaving them while raping their planet of its natural resources before departing and leaving the survivors to starve, *and* in the opinion of the galactic council we can achieve all this benignly, the council will designate us as the primary contact between the indigenous population and the rest of the known universe. Needless to say, this would be a valuable position to have."

"What have you got so far?"

"We sent out a clandestine exploration team to gather data about planetary conditions, language and culture samples, and, optionally, a collection of simple life forms. The data they brought back was somewhat problematical, according to our life-science and xeno-biology departments."

Vinellius thought for a moment, then said, "The usual procedure with something like this is to program the holographic chamber with data retrieved from the planet in question and direct the xeno contact group to practice in the chamber, the thought being that when we attempt to make contact with the native inhabitants of this newly discovered planet and establish a favorable working relationship, we'll at least understand language and custom. How far along are you on this?"

Styxal ruffled her feathers and shifted in her seat.

"Some progress has been made, but the project leaders and the head biologists are not communicating effectively. Both blame the other for the work stoppage, and now the High Seven are proposing to import specialized labor from the Mallorius System. This would not only drive the cost up exponentially, but would prolong the project to the point where a competitor will assuredly complete the required holo chamber before we do. Millions, perhaps hundreds of millions, of credits would be lost. Being Most High Chair, I'd be blamed."

"I see. Very well, set up separate meetings with the head biologist, the xeno culture engineer, and the chief project leader—and I don't mean the official project leader, either. I want a meeting with the being that's actually doing the work. Moreover, I neither want nor need more than one meeting with each. After that, we'll make some decisions on how best to fail this credit-burning wormhole."

"You believe you can fail it?"

"It's a certainty."

Neither meeting took as long as Vinellius thought they might. Wezzin, the director of the Biology Department, arrived with three personal assistants and a small entourage of commercial media workers, all of whom Vinellius curtly dismissed before the meeting started. Wezzin turned out to be an egomaniac with delusions of competency and had decided that this meeting with Vinellius warranted taking precious time away from his many other responsibilities. Vinellius sat patiently and was treated to a lengthy description of the project and the impossible life form specifications he'd been given, which segued into an extended lecture where Wezzin described his professional accomplishments, beginning with his graduation from an enormously prestigious school that Vinellius had never heard of. He went on to describe his personal contributions to the rebuilding of the civilian medical care system on Tinnularis, which were as significant as they were numerous.

Vinellius was familiar with this project—a system that had not only gone bankrupt but had destroyed the entire planetary economy with an efficiency that was as silent as it was brutal. The system was now cited as a textbook case of basic economic theory and the failure of government offi-

cials to understand it. Vinellius quietly excused himself, promising to return shortly.

He made his way down to the holographic engineering department and discovered that everyone was taking a scheduled relaxation period, leaving only Director Rallis and a few socially unpopular subordinates to handle whatever problems arose. Rallis beckoned him into his personal workspace and flipped the privacy screen on. The door and windows immediately darkened to pitch black.

Vinellius introduced himself, stating that he was a consultant working directly for one of the High Seven.

"Consultant? What do you consult about?"

"That's not pertinent to this discussion. What I'm here to find out is the cause of the delay in the holo project and the feasibility of the environment you're going to create."

"Pertinent? I'll give you pertinent. I know why you're here, and I know just who hired you. It's that Wezzin. He's behind all of this, and if you're smart, you'll find a way to get rid of him and make it look like an accident. You'll be doing the universe a favor, believe me."

"As I said—"

"What he claims he wants can't exist on the world he's describing. It violates the known laws of physics and substitutes a few new laws that are supported by superstition and ignorance personified."

"Assuming Wezzin is responsible, he has to have some sort of evidence that what he proposes actually exists on another world. I presume that the exploration team passed everything they discovered along to him?"

"Exploration team. Is that what he said? If those—have you spoken with them?"

"No, I saw no reason to. Until now."

"Until now is right. I think there are two of them left on-station. The rest departed for parts unknown on the first freighter that could be cajoled into taking them."

"Why didn't the other two go with them?"

"Both are being detained by security for disorderly conduct in public, extremely impaired judgment, and destruction of personal property. Until someone pays their fines and compensation to the injured parties, they aren't going anywhere."

"I understand. Or at least I think I do. Well, I thank you for your time and cooperation."

Gordillion, the security officer in charge of the detention area, rolled his eyes and shook his head.

"The two higher learning types? Calling themselves bioengineers?"

"I would suspect so," Vinellius said.

"Arrested and detained by OS2 security and officially charged with conduct comma disorderly, personal property comma damage and destruction of same—"

"That sounds like the two I'm looking for."

"—public disturbance comma creation of, assault comma minor, resisting arrest—"

"Shouldn't that be arrest comma resisting?"

"—along with a list of other charges, including throwing food at an official security guard, namely me."

"I wasn't aware there was a law against that."

"If there isn't, there oughta be. The little one threw a Faustarian slush-dump pie at me and ruined a brand new uniform shirt. Brand new. You want to talk to 'em, the next vistin' period is in 31 hours, galactic. You can see 'em then."

"I'm a consultant working directly for The Most High Chair of Transformix on a project of considerable importance, and time is of the essence."

"Sure you are. And I'm Lord Admiral Hockenhunny, commander and chief of Pursurvian Intergalactic Starship Security."

"Shall we raise her on the local vid link and see?"

"Nope. Both you and her grand high whatever can wait."

Vinellius pulled out his personal communications device and activated it. When Styxal accepted his request for assistance, he switched the mode to public communication and outlined his problem in a few words, describing the security guard as reluctant to cooperate. Styxal delivered a terse set of instructions about cooperation and the lack thereof being directly related to Gordillion's future, and the bleakness of same. In very short order, Vinellius was seated in an interrogation room with the two criminals sitting across the table from him. Both were Alexians, one male and one female. Vinellius found the female to be somewhat attractive in spite of her one-piece prison garb and lack of cosmetic ornamentation.

"I've got an electric energy prod you can use if you want it," Gordillion said. He'd been tripping all over himself, trying to co-operate and be helpful since his brief conversation with Styxal. "Or I could just slap 'em around a little. Get 'em softened up for a good I-session."

The two looked alarmed and backed away from the table as far as their restraints would allow.

"I'll let you know if I have to resort to anything like that," Vinellius said flatly.

"Well, don't hesitate to request assistance," Gordillion said as he departed, closing the door behind him.

The area was featureless except for a suspicious-looking floor drain in the center of the room. It was illuminated by concealed lighting and had no furnishings except for a table, solidly anchored to the floor, and three chairs, similarly anchored. Vinellius made himself comfortable, then gestured for the other two to sit down. They did so, somewhat gingerly. The Alexians were small, and they looked frightened.

"You," said Vinellius, staring at the female, "are called Vindy-Loo. Correct?"

"Yes."

"And you," he said, switching his gaze to the male, "are Sassalass. Truth?"

"Yes."

"You two were a part of the Transformix clandestine exploratory team. Is that correct?"

"Yes," said Sassalass.

"Tell me what happened," said Vinellius, settling back in his chair and focusing his recorder.

Both started speaking at once, protesting their innocence of wrongdoing and malicious intent. Vinellius held up his hand, and both stopped.

"We'll do this one at a time, turn and turn about. Vindy-Loo, since you're the most attractive, you'll go first. Sassalass will follow, verifying your summary and adding insightful comments inspired by his own experience. Also, please confine your summaries to the exploration of the planet in question, leaving your alleged criminal conduct at the station for another time."

Sassalass made a sour expression and remained silent. Vindy-Loo looked smug.

"A wise decision on your part, if I may say," she began.

"You may, but that's the final remark of adulation I'm going to allow. Future remarks of this nature will be treated as prevarication, which may result in my summoning Gordillion and his energy prod."

Sassalass snickered quietly, and Vinellius stared at him with a stern expression. Sassalass dropped his eyes and regained his sour expression, staring silently at the floor.

"Aasemp and Fortus were in charge of the expense account, the rule being that both would have to approve any expense before the company would cover it, thus preventing unnecessary or wanton expenditures. Well, I don't know if you are aware of this—"

"Let's just assume I'm ignorant," said Vinellius dryly.

"As you so order. It seems that this newly discovered solar system... well, the ship's astrogator informed us that the path intersects with Zephalon Three, and—"

"Zee-Three?" Vinellius leaned forward with interest.

"That's the one! Do you know it?"

"Of course I know it. There *is* only one Zee-Three, for which this quadrant of the known universe can be thankful. Please inform me that you didn't stop there for a short layover."

"I thought you wanted the truth," Sassalass interjected.

"I was being somewhat facetious. Continue, Vindy-Loo."

"So we, ah, well, that is Aasemp thought it wouldn't hurt, and Fortus said it could only help, so we dropped out of FTL drive and put in to orbit. They have a special luxury class shuttle—"

"I know all about their shuttle service. Didn't it occur to any of you to ask yourselves just who might be paying for this service, or how they ever remain solvent?"

"Well, no."

Sassalass snickered.

"What's so funny?" Vindy-Loo snapped.

"You are, if you want the truth," Sassalass replied. "You had the magic touch; you just couldn't lose, oh, no, not you. How long did you last?"

Vindy-Loo was silent.

"Enough," said Vinellius. He took a deep breath and briefly regretted taking this assignment, knowing he had to stay and hear the rest of the story.

"Tell me, how long were you on Zee-Three?"

"Three days. They give you that in case you run out of credits," said Vindy-Loo quietly.

"How reassuring. What could possibly go wrong. Tell me, what did you play?"

"She played the wheel and plaques. She made five straight passes and blew it all on the sixth," Sassalass volunteered with some enthusiasm.

"And the rest of you?"

"Oh, we played various games. It didn't take long before the expense account ran out," said Vindy-Loo.

"How did you get the data you collected?"

"Well, we had a large amount of surveillance gear that the corporation gave us. We used it as collateral for a short-term loan, and from there we hired a freighter—"

"Stop right there," said Vinellius with impatience. "This is a newly discovered planet and was just registered with Empire Central. Ergo, it's interdicted. There isn't a skipper in the sector that would... wait. You already had passage on the corporate ship. What, exactly, did you do?"

The two were silent, staring at the floor.

"Ordinarily, I'd say that the one thing I have is time, but the more I hear from you two the less inclined I am to believe that to be the case. Now, let's hear the entire story, or I'll have Gordillion adjust your attitude into a new and much more enthusiastically cooperative configuration."

Silence.

"Vindy-Loo, I'm serious."

"Well, we... I guess, technically, it was Aasemp and Fortus who did it, but we sold our passage tickets. Aasemp got the idea that he could win at the speedball table, if only he could get to the third quadrant in time, then there would only be one move left, and the game would end leaving him the victor."

"But he didn't, and it did, and he wasn't, so you lost. Again," said Vinellius.

Vindy-Loo nodded silently.

"Then?"

"Then we got the short-term loan, but it was only enough for two, plus passage back here for the rest of us. So Aasemp and Fortus went, and they came back with a pod of hard print data, and a few trillion bits of data on some form of magnetic medium."

. "Right. What's the name of the astrogator who suggested this little holiday?"

"Zalti'tolium. He's from Coover 3."

"Is he now. And the name of the freighter that Aasemp and Fortus booked passage on?"

"The Fourth Pass."

"Wonderful. Now then, about the data you gathered. Where is it?"

"The Department Of Prototype-biological Engineering took it and fed it into their AI system."

"Again, where is it?"

"I don't know. I suppose the Department Of Prototype-biological Engineering still has it."

"I see. Not that it really matters, but how much experience do you two have with xeno-surveys?"

"This was my first real assignment," said Vindy-Loo.

"Mine too," said Sassalass.

"How about the others on the team?"

"They didn't say. It just never came up," Sassalass replied.

"Very well. Now, finally, just how did Aasemp and Fortus get the survey data?"

"They didn't say. They, that is to say *we*, just dropped everything off, got our final reimbursement, and went out to celebrate," said Sassalass.

"He's right," said Vindy-Loo. "We ate some Tasian doodle-flowers, then everything got a little blurry."

"Blurry? She was swimming naked in a fountain. The one in front of the *Three Delights*," Sassalass said. "Then she yelled that she was drowning, and everyone piled in to rescue her, and somehow we all ended up here."

Vinellius rose to his feet.

"I have work to do. I'll pass along the generalities of your situation to the proper Transformix administrative personnel, but if I were in your situation, I wouldn't worry about my future too much," he said, reflecting on the fact that he, personally, wouldn't be in this situation to begin with. He signaled Gordillion, and the door opened for him. He left, the pleas and entreaties for help from the two unfortunates fading away in the distance.

He returned to his personal quarters and opened a private communications link to Transzan, Wezzin's personal business assistant. He requested access to the collected data from the survey, and was denied. When he asked to speak with Wezzin, Transzan informed him that Wezzin was much too busy to speak with him just now, and his schedule was sufficiently tight so as to preclude any communication whatsoever until further notice. Vinellius suggested that Styxal be consulted, and after a short pause was curtly informed that he would be granted access in three cycles. He stated that his request specified immediate access, not delayed access. There was another, longer pause, and Transzan acquiesced. Vinellius responded that Transzan's performance was adequate.

He settled back and reclined his chair, and began reading various sections and pieces that piqued his interest. He hoped the AI had translated accurately, but he knew the translation depended on the usage, and with a xeno culture... he sat up suddenly as a title caught his attention.

A non-historical or unverifiable life form comprised of multicellular organisms that have a well-defined shape and usually limited growth which can move voluntarily, actively acquire food and digest it, combining features of...

He smiled and continued to read. Hours later he retired, but not before leaving a message requesting a private meeting first thing in the morning with Styxal.

Styxal left a return message, again specifying level seventy-three, subsection twenty-seven, unit eight point three. The three Messtoovians stood guard, one of them evidencing a notable tremor in his tail and ears. He presented his galactic identification and was admitted, finding everything as it was on his previous visit. Styxal's feathers were down, indicating a peaceful frame of mind.

"You have news?"

"I do. I can fail your project on several different levels, and at the same time expose corporate sabotage."

"How so?"

"Your clandestine data collection mission was preordained to failure by the decision to employ inexperienced and immature team members, two of which are currently incarcerated on various minor criminal charges. When their fines are paid and restitution for damages made, they'll go free. Their story is simple enough to verify, and once heard, it should have been enough to stop the project immediately. It wasn't, and as a result of this and a few other errors, the data from this newly discovered world is not only faulty, it's completely fictional."

"Fictional?"

"Indeed. The video segments do not depict history or recent events. They're fiction. Stories made up and designed to entertain."

There was a long silence as Styxal pondered this.

"And the rest of it?"

"From what I've examined, I can't say for certain, but I'll give you an educated guess if you like."

"Go ahead."

"It's a game. A game of storytelling and make-believe and has nothing to do with reality."

"A game."

"Truth. Its name translates into something along the lines of *Underground Passages and Giant Supernatural Beings*."

Vinellius stared at his communications device for another minute, watching as his fee and a suitably large bonus were moved from Transformix to his account with P-Bank Three. This had been one of his more lucrative failures, and included the complete ruin of several careers; hence his eagerness to leave the area with all expediency. The transfer completed before he boarded the shuttle, which took him from Orbital Station Two to the luxury FTL transport, *Moon Chaser 1*. His communicator vibrated silently, and he looked at the message. An upper-level manager working for *Farthinghouse and Ollet Development* had been referred to him by Styxal. Apparently, a new construction project required the attention and expertise of a being of his particular talents.

Failure was still a good business, and it seemed to be picking up.

Epilogue

Ray awkwardly held the dustpan in one hand and the push broom in the other, trying to sweep the small pile of broken glass and other, less recognizable debris into the dustpan.

"Here, let me give you a hand with that."

"Thanks," Ray said. He relinquished the dustpan and carefully swept the dirt into it, then looked around his shop again. He shook his head in disbelief.

"No problem. Who says there's never a cop around when you need one?"

Ray smiled, but he still felt shaky and a little sick to his stomach. He'd gotten a call at six-thirty in the morning from the owner of the greasy spoon next door, telling him his place had been broken into and the cops were all over it. Ray pulled on his clothes and got over to the store as quickly as he could, not even stopping for coffee.

The back door was missing. Gone without a trace. It was a steel fireproof door, and the only thing left was half of the hinges. The other half, which were attached to the door, had vanished. The security system was new. The alarm should have sounded as soon as the door opened, but it didn't. Ray sighed. Detective Regis had his notebook open, pen poised to take notes.

"What all was taken?" he asked.

"All the DVDs are gone. There weren't that many, maybe thirty or so. All of 'em were used junk."

"Got a list of the titles?"

"I will have just as soon as I run an inventory report," Ray said, looking at the empty shelf.

"Anything else?"

"Yeah, all the T&T stuff is missing. Nothing else, just T&T."

"T&T?"

"Tunnels and Trolls."

"Huh..." the detective scribbled. "What's Tunnels and—whatever."

"Trolls. It's a role playing game."

"Oh, sure. Is that anything like that, I don't know, something about dragons."

"Dungeons and Dragons, yeah, like that. Only better. I just can't figure it. Nothing but the T&T stuff."

"Well, probably kids then. I'll give this to the juvenile division, but honestly, I don't think we'll find much."

"No dice, no board games, nothing else was stolen. Just the T&T stuff. And hey, what about the door?"

"Well, you know, kids. They might have unbolted it somehow."

"They didn't. Look at the hinges. They've been cut off flush with the frame, and not with a cutting torch, either. I used to work at a junkyard, and you can't get cuts that clean with anything. They're cut so clean, I could shave with those leftover pieces. And the door? What about the door? Who would want a forty-pound fire door?"

The detective shrugged and scribbled something on his report.

"Just one of life's little mysteries," he said on his way out. "Like that UFO business last night."

In memory of Rick Loomis. Special recognition to Mike Hamann and Donnie Hale.

WL Emery is a semi-retired curmudgeon who used to be a lot of fun at parties. For his sins, he lives in Columbus, Ohio, where he spends his time drinking, dancing, and writing - fantasy and science fiction. Find his website at www.WLEmery.com.

Thorwynn Stapledon and "The Mellifluous Phoenix"

By SU-RA-U

It was supposed to be a drug-fueled science fiction anthology alleging to recreate the human brain! But what was the sinister truth behind The Mellifluous Phoenix?!

Perhaps the best place to start my story would be at the very beginning, with Thorwynn Stapledon.

As most people familiar with the history of science fiction know, Stapledon was one of the founders of science fiction fandom. This of course was a most peculiar circumstance since very few people, that is until the early 1970s, had ever even seen him face-to-face. No pictures are known to exist until 1972, and no information about his life until he was in his early 20's has so far been unearthed, though there are rumors he was born in Lithuania and brought up in Poughkeepsie, New York.

Despite being highly reclusive, he was, even by the standards of the time, a voracious letter writer—back when this meant putting pen to paper, folding the finished document, placing it in an envelope, pasting the stamp, and finally putting the sealed envelope in a mailbox, all astonishingly without pressing a single button. Stapledon in his prime was famous for keeping a running correspondence with hundreds of fans, friends, business partners, acquaintances, and at times even his enemies; and he could shoot off over two-dozen letters all before most people had finished breakfast.

All movements need such eccentrics, and Stapledon played a pivotal role in coalescing the nascent science fiction underground of the 1930's and 1940's. Through his vast network of contacts and with liberal donations of funds—another rumor claims that as the grandson of a turn-of-the-century German shipping magnate, he had a sizable inheritance and spare cash waiting to be wasted—he was instrumental in founding early science fiction fan clubs, publishing magazines, and organizing some of the earliest science fiction conventions in North America. He also discovered such writers as Frank Cliburn, Joe Kleitz, and P. J. Irving.

There wouldn't be much more to write about if it wasn't for Stapledon's grand entrance into the halls of the Galaxy Science Fiction Convention of 1972, setting in motion a series of events that would eventually touch Gloria and me.

It should be noted that his letter-writing had declined from the prodigious levels of the middle of the century to barely a trickle by the early 1970s. He had no known family members, and during the previous ten years, he seemed to have had no physical contact with anyone except for a buxom 30-year-old woman who claimed to be his secretary. Yet here he was, in front of an audience, probably for the first time in his life.

Pictures from the convention show a short, bespectacled man, who was bald except for a white fringe of soft hair at the back and sides of his smooth, shiny head. His back was a little hunched and his stomach bulged. He wore an olive-green jacket and slacks with a yellow shirt and black bow-tie. He looked like the epitome of a nebbish college professor.

In the packed main hall of the convention center, he had spoken, according to a news article, in a monotone but steady voice about a new project to be funded by him and other "high-minded benefactors" that would "revolutionize human consciousness" as "we explored man's last frontier—The Human Mind!"

I'll admit the idea was fascinating—yet at the same time utterly crackpot. Stapledon had announced to the hushed audience a project to recreate the human brain; not, he had explained, with a machine or through a computer simulation, but (get ready for it) in the form of a collection of short stories. Stapledon's plan was to gather a hundred of the world's greatest science fiction writers—of course, this meant mostly hacks and amateurs from the US and Canada—who were each expected to write a two-to-five-page short story on a topic provided to them by Stapledon: topics such as the "Thalamus," "Emotions," "Data Analysis," "The Regulation of Breathing," "Cerebrum I-IV," "Speech," etc.

I can't say I can really get my head around the concept, but from what Gloria has told me, the stories in the book weren't meant to describe the various aspects of the brain and its processes, or to even convey metaphorically the specific characteristics of the mind. Rather the aim of the book was to cause any person who read the collection from front to back to somehow personally experience the human brain in all its totality. One would, for a moment, according to the publicity material, "become a Brain". As I said: utterly crackpot.

The announcement created a flurry of excitement among science fiction writers and fans, with Stapledon receiving thousands of applications for the project. This was naturally the result of Stapledon's willingness to offer cold, hard cash for each story at rates above those offered even by the upmarket slicks.

Yet, there was one catch. Each writer, before writing his story, would be administered a mild hallucinogenic drug to aid them in the creative process. The writers were also expected to sign a waiver absolving Stapledon and his backers of all legal liability. Over a third of the selected writers backed out—which I think is quite a small number, considering the conditions imposed, but this was, after all, the 1970s—so the selection process had to be restarted to find 38 new writers willing to take the drug.

One final matter that should be addressed was the unconventional manner by which each author was assigned a topic. Blood was extracted from each participant and tested to match the author with a compatible topic. If there was no match, the author was disqualified and a new writer selected. What the criteria for compatibility were or what each author's blood was tested for were never made clear by Stapledon or others involved in the project. My belief is that, for most of the participants, any concerns about the drug or the blood test were far outweighed by the generous compensation they expected to receive from Stapledon, especially since most of the authors, I am certain, lived from paycheck to paycheck.

The project commenced in March 1975, and the last short story was completed seven months later in October. The book was to be released in the spring of 1976 with the title *The Mellifluous Phoenix* (???). The science fiction community awaited the release of the book with great anticipation, but then, with no warning, the release date was pushed back, first to the winter of 1976 and then to some unspecified date in 1977. Finally, it just disappeared. Stapledon made a couple of announcements that everything was on track and that after some fine-tuning the collection would be released, but after 1978, nothing was heard from or about him for the next 20 years until his obituary appeared on September 14, 1998.

It seems that some copies of the book were printed before the project was terminated. Though they were never distributed, Carl Heinnes, Gloria's father and one of the authors chosen for the project, had somehow procured three copies before, according to Gloria, the rest were destroyed. Gloria doesn't know what happened to two of the copies, but one passed from her father to her and now lies at the corner of my desk as I type this up.

The book isn't much to look at. The front cover is bright red with two thin green stripes stretching from right to left, starting about a third and two-thirds of the way down respectively. The space between the green stripes is shaded light blue with a yellow dragon—not a phoenix as one would expect—right in the center. At the bottom is the title of the book in a fat black serif font. The back and spine are red and devoid of any text or illustrations.

I had a chance to read this fat compendium of drug-induced fiction over the last week, and I can state without hesitation that, with the exception of a few stories, I found it to be an inscrutable mess. The book is a mishmash of gibberish, directionless stream-of-consciousness meanderings, and trite narratives wholly unconnected to the theme of the book. Most importantly, the book, despite claims to the contrary, never caused me, even for a fraction of a second, to "become a Brain".

In some of the stories, the authors seem to have suffered a catastrophic impairment of their ability to form not just sentences but even the simplest words—a product, most certainly, of the drug they had consumed. This is a sentence from the story "Motor Skills": "skPrz aogbn Fsallmqet BBSdoljeuc moRHOzY." The first paragraph of "Touch and Temperature" is: "Sil;397zb N+32e!" An excellent password, I'm sure.

Other stories, such as "Occipital Lobe," do not exhibit such an extreme breakdown of language but are still composed of sentences such as: "Long oblong discernment at eels in the dimensional finger stung been." Another set of authors seem to have experienced attacks of mild-to-severe paranoia. A representative example is "Cerebrum III." The author starts with, "My hands, my hands. What grows on my hands?" and ends three pages later with, "Get me out of here. Pull the lever, PULL the chain. I want out!" At least he was lucid enough to add that exclamation mark.

It makes me wonder what kind of bad trip they were on when the authors wrote their stories and what the long-term side effects were of taking what I believed (at least before reading Heinnes's letter) was a very strong mind-altering drug. I was able to find information about 81 of the writers who participated in the project, out of whom 32 are still alive. Of the 46 who have passed away and I know the cause of death, eleven committed suicide, eight died from strokes, and twelve succumbed to cancer, which includes seven cases of brain cancer. I am not certain if this is statistically significant, but you can be the judge.

The majority of stories, though, are surreal, tripped-out narratives that at times appear to be on the brink of collapsing but somehow manage to make it to the end in one piece. One story ("Medulla") is about an old man trapped in a giant fist: a right fist, he presumes. The old man then notices his right hand is also clenched in a fist, and he starts to wonder what could be trapped between his own fingers and palm. Another story ("Amygdala") is about a boy climbing a hill: "Oh the yellow sun, yellow flowers, yellow bunnies. I shall blow yellow. I shall burst this yellow. Up I go." Still another ("Visual Processing") is about a bear who falls in love with the Pope.

The oddest story in the book isn't a story at all. Instead, it is a scientific treatise describing the brain's role in the process of "Homeostasis." Five pages are filled with the kind of medical and scientific jargon only a trained professional could understand. For example: "Brain homeostasis is in part controlled by a variety of capillary endothelial cells consisting of apical junctional complexes that form the blood-brain barrier and can be impacted by a number of etiological factors."

What makes this so odd is that the author, Lukas Miller, had only a B.A. in Geography and had spent most of his decade-and-a-half-long literary career writing for home decorating and body-building magazines. How did an author, who exhibited no interest and had no training in medicine or any of the other hard sciences, write what is technically a work that belongs in a medical journal or textbook? Not only did he include two charts and a table in his story, this lightweight was also able somehow to construct sentences containing words like homoeothermic (warm-blooded) and phylaxis (protection against infection) while stoned out of his mind. I don't know if this is relevant, but Lukas Miller blew his brains out in 1986. Even worse, before committing suicide, he fatally shot his dog, Cuddles.

I've had to provide this background information about Stapledon and *The Mellifluous Phoenix* so the reader can understand what happened to Gloria, and why I'm dumping all these documents on the Internet.

About one month back, I got a call from Gloria after almost three years. Gloria Watson—she took her mother's maiden name—and I have been friends for more than twenty years, going all the way back to our first year of college. I never met her father, but Gloria had often talked about him, especially when she was drunk or feeling depressed—sometimes both at the same time.

Carl Heinnes, she often lamented, had abandoned her and her mother when she was only five years old. Though she had reconnected with her father for a couple years when she was in her mid-twenties, a fight with Heinnes's second wife—Gloria never referred to her as her stepmother—had caused a strain in their relationship that had sadly never been resolved.

Gloria's father had died four years ago, and a year later, her mother had been diagnosed with throat cancer. It was one month after her mother's death that she had gotten an offer to make $20,000. That's when she called me.

Gloria told me over the phone that she had been contacted by representatives of the Thorwynn Stapledon Trust. They had informed her that they were restarting the Mellifluous Phoenix project after it had lain dormant for 40 years. Following a lengthy investigation, they had discovered that her father, along with some of the other participants, had chosen not to take the drug while writing their story, resulting in the failure of the project. One by one, each of the stories had been rewritten by either the original author or someone who had passed the blood test, usually a close relative. "Ganglia," Carl Heinnes's story, was the last story that needed to be rewritten.

Gloria was in a bit of a bind since her father had strongly warned her to keep away from anyone claiming to represent Thorwynn Stapledon and not to even consider writing for *The Mellifluous Phoenix*. On the other hand, Gloria still had her mother's sizable medical bills to clear, and she was, at that moment, unemployed. She had been warned that if she rejected the offer, the Thorwynn Stapledon Trust would just select another writer, and she would be out $20,000.

My involvement, except for encouraging her to write the story, would have ended there if Gloria hadn't asked me for a favor. While she was in contact with Thorwynn Stapledon's minions, as she referred to them, she wanted me to hold some documents for her. A week later, I got a box of documents related to Stapledon and his project, including a copy of the book, various promotional pamphlets from the 1970s, and clippings about the 1972 convention. Please see the links below. The most important document Gloria sent me was a letter from her father posted shortly before his death.

Now, I want to make clear before I start discussing the letter that some of Heinnes's ideas were pretty batty. Just to give one example, he strongly rejected the theory that millions of years ago dinosaurs walked the earth. According to Heinnes, dinosaurs were originally a necessary evil created by a small band of early evolutionists to popularize the concept of Darwinism, but the "glorified dragons," as he called them, should have been given a decent burial after more rigorous evidence in favor of evolution had been discovered. The problem, according to Heinnes, was that kids couldn't get enough of tyrannosaurus rexes, pterodactyls, and brontosauruses, so there would have been too much lost goodwill and funding (and where would a scientist be without funding?) if biologists, and especially paleontologists, had abandoned the idea that giant lizards once ruled the planet.

Despite some of his unorthodox beliefs, he was still a respected member of the science fiction community. Though not a leading light, he had written some well-respected novels in the early 1970s that had sold moderately well. He had also edited a number of science fiction and fantasy anthologies in the 1970s and 1980s and published a series of books attempting to popularize chemistry (as if that's possible). Considering his life-long, though closeted, embrace of communism, it is ironic that over the course of his life, he had amassed a small fortune. However, Gloria had told me that by the end of his life, he was a lonely man with three wives and three divorces and a daughter whose love he was uncertain of.

Much of Heinnes's letter to Gloria is a pathetic, rambling attempt by a man in the last days of his life to reconcile with his only daughter. Much of this is of no real relevance to the reader or me—you can read the entire letter in the link below—but in the second half of the letter is a lengthy passage that I find most disturbing. Either it is an absurd conspiracy theory by someone who is seriously unhinged or a warning about the imminent doom of our planet. Since yesterday, I have been leaning towards the latter possibility.

Beginning in the second paragraph of the seventh page, he writes:

"Most importantly, I must warn you about Thorwynn Stapledon and his book *The Mellifluous Phoenix*. Both are exceedingly evil. You must never associate with anyone who claims to represent Thorwynn Stapledon or asks you to write for that wretched book. Thorwynn Stapledon was a deplorable human being who had no qualms about betraying the human race. This man had no compunction about being recruited by powerful members of the political and business elite who had formed an alliance with an alien race from another dimension. The aim of the alien race was to conquer our universe.

"I know the following may shock you, but please keep an open mind as I narrate the adventures of the idealistic and intrepid young man who was your father. When I was in my early twenties, I became a communist, and despite the more than half-century that has passed since then, I still unapologetically maintain my loyalty to the teachings of Marx and Lenin. You must remember that during my early adulthood, the Red Scare was still very much alive, and I was forced to keep my beliefs a secret, even from your mother. But this did not stop me from collaborating with the government of the Soviet Union beginning in the early 60's. I have no regrets about my association with a foreign government. I am proud of my service to a government that has been unjustly tarred by the worst imperialist propaganda and was instead a beacon of hope, freedom, justice, and equality for the whole world. We saved the world from almost certain destruction in 1975.

"I was called up by Soviet intelligence to infiltrate *The Mellifluous Phoenix* project shortly after it had been announced. My KGB handlers explained that Soviet intelligence had discovered a plot of literally earth-shattering ramifications. An alien race had promised key members of the capitalist establishment of America and Britain immeasurable wealth and power in exchange for their assistance in the invasion of our universe. Thorwynn Stapledon would serve as the point man for the aliens and their capitalist partners in their bloody quest to subjugate this dimension."

I will skip six paragraphs where Heinnes describes details of *The Mellifluous Phoenix* project already discussed above. He continues:

"The pill we were supposed to take was not a hallucinogenic drug at all. It was instead a capsule filled with microscopic alien spores that would, upon entering the human body, mutate into parasitic organisms and assume control of the host's nervous system for a short period of time. Based on the genetic makeup of the individual, a certain text would be produced by the parasites using their human host. The reason for the blood test was to find the appropriate host for each set of alien parasites, and thus each text.

"The combined texts, when organized in a set order, would create, in a sense, a linguistic key. When this key was read out loud by the 101st participant in the project, perhaps Thorwynn Stapledon himself, the vibrations created by the text would cause a rift in space-time or, to put it more accurately, a disruption in the music of the spheres, a celestial catastrophe that would open a dimensional portal through which an alien armada would be able to enter our dimension and conquer not just our planet but the entire universe itself.

"The Soviet leadership, in their supreme wisdom, decided the best course of action would be sabotage. I and nineteen other communist comrades applied to participate in the project, and five of us were selected as finalists. Our handler taught us a simple parlor trick by which each of us would be able to hide the capsule in our sleeve, and while pretending to pop it in our mouth, deposit the capsule in our pant pocket. We wrote our stories undetected and unaided by the parasites."

Heinnes then for no reason discusses the history of magic. After seven paragraphs he returns to the central narrative.

"The sabotaging of *The Mellifluous Phoenix* was just the first round in our on-going and fearless secret war against the aliens and their allies. The Soviets built an extensive espionage network, assassinated many of the human traitors, and fought hot and cold wars across the planet for the future of our race. Yet I fear all was lost with the collapse of the Soviet Union last year after their simultaneous defeat in the Kazakhstan War and the Baltic confrontation.

"I am certain you may be incredulous at my story and perhaps even consider the above confession the ravings of a senile, old man near death, but I assure you that I have told you the absolute truth.

"You must understand why I am making this confession. I love you dearly. You are the only non-communist to whom I have revealed my secret life, and as my only child, I fear the aliens may draw you into *The Mellifluous Phoenix* project, which I fear they will revive now that there is no force to oppose them. Whether you believe my story or not, you must never become involved with this damned project, with any representative of Thorwynn Stapledon, or with the aliens who are pulling the strings. I implore you."

There is one more passage I want to quote from Heinnes's letter, this time from the second to last page:

"I know you will resent my failure to provide you with an inheritance. I have always believed that a man reaps what he sows. We must make our own way in this world and live by what we can earn by the sweat of our brow. Depending on handouts will only deter us from maximizing our full potential. To hand over my fortune to you would be not only a betrayal of my principles but also a betrayal of my love for you. I know you are smart, talented, and a go-getter; after all, you are my daughter. You can even now still be successful, but you must take some firm decisions and endeavor to work as hard as I have.

"Furthermore, I see no greater service a man can perform than to help those who are most in need. By this I mean the dogs, cats, and other animals who freely offer us so much unconditional love. I hope when you make your fortune you will, like me, donate, if not completely, at least a part of your life savings to the American Humane Society."

I know the passage above has nothing to do with aliens, Stapledon, or his book, but I've quoted this part of the letter for a reason. I now wonder if things could have turned out differently if she had gotten some money from her father and had not been so desperate for cash, because two weeks after my initial conversation with Gloria, she told me she had accepted the offer. I would have supported her wholeheartedly—after all, it was a hell of a lot of money just to write a five-page story—but after reading the documents she sent me and learning about the possible side-effects of the pill, parasite or no parasite, I couldn't help feeling apprehensive about her decision.

I wish I had told her this a bit more

strongly. I really wish I had seen her one last time, but she's in Tampa Bay, Florida, and I'm on the opposite coast. I'm sure most of you have heard by now what happened in Tampa Bay yesterday, and that's why I wrote this down and posted it here. From what I saw on the news, Gloria's house seems to be the epicenter of the gas line explosion that destroyed four blocks of the city. I saw where her house had been in the helicopter footage, and all that remained was a black hole.

I read on the Internet that the military has now sealed the area. They have banned all civilians from coming within a one-mile radius of the explosion site and restricted the airspace around the area to only military aircraft.

I can't help going back to Heinnes's letter without doubts starting to form about the official narrative. Maybe he was right. Maybe there is a plot against our planet. Maybe we are facing an alien invasion. All I'm certain of is that Gloria hasn't called me for the last two weeks.

Or maybe I've just spent too much time with Thorwynn Stapledon, *The Mellifluous Phoenix*, crazy conspiracy theories, and science fiction in general. I'm not even a fan of the genre. Maybe, in the end, a gas line explosion is just that: a gas line explosion.

Su-Ra-U chooses to remain anonymous.

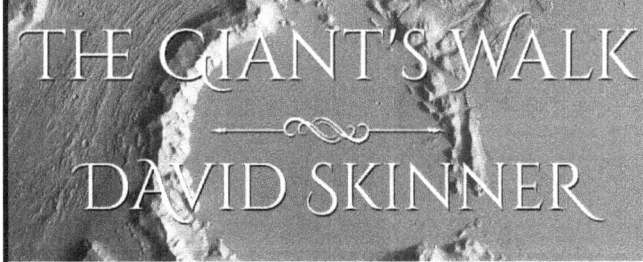

Harmonious Unity Burns

By Jed Del Rosario

The most diverse city in the Federated Alliance is burning! Riots and upheaval have necessitated the intervention of elite mercenaries—who is behind the chaos?!

Though the city covered almost an entire continent, Ogut could still make out the burning destruction from space. The riots that convulsed Sector Harmonious Unity grew in visibility as the *Raider* transport approached its destination.

Ilm, the greatest city in the Federated Alliance, was a giant cosmopolitan wonder that covered one of the planet's continents. Massive tree-like spires kilometers long littered the city's central hub; sprawling hive structures filled every sector of the city; tens of billions of aliens from all across the known galaxy called Ilm home, a grand experiment in universal unity.

The residential spaces of this gargantuan city were divided into 17 Sectors: one for each of the member species of the Federated Alliance. These sectors were carefully planned and managed by the most sophisticated AI, where each species would have all its needs catered to, allowing it to not only survive but thrive in a multi-racial utopia.

In the midst of this perfectly managed stability, sector Harmonious Unity burned, its AI control nodes looted and in ruins. The sector, which was home to several millions, was the home of Ilm's Dikri community, a *developmentally challenged* race only (rela-

tively) recently allowed to join the Federated Alliance. The planet's administrators saw fit to isolate the sector, lest its destruction spread to other parts of the city.

The center of the sector was filled with flames, smoke, and dirty light, as its inhabitants had seen fit to burn down their own homes. Hundreds of small groups of rioters fought each other in the streets; some sought to murder the recently elected Dikri Tributurine-Representative, Harrack; others called for the head of his electoral enemy, Carrack. Others simply rioted because they wanted to loot and destroy.

LADAR scanners identified more than 23 skyscrapers on fire and several more in the process of being looted by rioters. Ilm's Fed-All security forces could easily defeat the rioters, but they were ordered to stand down and hold position in the adjacent sectors—Sector Serene Repose and Sector Bright Joy. The delicate situation required a more subtle solution.

As the cylinder-shaped *Raider* shuttle made its approach, smoke from the sector's destruction concealed its bulk; allowing the transport to deploy its assault team with relative ease on top of a skyscraper's wide balcony, right across the target building, the Harmonious Unity Central Administration Node. The vessel quickly disgorged three "human" mercenaries—each of them belonging to a warrior gene-breed.

"Remember, our client needs Harrack and the data in one piece," Horton, the company leader, yelled from the transport, as the mercenaries secured their drop zone. His skin shone bright gold despite the smoke. "I'll meet you with our *other guest* when you're finished. *Don't fail.*"

All three nodded their head, after which the *Raider* closed its doors and soundlessly flew away.

"Hold fast," Toshir, the team leader, told to two others of his team the moment the *Raider* had disappeared. "We're not moving an inch until the *signal.*"

"Easy fer ye to say," his longtime partner Park muttered as he swatted away the smoke from his face.

Ogut—a recent and temporary addition to the team—didn't say anything. He merely took his position and waited for the order to begin.

In the midst of the smoke and turmoil, a loud voice spoke across a hundred echo drones scattered all around the sector.

When we come to Ilm, council promised prosperity! Bah! Dikri lived on Ilm for thirty years, and Council treat Dikri like slaves. Fed'rated Allans claim we have voice, we have power. Lies; Excrement! They trick Dikri! They look down on Dikri! Now, Dikri burn down Fed'rated Allans!

The humans' translators didn't fully catch the meaning of the words, but even they recognized the speaker's identity.

"That's Carrack's voice," Park said.

"Which means he's nearby," Toshir added. "Ogut! How are you holding up?"

"I'm ready," Ogut answered mechanically. "I'm ready."

Park and Toshir said nothing, but Ogut felt their unease—their suspicions. He knew what other breeds thought of his kind, and frankly he couldn't care less. Berserker genes were designed to eliminate the vast majority of human emotions, those worthless relics from obsolete versions of humanity. His kind were designed for war.

That's all that mattered.

As per his gene-breed's patriarch's orders, Ogut quietly observed the other mercenaries. Toshir, who led the group, was a *Taira* breed, a race known for genetically tampering with all kinds of dangerous toxins and artificial viruses.

Toshir had the characteristic porcelain-white skin and slit-like eyes of his kin. But Ogut knew that underneath his sanitized exterior lay glands that stored the most exotic toxins, enough to kill a small army.

The *Taira* had once fought Ogut's kind back in the Purgation Wars many centuries ago, when humanity's many breeds exterminated one another. But the conflict never escalated beyond a few skirmishes. Only a couple million killed on both sides. Nothing to hold a grudge about.

Park, on the other hand, was a bit of a mystery. A *Doric* breed, his kind rarely interacted with *Berserkers* and their High Patriarchs in the Purgation Wars. What little

Ogut knew of the breed is that they were forged for front-line attrition.

Looking at Park, he didn't doubt their gene-breed's reputation. Both he and Toshir were masses of muscles, but Park simply had more of them. And Ogut knew that his strange bluish-orange skin was almost hard as stone. There was also an aggression enhancer buried slightly inside his neck. Interesting.

All of them were of a similar kind—war breeds: humans bred, trained, and designed for war. But unlike Park's hardened rock-like orange skin and Toshir's pale toxin-filled flesh, Ogut's features were closer to the skin of ancient Fricans from before the age of expansion, when breeding and begetting was left to chance. He also had a flat nose, wide lips and, unlike other war breeds, a body not that different from pre-spaceflight humans. But to think that the Berserkers, like Ogut, are barely different from their pre-speciation ancestors would be a mistake.

Ogut flexed the hidden claws within his body, and a couple of them bloodlessly emerged from his hand. Sophisticated *mods* then began to pump synthetic substances designed to boost his strength and speed. He was ready for the coming slaughter.

Then echo drones interrupted Ogut's thoughts, forcing him back to reality.

When Fed'rated Allans find Dikri many stars ago, them promised many things; promise equaliteee. Fed'rated Allans promised wealth, honor, and dignity. Them promised justice? Lies! Many stars pass, and them treat Dikri like fools; force Dikri to serve selfish

Council!

The sound of propaganda was soon followed by the whirl of a nondescript delivery drone, which was then followed by Toshir's cold, baritone voice.

"Eyes front. Our equipment's here," Toshir barked, and Ogut saw the drone land in front of them. Without wasting any time, the machine opened its compartments, revealing a series of jump packs designed for the mercenaries to use, all of them Fed-All design but customised for human users. There were also two Guardian Drones, their mass accelerators adapted for urban conflict.

The mercenaries quickly put on the jump packs then double-checked the rest of their gear. Toshir then opened a nondescript box from one of the drone's smaller accessory compartments.

Inside were several pieces of cloth. Toshir smelled them deeply, ingraining each scent in his mind. He then handed the rags to Ogut, who did the same. After he finished, he returned the cloths back to Toshir, who burned them to erase the evidence.

Toshir nodded, then turned to their equipment and made sure that their weapons and armor checked out. Aside from the jump packs, the team's gear consisted of alien-made law enforcement weaponry and full-spectrum *mimicell* cloak projectors for stealth. It was not the sort of weapons they were used to; human-made weapons typically caused maximum damage, but the mission called for subtlety, not slaughter, so they would suffer these tools for now.

The mercenaries also wore multi-layer

hyper-Graphene vests to withstand mass accelerators, as well as combined ceramite plate armor to hold back heat and energy-based weapons. They also brought along personal phase shields as an extra precaution should they encounter more than just rioters or looters in their mission.

Having finished the equipment check, Toshir quickly looked out at the riots. They were getting worse. Even at this height, and with smoke rising from different places, he could still see the masses of rioters fighting in the streets below. They were primarily targeting properties owned and controlled by the Council Species—the Hithraki, the Mit-Mit, and the Keramlik—except the rioters were focusing on Hithraki and Keramlik buildings and were actively avoiding Mit-Mit property. None of this surprised Toshir. He knew how politics worked in Fed-All space.

Swatting a cloud of passing smoke, he stared at the building right across from them. Their VIP was located somewhere inside, and they only had a little time left to extract him. Smoke and dirty light already surrounded the once-graceful structure, turning it into a pyre of metal and glass. In a little while it would collapse.

Toshir turned to Ogut, his porcelain-like face fixed into a scowl. "Ogut," he said, "there's been some *new developments* regarding the mission."

"There're always new developments for *these* kinds of missions..." Ogut replied tersely but added nothing more.

Toshir and Park paused briefly, as though caught off guard by the comment.

Park chuckled and muttered something about a 'cheeky pisser.' Toshir remained quiet.

"The political situation in this sector is sensitive," Toshir said, stating what Ogut already knew from their *imprint-briefing*. "Those rioters want to kill their recently elected Tributurine, their species' local representative in Ilm's senate. Fortunately, the riots are a small, violent minority, quite separate from the majority of Dikri Fed-All citizens..."

"They do'an seem like a small minority at all," Park snorted at Toshir's declaration and peered at the devastation on the ground, finding the streets filled to the brim with rioting Dikri.

"Park..." Toshir growled at his partner, then turned back to Ogut. "As I was saying, the political situation is desperate. You know about Harrack from your imprinting. What you don't know is his political opponent, Carrack..."

"I know about Carrack," Ogut cut off again, wanting to end the little *off-the-record* conversation as soon as possible. "About Carrack. He was a popular candidate during the Tributurine election; more so than Harrack—polls expected him to win. He campaigned on giving the Dikri a seat in the Fed-All council. Fed-All council. Quite impossible, of course, but he was riling up a lot of Dikri, and the other client races supported him. Supported him. A mass movement like that... would have been a disaster for the Fed-All Council. The Fed-All Council. The Mit-Mit, the Hithraki, and the Keramlik."

Ogut became quiet again and turned away to look at the riots below. But Toshir was frowning; Park grinned.

"You're extremely well-informed on Fed-All politics," Toshir said. "That's not always a *good thing*. Did the Berserker Patriarchs tell you that?"

A silent smile was all the answer Ogut was willing to provide.

Ogut, Park, and Toshir burst through the 143rd floor of the target skyscraper. Imprint-briefing reported that Harrack's panic room was located in that area, so that's where they would start their search.

Broken synth-glass and ultra-plastics greeted their approach. They navigated their way through debris-covered corridors and half-shattered hallways. Through the chaos, Toshir and Ogut had little trouble tracking their target, Harrack's scent fresh in their minds. Harrack had fled through this floor, guarded by his bodyguards and followers.

For the first few minutes, they encountered nothing but trash, damaged electronics, and alien graffiti. It wasn't until after they reached some sort of lobby that they encountered possible threats. The area was covered in alien corpses, most of them Dikri.

Ogut paused briefly at a particularly grotesque scene: a lynched Dikri, its six limbs pinned to the wall by cheap plastic spikes and the contents of its torso spilled out onto the floor. The creature's face, a mixture of a ferret and a large fish, exuded only suffering even in death.

Toshir looked at the bloody graffiti written next to the lynched corpse: "Species Traitor," Toshir said. "Written in common Hithraki, not Dikri. Someone wants publicity."

"Imprint-briefing said that this area was supposed to be clear." Ogut said. "To be clear."

"Obviously. They be wrong," Park growled, and he turned to his partner, voicing what all three were thinking. "We're here fer Harrack. Wot're we gonna do if he's already dead?"

Toshir didn't answer.

As they progressed, they found more signs of vicious fighting, including several dead Dikri, their bodies visibly tortured, their clothes torn off or their limbs severed in the most gruesome ways. At least one of the xenos lived, and it cried for help.

Naturally, they ignored it.

As they made their way deeper into the building, they were greeted by more propaganda, this time coming from audio devices from within.

Council look down on us! Look down on ancestor! Think Dikri primitive, stupid race. Council say they help ancestors; give knowledge. Lies! Dikri having rich and noble culture; not lesser race, like Vorogogzy or Motoi...

"Ye are nae different from the Vorogogzy or the Motoi," Park said derisively, now angry at the constant noise from the propaganda speakers.

As they crossed closer to the center of the building, the devastation became worse, with some of the bodies sporting weapons and miniaturized shields.

"Contact," Ogut said laconically as they made a turn. And he sniffed the air for a whole minute before growling to himself.

Toshir turned to him. "Harrack?"

"No," Ogut said. "Dikri. Plenty of Dikri." He tilted his head to one side. "Of Dikri."

Park and Toshir looked at each other, clearly perturbed. "Stay here," the latter said. Toshir signaled his team to hold their position while he reconnoitered the forward area. He activated his *mimicells*, turning him into a living blur, his scent concealed by artificial pheromones.

Toshir was gone for only a little while before returning. He was frowning when his *mimicells* shut off, xeno blood covering his hands. "Panic room," he explained. "Harrack's inside, and a group of rioters are trying to get it open so they can lynch him. Had to kill one of them to keep it quiet, but it's only a matter of time before the others find the body…"

A muffled explosion interrupted him, but there was no need to explain what it was.

"Damnation. Those ram-ranchin' fellats!" Park growled as he realized what the Dikri were doing.

Toshir wasted no time explaining his plan. The panic room was located two rooms from where they were. There were eight Dikri, armed with cheap chemical propellant ammunition that could do little to harm their shields.

The only problem was that there were other Dikri a few floors below, busily looking for Fed-All loyalists to lynch. One mis-

take, and they could end up facing an army.

"Move into the room adjacent to the Dikri," Toshir snapped. "I'll head for the rear. When I give the signal, kill every last one of the fellats. Move!"

Ogut obediently followed Park, sneaking to where their targets were. They found the Dikri assault team—less than a dozen of them—exactly where Toshir said they were: in front of the Panic Room, trying to blow it open. The xenos seemed to be in a hurry, and more than a little tense, if Ogut had to guess. They appeared to be rabble, too; all of them crowded around like a mob, leaving their perimeter open to attack.

Park crouched low and activated his *mimicells*, rendering him partly invisible as he approached the Dikri. His massive body was surprisingly quiet as he positioned himself for the attack. Ogut, meanwhile, used the specialized claws in his hands and feet to silently climb the plastic-like ceilings like some primal arachnid eager for its meal.

One minute passed, then another… Suddenly, the xenos began to panic. Some of them started to screech as an unseen toxin began to devour their skin, while others called for help as the chemical began to damage their lungs. Fright turned to terror, and they quickly scattered, believing that the toxin had come from the panic room.

It was at this point that Toshir struck. Like living mist, he leaped at the aliens seemingly from nowhere; his flesh, the source of the toxins; his steely limbs silently cracking alien bodies. He struck opposite where Park and Ogut had entered, forcing the Dikri to retreat into a trap.

At the same time, Park stormed the reeling group of Dikri, an invisible wrecking ball that caught the rabble by surprise. In that brief instant, he and Toshir had killed half of the aliens and mutilated a few more. The aliens managed to fire a couple of shots at their unknown attackers, but that's all they managed to do. A third monster burst from up above, eviscerating one Dikri and maiming another by slicing off three of the creature's four feet.

One Dikri caught sight of his attacker's face, and it filled him with primal fear—a long-buried terror at the nameless predator. Ogut's face froze in a grotesque smile. He said nothing, but his lips flared and his teeth seemed as though they were larger than nature intended.

And then the claws emerged all over Ogut's body, turning him into a monstrous ravager. More hormones flowed through his body, numbing all sensations of pain. Ogut leapt forward, slaughtering the remaining Dikri rabble with ease. The dozens of steel-like claws turned him into a living blade. He pounced on the Dikri like so much meat, easily ripping them open.

Park came from behind him, not bothering to fire his non-lethal Fed-All weapons and merely using his massive fists to butcher the maimed Dikri that Ogut hadn't slain yet. Fists strong enough to smash through cement crushed xeno skulls, their physiology no match for the monstrous biology of human warrior gene-breeds.

Finally, the last Dikri fell, its skull broken by Park's prodigious might, its lungs liquefied by Toshir's toxins, its limbs sliced off by Ogut's claws. As soon as all the enemies were confirmed dead, Toshir ordered them to check the corpses for any critical information. Ogut found two data mnemonic imprinters; Park found another. They immediately gave these to Toshir.

He then walked over to the panic room's door and tapped softly. He leaned towards the structure's external cam, showed it something, and ordered his team to get ready in case of a surprise. It took a few minutes for the panic room's door to open, but at last the recently re-elected Tributurine of the Dikri species on Ilm, Harrack, emerged. His ferret and fish-like face was funny, as far as the humans were concerned. Even the alien's six limbs—four legs, like those of a quadruped, plus the two human-like hands—looked weak and ridiculous.

Ogut couldn't tell what the Dikri Tributurine was thinking, but he was clearly tired, and if he had to guess, slightly injured.

"You late! You come rescue me earlier, human," Harrack demanded as soon as he got out of the panic room, his linguistic skills barely understandable even with the aid of an upgraded translator. "And where is Hithraki Justicar?"

That was news for Ogut. Justicars were the elite of the Federated-Alliance, not only for their skill and experience but also for their political loyalty. Or at least, that's what he had learned from the official information.

Ogut was not the only one perturbed by the information, though. Both Park and Toshir frowned at Harrack's question, and the latter jerked his head to activate his subdermal.

"We have the target. He's asking about a Hithraki Justicar," and paused a moment to listen to the response. He briefly glanced at his team while listening to the other end, his eyes telling the others everything they needed to know. At last he asked, "Are you sure? Right. Keep us posted," and cut off his subdermal link.

"*Where Justicar?*" Harrack whined, the translator having a hard time conveying his emotions. "*They said they would rescue me! They said…*"

Toshir grabbed the alien and hissed something in what appeared to be the creature's ear in his neck. That did the trick, because Harrack became quiet and went back inside the panic room to retrieve several sealed cases.

"Is that all of it?" Toshir asked, even as he checked the cases' contents.

"Yes! Yes, all please! We leave now? I promise to…"

Harrack's panicked voice was interrupted by a feral snarl from Ogut, his calm, indifferent features taking on a more animalistic nature.

"Wot is it?" Park asked.

"I don't know," Ogut answered with a twitch and an inhuman hiss. "Don't know."

"Mo'ar Dikri?" Park asked.

"It's not the Dikri," Toshir said, his nose suddenly filled with a well-known scent. He grabbed Harrack by his neck, his slit-like eyes opening to become black-within-black orbs filled with fury.

"Tosh!" Park growled.

But Toshir ignored him. The *Taira* looked as though he wanted to say something, but his self-discipline took over at the last moment, and he released the Dikri, who fell down, clearly injured. Toshir ordered Park to pick up Harrack, and the *Doric's* tremendous strength allowed him to bear the alien easily.

"Change of plans. We're taking an alternative exfil point," Toshir snapped. "Ogut, you take the rear. Park, you take the lead—max phase shields."

"What going on," Harrack stammered, suddenly afraid of the humans.

"Arquin! There's a damnable Arquin," Toshir snapped at the Dikri.

Arquin were military-grade weapons servitors, bred by the Federated Alliance for *peacekeeping* missions, though how a breed of semi-sapient assassins could help the peace, only the ghosts of old Terra could answer.

The mercenaries made their way through the debris-covered corridors, doing their best to reach their exfil point as soon as possible. When they hurried past a burning office, Toshir jerked his head to the right, as new, coded information flowed into his subdermal. As the information was translated, he cursed under his breath and looked at Park and Ogut with clenched teeth.

"We have another problem," Toshir snapped. "There are anti-air assets nearby. The *Raider* can't extract us until they are removed."

"And how'd those fellats get them? Yeah?" Park snarled, not slowing his stride, as the team passed through several dead

Dikri. "The *Toffies* in int'ligence said nothin' 'bout them."

"What you talking, Human? Use translator, yes?" Harrack asked, clearly perturbed by the anxiety in Toshir's voice. "Human?"

Another data burst came in, and Toshir quickly motioned for all of them to halt. He ordered Park to put down Harrack. The Dikri looked like a cornered deer; its legs lowered as though to flee from three predators.

"We do'an have time Tosh," Park said, but he obeyed.

Toshir activated his translator while holding Harrack's neck with his left hand. His grip was loose but there was no mistaking his intentions. "Where are the Mit-Mit?" Toshir asked ominously.

Ogut frowned at Toshir's sudden question but kept quiet, waiting patiently for what would happen next. The bat-like Mit-Mit controlled most of the manufacturing industries throughout known space. *Rumors* and *conspiracy theorists* claimed that they secretly controlled the Dikri through their elected leaders, though of course, that was just nonsense.

"What Mit-Mit?" Harrack protested. "I know no Mit..." He gasped as Toshir's fist tightened despite the Dikri's struggles.

"Let's try that again!" Toshir snapped, then continued in a slow, deliberate voice. "Where are the Mit-Mit? How did they smuggle in an Arquin? How did they know my team was here?"

"Don't. Know."

Now, Park and Ogut decided to join in. Park's rock-like fists held Harrack's arms, ready to break them at Toshir's orders, while Ogut showed his right hand, covered in claws.

"Ye goin' to make us tear off yer head an' look fer the words in yer neck."

The Dikri's terror was palpable, though, to his credit, he hid it well. "I tell," Harrack's voice rasped through the translator. "No hurt. No use hurting me, yes?"

The humans released Harrack, but they continued to surround him like vultures. The Dikri quickly explained his story; the Arquin was sent in to eliminate him, not Carrack. This surprised Toshir, who expected he was rescuing Harrack for his Mit-Mit masters.

According to Harrack's admission, he served as the Mit-Mits' puppet for several years—until recently, when their power had begun to decline. In light of the new circumstances, he had seen fit to reach out to the Hithraki Kritarchy, another council species and one with significantly better PR.

The latter information surprised the humans, especially Toshir. They thought their employers were interested in propping up Mit-Mit interests in Harmonious Unity. But now, the Dikri Tributurine was claiming that he worked for the Hithraki, which could only mean that the Mit-Mit wanted him dead. That explained the Arquin and the advanced weaponry.

Two Federation Alliance council races were engaged in a proxy war with the Dikri as their pawns. Whoever won gained control of the Dikri's voting rights and consumer market, both on Ilm and elsewhere. They also began to piece together the mystery of the dead Hithraki Justicar, and that their client neglected to mention that the Hithraki now secretly controlled the newly elected Tributurine.

All this was academic for the human mercenaries, though. They were in a burning skyscraper, filled with rampaging aliens, a gene-forged killing machine tracking them, and they were being prevented from exfiltration by a black-ops team.

"You got all that?" Toshir said, a finger on the subdermal. "Looks like they forgot to mention the part about the Hithraki and Harrack. Right. We'll get it done."

"Who's side're we on 'ere, Tosh?" Park said as soon as Toshir finished speaking to his subdermal.

"Our own," Toshir said grimly. "The mission stays the same. We're paid to get this xeno out."

"We're goin' to have to take out dem Anti-Air assets first."

Unfortunately, Harrack did not have that information, and time was running out. Ogut and Toshir could smell the Arquin drawing closer, and the fires were beginning to spread on this floor.

"Ogut," Toshir turned to the Berserker, his porcelain-colored skin looking alien in the dirty light. "We need to find those anti-air assets…"

"I will take care of the Arquin. The Arquin," Ogut cut him off, steel-like bone claws already emerging all over his body; his face became more grotesque as he readied himself for the battle. Harrack said something, horrified at the recently trans-

formed human, but the mercenaries ignored him.

"The situation is…"

"I will take care of the xeno construct!" Ogut snapped, and he began to smile predatorily. "Xeno construct."

"We'll keep in touch through yer subderm," Park said. "Once we kill dem fellats, ye retreat to us, ya hear?"

Toshir nodded silently. Park quickly picked up the Dikri Tributurine, and both he and Toshir hurried way to the terraces, the most likely location of the Mit-Mit anti-air assets.

Ogut watched them go, knowing that he was on his own. But such thoughts did not bother him. He was bred for slaughter, and his cells affirmed this. His enemy was close now.

The Arquin was alarmed that the humans left one of their own. It was trying to reach one of the building's numerous recreational terraces to pursue its prey and knew that Ogut was there to act as a rearguard and keep it from pursuing. It slithered through crevices and scaffolding, doing its best to avoid Ogut, but the latter kept pace. Ogut tore off his armor and cast aside his weapons, leaving only his phase shield as he chased after the Arquin.

The minutes ticked by, both creatures locked in a game of cat and mouse, evading one another across burning corridors and shattered walkways. As Ogut pursued his target, he saw rasping radulae and smelled the pungent stench of vat-bred flesh. The Arquin kept trying to reach the terraces, but the Berserker was always one step ahead of him, his claws allowing him to climb walls and tear through barricades.

Amidst their skirmishes, the words of Carrack boomed through echo drones and audio speakers: *Remember insults to Dikri! Allans Council claim they lifted Dikri out of poor; that we primitive... Lies! Dikri build great empire. Dikri wise and great. Allans oppress Dikri, steal wealth and knowledge. When Dikri rise up...*

Suddenly, the audio turned to static, and Ogut knew that something had happened. The Arquin felt it too; its limited sapient mind was alarmed by the sound of static from the nearby echo drones. Its unseen masters heard what the Arquin heard, saw what it saw, and now, they too were alarmed by the lost broadcasts.

At the same time, a subdermal message from Toshir came through. He and Park were using their jump packs to jump from one terrace to another, hunting down the black ops team consisting of Mit-Mit soldiers and Dikri militia. They had already eliminated one team. Only two more to go.

Park had stashed Harrack somewhere close by, guarded by two drones, while they hunted down the rest of their targets. Toshir transmitted a series of rally points that Ogut could go to for rendezvous once the anti-air teams were neutralized.

Ogut felt the Arquin pause, its prodigious mass suddenly still as it waited for its master's orders. With a noiseless shudder, it turned towards the human. The creature smashed through the walls that separated it from its new target. No longer hunting Har-rack, it saw no need to conceal its form.

Ogut braced himself but was still overwhelmed by his enemy. He was hurled into the nearby ceiling and then cast from side to side by the Arquin's radulae, his phase shield absorbing some of the impact. Though lying on his back, the mercenary retaliated with his claws, tearing into the Arquin's appendages and severing two of the creature's radulae.

Ogut quickly got up, and summoned every claw in his body. His blood became toxic from all the noxious hormones flooding through him. His flesh clung to his bone, his muscles tightening unnaturally. His ribs and limbs shifted, appearing like knives. Even his flesh seemed to change and became part of the knife-like bones.

Ogut faced the Arquin, claws out and his feral features completely inhuman. He grinned at his enemy, a primordial mien allowed to full expression in this time of fury.

He and the Arquin were of a kind, bred to kill and be killed, facing one another with something akin to joy. Here among the chaos and destruction, they were allowed to reach the pinnacle of ferocity; to kill or die without reason or purpose.

The gene-forged fiends leaped at each other in silence. Claws cut into flesh; tentacles crushed bones; both the human and the Arquin tore at each other with unnatural fury. They clung to each other, wrestling on the ground, eagerly seeking the slightest weakness.

The xeno-born monstrosity spat something at Ogut, an acidic substance that caused Ogut's outer skin to boil. Were his flesh that of an Atavisti, a non-speciated human before the age of gen-forging and mass eugenics, Ogut would be nothing more but a pool of blood by now.

But Ogut was of the Berserker breed, and as the pain shot up through his body, the more he desired to tear through his enemy, to rend it with his claws. Aggression hormones rushed through his nerves, and his body grew prodigiously, more inhuman. Ogut's flesh became thicker, his muscles coiled, and his claws filled with an odourless fluid.

They fought across smoke-filled corridors, ignoring the falling debris. Soon, primitive chemical propellant ammunition began firing, and Ogut knew that some of the Dikri had found them.

Now, the battle continued with the addition of Dikri bullets flying. They fought in the noxious corridors of the burning building until one of the Dikri militia accidentally shot a large fuel line, destroying most of that floor.

Ogut quickly recovered from the fall. Various parts of his body were covered by burns.

He was in an antechamber, next to one of the building's wide-open terraces. The Arquin lay on the terrace ahead of him, clearly injured from the explosion. Ogut was also wounded, but that did not prevent him from launching himself at the Arquin. Amidst the smoke surrounding the terrace, Ogut leapt onto the monstrosity and stabbed his claws deep into its back.

The clear light of day revealed the Arquin's bestial form. It was four times the size of a human and was composed of a mishmash of radulae, tentacles, and scaly limbs. Ogut found it difficult to visualize how such a creature moved so fast, and yet it did. Its tentacles slashed at the human, wrapping themselves around him as it tried dislodge him.

But Ogut clung on. He ripped off the creature's appendages, but it didn't seem to have any effect, and the Arquin had several more tentacles and whip-like radulae to spare.

Then Ogut slipped his footing, allowing the Arquin to hurl him off. He was thrown into a pile of debris, his mind whirling from his injuries and the toxins of his enemy. He quickly got up, just in time to catch the hurtling mass of the Arquin. The creature's momentum broke something inside of Ogut. The crack of steely bone echoed through his ear.

The Arquin smashed Ogut against walls. Even so, Ogut clung, and he dug his claws deeper and deeper, some of them digging into the Arquin's inner organs. The two antagonists flung away all thought of survival—all that mattered at this point was to kill the other, no matter the cost.

And then a terrible scream from the *Raider* shattered the wind's serenity. The sleek transport aimed one of its turrets at the creature. The Arquin tried to escape, but Ogut would not let it. He dug the claws on his feet into the ground and tightened his grip on his prey.

The *Raider's* forward turret glowed ominously as it charged to fire...

The *Raider* extracted Ogut, his body a wreck from its injuries, before it flew to the exfil point a few floors up. It floated placidly near a balcony, where Park, Toshir, and the VIP waited for their extraction. The building's upper structure was collapsing, so they didn't have much time.

Harrack in particular looked relieved by the transport's arrival; that is, until the vessel opened its doors, revealing its passengers. There was golden-skinned Horton, the mercenary's leader, and a few other human mercenaries, clearly injured from recent fighting. Ogut was plopped on a chair, his arm torn off, his body covered in blood and ichor, but otherwise, alive.

But the biggest surprise and the source of Harrack's sudden terror was...

"Carrack," the Dikri Tributurine muttered, and he started to back away suddenly.

"Get in, please, Tributurine," Toshir said and gripped his arm to push him forward into the transport.

"What's going on here?" Harrack demanded even as he was forced to sit on chairs designed for bipedals. "Unhand me."

"Quiet!" Horton snapped, then turned to face Toshir. "You have the data?"

Toshir nodded and handed the cases Harrack gave him earlier. The lead human scanned the data inside the cases and nodded his head. "They're still sealed. Good."

As the human leader inspected the case, Harrack looked at his nemesis, Carrack. He was covered in bruises and injuries and restrained by primitive handcuffs. Carrack looked at Harrack briefly with a tired, broken expression, and lowered his head once more. It took him another minute to realize that Carrack's vocal organs had been removed.

"You animals!" he muttered. "The council will—"

The human leader's menacing smile gave Harrack pause. "It seems your patrons have abandoned you, Tributurine. Propping you up is just too much trouble..."

The Dikri riots, officially called the Harmonious Unity Protests, finally ended when news of Carrack's death began spreading among his supporters. Apparently, the would-be political revolutionary had been killed by a stray shot from one of the rampaging mobs. At first, his supporters refused to believe the news, and continued to hold the streets, but exhaustion and infighting among Ilm's Dikri population prevented them from doing so.

Two standard days later, news emerged that Harrack—the legally elected Tributurine—was also dead, killed by rioters. Unfortunately, his killers were never found, and the planet's council had to quickly put the matter to a close. With both Harrack and Carrack dead, and *Harmonious Unity* in ruins, the Dikri silently faded back to their homes, which they themselves had burned down.

To restore order and maintain social cohesion, the Ilm government ordered an emergency program where the various alien species on Ilm would help the Dikri in their time of trial. Certain citizens complained that they shouldn't be made to help a race who burned down their own homes, but these vocal minorities were few and far between and were ignored by the vast majority of citizens.

The conspiracy theorists claimed humans had abducted and executed Carrack and Harrack. Moreover, they argued that segments of the Mit-Mit and the Hithraki, both Council Races, supported Carrack and Harrack respectively, and that the human intervention was ordered by other segments of the Federated Alliance government to prevent the proxy conflict from escalating. Fanciful theories, to be sure, but such theories tend to appear after great tragedies.

The human mercenaries denied such claims, of course; arguing that they only sought to help the Federated Alliance against *all its enemies,* secessionists, traitors, and conspirators. And, of course, the murdered Dikri are clearly none of those things… clearly.

Thankfully, and with the full generosity and support of the Federated Alliance Council, a new Tributurine had been quickly elected, one fully supported by the Dikri people and the galactic community. The fact that the new official faced three different assassination attempts within a month was irrelevant.

As for Ogut, he did well, even if he had to undergo three weeks in a *Blood-Song* Cell. He had pleased the Patriarchs of the Berserker gene-breed as well as the company. His breed could expect substantial favors from the company in the future, and the company could expect more Berserker recruits.

Ilm was entering a time of sacrifice and loss, but for the human mercenaries, it was a time of great opportunity.

Jed J. Del Rosario is a Philippines-based journalist and freelance writer. His articles have appeared on Panay New Inc., Rappler.com and the US-based Manila Mail. He draws most of his inspirations from classical literature, like the Ramayana, the Iliad, the Mahabharata, the Romance of the Three Kingdoms and many others. His stories have appeared on Terrorhousemag.com and on DMR Book's Death Dealers & Diabolists.

My Name Is John Carter (Part 10)

By JAMES HUTCHINGS

[Editor's Note: Continued from Cirsova Vol 2. #6]

"Many secrets were known by my labors alone
when this place and our home held their truce.
It is bitter indeed that this hour of need
finds my talents bereft of all use.

"Still I gather my hints from each merchant and
　　prince
hoarding seeds that can never bear fruit.
I am caught in that dream where I struggle to
　　scream
when some power has rendered me mute."

"You shall soon speak again," Dejah answered.
　　"And when
all is done," she said, turning to me,
"you shall hear yourself praised by the crowd, and
　　be raised
to a lord of the highest degree."

Inarticulate print, that conveys not a hint
that bright words may be naught but disguise.
None who heard Dejah's voice could be moved to
　　rejoice
nor who saw the despair in her eyes.

When I think of it now I must ask myself how
I acceded. For what or for whom
did I curb my dissent while my only love went
to unknown and unbearable doom?

Well I know that to fret with such fruitless regret
changes naught—yet I fret all the same.
He was cruel who designed us with reasoning minds
and then handed blind Instinct the reins.

Be he wise as the Sphinx, still the mariner drinks
from the sea when his thirst is grown keen
with a will no more free than a drop in that sea
or the gears of some grinding machine.

And perhaps every stone that is picked up and
　　thrown
thinks the thrower obeys its command.
Given speech I suppose it would tell how it chose
the direction, the speed, and the hand.

We are puppeted kings never seeing our strings
faithful servants who think ourselves master
and our life travels straight on a line drawn by Fate
and our blindness provokes him to laughter.

So at least I suspect when my mood grows deject-
　　ed.
If ever some deity grants me
greater wisdom, I pray I can figure a way
to tell insight from dolorous fancy.

But my sorrowful brain did not conjure the pain
that disfigured my love's noble face.
Heaven's halls turn to slums, and all beauty be-

comes
hard to look on when hope is erased.

We seemed lapped by the clock in one step of that
    walk.
We were filled with a terrible languor
every moment seemed slowed to a day on the road
to the seat of the lords of Zodanga.

In a while she emerged, with the face of one
    scourged
and worn down by the burden she carried.
"The vendetta is done, and two peoples are one
for myself and their king shall be married."

If the Devil were real and inclined to make deals
and Barsoom were a part of his writ
and he chose to appear in that moment, and sneer
of some evil he'd have me commit,

and that crime were so vile that the length of the
    Nile
lacked the water to wash out its stain
and he said, "By this deed, Dejah Thoris is freed,
for the king, her betrothed, shall be slain,"

then he'd have little sport, for the hunt would be
    short
and the quarry content to be snared—
but naught happened. And I made no word of reply
and at last Dejah Thoris declared,

"Well I know ye, John Carter, and know that thy
    heart
writhes in pain, though thy visage is placid,
and to face me thus, frozen in stoical pose
seems to boil thee within like an acid.

"And I know ye would slay all who wound me,
    though they
did not seek for that harm, but were sought,
and I long to permit my lord's throat to be slit
and be free from the trap I have wrought.

"How abundantly loathed is my royal betrothed
that two planets bore people who hate him!
But if I were released, it would shatter the peace
I have bought with this damnable mating.

"Therefore go, ere the sight of thee tempts me de-
    spite
kin and city, and dying Barsoom,"
and with that my poor soul, that was stable and
    whole,
was as splinters the axeman had hewn.

The next weeks have grown blurred. I suppose
    things occurred,
and days passed at the usual rate,
and all time did not halt, that the gods might exult
at the consummate woe of my fate.

The abode of the spy held my body while I
stayed imprisoned inside of my skull.
With my burdens as sentry the world gained no en-
    try
and future and past were annulled.

And my thoughts seemed to run like the course of
    the Sun:
never still, but forever repeating,
and each circuit would end with two lovers con-
    demned
by the words of our last, dreadful meeting.

She was right, in a way, for I did long to slay
every prince in this pestilent place,
but she strayed from the facts when she claimed I
    would act
out of love, for my motive was base:

just to have solid foes, not insoluble woes,
and to meet them with sword and with shot,
and to feel the red rage and slip free from the cage
that the hopeless man builds from his thoughts.

When your talents are few and the one thing you do
with great skill is your worst, fatal vice,
and to act would mean war, and the one you adore
begs you hold, and you know that the price

would be death, you refrain, and live on, though you'd fain
never wake, though all solace deserts you.
Yet all will must grow weak among people who speak
of such slaughter as noblest virtue

where one word of disdain, and the speaker not slain
would dishonor the lowliest tiller,
and the mother who grieves that her children are thieves
would rejoice to discover them killers.

Like a glutton who wakes in a kingdom of cakes
with an ulcer that stops him from eating,
I reflected, and smiled, and the ocean of bile
in me ebbed, though this respite was fleeting.

It took hours to sift through the torrent of gifts
Dejah sent: beasts to pet and to ride,
raiment silken and sleek, furs as soft as her cheek,
all the riches that Mars could provide.

Had I been one of those who grow calm in repose
and more wise with more time to reflect,
I'd have swallowed my pain, seen that struggle was vain,
and lived safely and well, I expect.

But for me, to whom ease was a noxious disease
and long used to hard living thereby,
all the things that she sent me did little to tempt me.
I gave them away to the spy.

"For the food, and the bed, and my presence," I said,
"for I know I'm not easy to bear."
Save a mute or a saint, few would make less complaint
than she made as I soaked in despair.

And I left. All unknowing of where I was going
and owning no more than I carried
and a plan that consisted of no more than this:
wed the woman you love or be buried.

James Hutchings lives in Melbourne, Australia. The nostalgia of things unknown, of lands forgotten or unfound, is upon him at times.

Stealing the Alchemist Stone

By RICHARD RUBIN

Burke Fletcher and his wife Llana have just absconded with an Alchemist Stone! But the baron they stole it from is not the only one who desires its arcane powers!

A blare of klaxons wailing behind him, Burke Fletcher raced down the corridor leading to the stairs that would take him to the landing pad on the palace roof. Without breaking stride, he jammed the precious stolen object deep into his pants pocket. He heard rapid footfalls from behind, but it sounded like his pursuers weren't that close yet—he could still make it.

Rounding the corner, he came upon a lone sentry posted at the foot of the staircase. The startled man's eyes locked on Fletcher's as his hand went for the holstered blaster at his hip. But before the uniformed soldier could level his weapon, Fletcher smashed his right fist into the man's face, sending him sprawling senseless to the floor. Fletcher bounded up the stairs and burst through the roof door of Baron Amalrik's palace. Llana awaited him in a swift two-person flyer, its radium engine purring softly, primed for flight. In laying their plans, the couple had thought they would be able to take off at a leisurely speed so that their small craft passing through the barony's

sky would appear to be no more than a routine pleasure or business flight. But the time for such pretense was gone—the alarm had been triggered!

Fletcher flung open the door of the flyer and dropped into the copilot seat. "Get us out of here, fast!"

As his wife engaged the controls, Fletcher saw two palace guards dashing toward one of the plasma-ray cannons mounted on the roof. The flyer shot up sharply and soared away at full throttle out into the red-tinted sky of Rigel IV. A few moments later, a burst of white-hot plasma darted out at the fleeing ship. Llana threw the joystick over hard, sending the flyer into a barrel roll, barely dodging the flame of destruction. As the cannon repeatedly blasted at their frail craft, Llana continued evasive actions, dodging and weaving to elude the deadly energy discharges.

Without turning, Llana asked, "Did you get it?"

"Yes, I accidentally tripped an alarm, but we have it."

It was an Alchemist Stone—*one of only*

three on the entire planet—a powerful talisman that would greatly enhance Llana's fledgling powers of alchemy. Now it was theirs, if they could just manage their escape. Llana was a member of a select class of Rigelians who practiced an amalgamation of magical and scientific wizardry resembling nothing encountered on Fletcher's homeworld of Earth.

Her apprenticeship as an alchemist had been cut short two years ago when her mother had been killed in a blood feud with a rival mage, but Llana continued to refine her skills as best she could on her own. A week ago, she had learned that Marta, the ancient master alchemist who had served Baron Amalrik's family for well over two hundred years, had finally succumbed to death. And, as Llana had suspected, although the baron had kept Marta's stone on hand in hopes of passing it on to her eventual replacement, the precious object had been left relatively unguarded within his palace.

Fletcher removed the radiating sapphire talisman, the size of a hen's egg, from his pocket and set it on the dashboard to admire.

Ten years ago, Fletcher had served as a lieutenant in Earth Space Navy. He had been on a solo long-range survey mission when his scout craft encountered a solar storm, causing him to crash-land on Rigel IV. His comm unit was destroyed. Still, for a few months afterward, he held out some hope that an Earth vessel might show up to rescue him from this barbarous world. He finally came to realize that those hopes were foolish, and accepted that he would never see his home planet again. He resolved to make his way in this weird, war-torn world and had thrown in his lot with an itinerant mercenary band, a group of blue-skinned humanoids.

Fletcher, who'd always been athletic—he had been an amateur fencer in college—quickly impressed the mercenaries with his fighting skills and courage. They in turn taught him the language and customs of Rigel IV. Then he had fallen in love with and married Llana, a young alchemist. His mercenary band was now gone, slain in battle except for himself, but for what it was worth, this savage planet was now his home.

An hour after their flight from the palace, the small flyer cruised over a jagged mountain range. Gazing below, Fletcher made out a tall, ruined tower thrusting up from a bank of fog. Strange—he had never heard of any stronghold or keep situated this far north of Amalrik's freehold.

As they passed above the tower, the Alchemist Stone began to hum and vibrate, then it suddenly flashed a blinding white light. Fletcher cried out in alarm, shielding his eyes, but a few seconds later the humming stopped, and the light faded from the sapphire talisman.

"What just happened?" he asked.

"I don't know. Alchemist Stones possess many weird powers, and I'm far from comprehending all of them."

Llana frowned at the control screen, then said, "A black gunboat just appeared behind us, approaching fast."

"Is it one of Amalrik's?"

"Doesn't have any markings—no identifying insignia at all."

Looking over his shoulder, Fletcher made out a jet-black gunboat flying toward them at high speed. "No way to know for sure whether it's hostile or not," he said. "But it hasn't activated its comlink, so this doesn't strike me as a prelude to a friendly encounter."

"Let's lose it."

Llana attempted to speed away, driving their flyer fast and hard, taking advantage of the low-hanging clouds and mountains they were passing through, but it wasn't enough to shake the fleet pursuer off their tail.

The gunboat drew within range of their stern. A moment later, it discharged its forward laser. Dodging the blast, Llana spun their flyer about to engage the enemy, firing their own laser blast at the mysterious craft. The enemy dodged and weaved at full tilt, making it impossible for Llana to take careful aim or obtain a weapons lock.

Llana's flyer was nimbler at close range than the larger gunboat, however, and within a matter of seconds, she raked its nose, banking hard to the left while executing a roll and getting off a burst of laser fire at the foe. The opponent took some damage but ducked and dove, managing to escape the full brunt of Llana's discharge at the last moment. The gunboat then climbed, shooting a laser blast at their underside. Llana anticipated the move and countered quickly, looping around and firing at the gunboat's rear. She hit one of the enemy's wings, shearing it clean off. The enemy ship accelerated and spun wildly. A second later, it slammed into the side of a mountain.

The pursuing craft had been destroyed, but something was very wrong: their flyer was losing altitude and veering rightward. "By the Seven Hell Demons of Rigel!" Llana cursed.

"What's happening?" Fletcher asked.

"We've been hit. That bastard must have damaged our left stabilizer strut. I'm going to try to land before we end up crashing. I think I saw a safe spot but can't tell for sure because of all the damned fog below. Brace yourself, love, this one could be rough!"

Jagged terrain, obscured by fog, lay below, but Llana directed the flyer toward what appeared to be an extended smooth plateau. She dropped altitude, leveled the craft, and skidded its landing skis along the rocky surface.

As the flyer reduced speed, Llana released her breath. It looked like they were going to be all right, Fletcher thought, just before a giant boulder loomed up in their windshield.

The tiny craft upended and rolled end-over-end atop the huge rock, finally plowing into the ground with a resounding crash. Fletcher threw up his arms to protect his head as the windshield shattered and he flipped out of his seat. He groaned as his elbow struck the metal dashboard, just before his body landed on the steel door, which now lay on the floor of the craft.

Looking to where Llana had been, he saw that the pilot-side door had sprung open. His wife lay nearby on the ground, thrown clear of the wrecked flyer.

"Llana!" he screamed.

In pain, he climbed out of the wreck and dashed to her side. She was unconscious, her breathing labored.

Fletcher didn't think it wise to move her—she could have internal bleeding. Peering westward, he made out the ruined tower he had seen from the air. Set on a rocky crag, it lay several miles away through a precipitous mountain pass that appeared to be accessible from where he stood. The tower had looked abandoned, but perhaps he might find an old hovercraft or flyer there he could render operable.

He dreaded leaving his wife alone, but there was little he could do for her if he stayed. He went back to retrieve the Alchemist Stone from the flyer. It was wedged in the smashed wreckage of the dashboard, but he was able to extract it with his boot knife. He returned to Llana and pressed the sapphire talisman gently in her palm. He didn't understand its alchemical properties, but perhaps it would give her strength to heal.

He set out on foot, armed with the raygun and sword that were the tools of his trade as a professional sellsword. Soon he came upon a worn trail that wound its way through a series of steep mountain ridges going in the direction of the tower. When he was about halfway there, Fletcher stopped at a high vantage point to drink some water from his canteen. Shielding his eyes from the twin suns in the red-hued Rigelian sky, he surveyed the narrow pass below. There lay rugged, barren terrain, lacking any sign of roads or habitation.

A shadow crossed over him. Fletcher glanced up to see a crimson bird, twice the size of a man, circling in the sky. It was the creature Rigelians called a roc: a fearless and vicious man-eating predator. It hovered above, clearly contemplating its attack. Fletcher drew the raygun holstered at his hip, took aim, and fired two blasts at the creature. The shots struck the roc's feathered underbelly but to no discernible effect. The creature released a blood-chilling roar and soared down. As it made its approach, Fletcher quickly reholstered his raygun and drew his sword. The roc flew directly at him, its fierce, yellow beak aiming straight for the mercenary's throat.

Fletcher ducked his head just in time to avoid the razor-sharp bill of the hell-spawned creature. The roc flapped its mighty wings and flew a short distance away, then turned back for a second pass. As it closed in, Fletcher swung his sword and feigned a forward thrust at the approaching roc. Then, as the great red bird failed to react, Fletcher pulled back his blade and struck a savage blow that should have cut through the bone and muscle of the creature's left wing.

But the mercenary's blade bounced off the hide of the beast as if he had struck hard metal rather than yielding organic flesh. A numbing pain shot up Fletcher's sword arm as he stumbled back, recoiling from the deflected sword strike. The roc swept out its huge tail and lashed it behind Fletcher's legs.

Frantically, he fought to retain his purchase, then lost his footing and tumbled into the gaping chasm below. Fletcher released a curse, expecting to die the next moment, but giant talons reached around his waist and seized him.

The avian beast lifted him into the air and began flying in the direction of the tower, the struggling mercenary in its firm grasp.

Fletcher felt impotent rage as he dangled helplessly, carried above the rough trail carved through the mountain pass. He wondered if he would ever see Llana again. The creature was taking him to the ruined tower in the mists. Minutes later, Fletcher looked down on crumbling battlements as the roc flew over the tower's outer wall. The great bird finally landed, dropped Fletcher unceremoniously onto an oval cobblestone courtyard atop the structure, and flew off.

The courtyard was deserted, but Fletcher noticed two round metal doors at opposite ends. He picked himself up and started toward the nearest one. There was the whirl of machinery from behind, and he turned to see the opposite door irising open. Nine tall, gleaming metal robots glided hastily out to confront him. The robot in front, adorned with a bright red-and-blue sash across its chest, appeared to be the group's leader. Fletcher's hand instinctively went to the raygun at his hip as he waited to see how this would play out.

The robot in the lead called out in a metallic voice: "Human, you are our prisoner. Lay down your weapons and come with us peacefully. We have been instructed by our masters to disarm you and bring you to them. You will experience avoidable pain if we are required to employ force to subdue you."

Smiling grimly, Fletcher responded by drawing his raygun and blasting a three-inch hole through the center of the lead robot's chest.

As their leader collapsed to the ground, the remaining robots rushed the Earthman. Fletcher managed to gun down two more of them before they got to him.

As they closed in, one of the mechanical men swung out a metal hand, knocking away the mercenary's gun. Reduced to his bare hands, Fletcher delivered a smashing punch to the jaw of the closest robot, dropping it to the ground.

But there were just too many of them; he eventually went down in a flurry of kicks and flailing punches. The surviving robots seized his hands and feet, rendering him helpless. Then they hauled the immobilized Earthman through the door from which they had come, down winding stairs, ending up in a large, lavishly furnished chamber. The robots took him to the center of the room and released him.

Fletcher found himself standing before a slender, blue-skinned woman sitting in a heavily jeweled, high-backed throne. She wore a light purple robe and had long silver hair adorned by a golden headband. There was something strange about her; she seemed lacking in emotion and almost too beautiful and perfect looking.

"My name is Radea," she said. "Welcome to the Tower of Vantor, where I rule. And who might you be?"

"I am Burke Fletcher, late of the planet

Earth. I am a professional mercenary, an honorable calling on this world. Why have you seized me and taken me here? Disarmed me?"

"There is no need for apprehension, Burke Fletcher. We intend you no harm."

"I find that hard to believe. Your robots, as well as your roc, have already attacked me. And I suspect that the black gunboat that fired on our flyer also originated from your tower."

"I apologize if we have caused trouble for you, but our present intent is to offer you an opportunity beyond your imagination. We of the tower have just awakened after over a thousand years of suspended animation. In fact, Lord Master Alchemist Vantor is still in the process of achieving full wakefulness."

She pointed to a corner of the large room; Fletcher looked over to see an open stasis cylinder set against a wall. During Fletcher's service in the Earth Space Navy, he had seen chambers like that used to transport colonists in deep sleep during long space voyages, but this was the first time he had seen one on Rigel IV.

"Long ago, our people fought a great war against our neighbor, Baron Amalrik," Radea continued. "We were defeated, our civilization destroyed, our lands rendered barren and radioactive. But in the moment of defeat, our ruler, Lord Vantor, conceived a great plan to exact a devastating revenge upon Amalrik's people and to forge a vast new empire.

"For forty years, Lord Vantor labored in secrecy behind the walls of what looked to all the world as nothing more than a ruined, abandoned tower. There, he crafted a seemingly invincible arsenal of war. When he was done, Lord Vantor and I were placed in stasis along with a massive army of fighter robots and advanced techno-weapons that he had built, including the mechanical roc and black gunship you encountered. This was intended to give us the means of launching a surprise attack upon Amalrik's freehold long after he and his wretched subjects had all but forgotten us. Lord Vantor programmed the systems in this tower to fully activate and awaken us after eighty years of cryosleep. Then we would take our revenge and go on to conquer a vast empire."

"But you say you've actually slept much longer—something happened?" Fletcher interjected, surmising that the "Baron Amalrik" she referred to was not the present lord but his long-dead ancestor.

"There was a breakdown in our machinery. Our surveillance and monitoring tech continued to function, but Lord Vantor and I remained asleep for centuries. Until today. Upon awakening, I looked to our scientific instruments and determined that the proximity of an Alchemist Stone shocked the systems of the tower into wakefulness—an Alchemist Stone carried in the very flyer in which you arrived. But unfortunately the long passage of time has taken its toll: only a handful of our robots and techno-weapons survived the centuries of dormancy in operable condition. We shall have to rebuild our capacities—that is where you fit into our plans. Come, I will show you why there is a place for you here by my side."

Radea gestured for him to follow her across the room. Fletcher did so, flanked by the surviving robots—the robot he had knocked down earlier hobbled behind its five counterparts. Fletcher wondered how he would manage to get back to Llana and help her before it was too late. He joined Radea alongside the stasis chamber. Looking within, Fletcher saw a small, white-haired, gnome-like man, naked and hooked up to various tubes and wires. Lord Vantor's eyes were open, he drew breath, his fingers even twitched sporadically, but he seemed to be in a subdued state, like someone coming out of a drugged sleep.

"This is Lord Master Alchemist Vantor, creator of this tower. As you can see, he has yet to fully awaken," Radea said. "No doubt it is because of his advanced age. I was to serve as his consort and second-in-command, but you can see for yourself that he is too old and weak to lead. Come, I have more to show you."

She guided him down another flight of stairs, with the six robots silently following them. A metal door irised open, and they stepped out onto a wide interior balcony overlooking a vast cavernous room. Below them lay seemingly endless rows of shiny new robots, lying side by side on flat metal platforms enveloped within mazes of wiring and machinery.

Radea waved her hand at the banks of robots and said, "They're all dead, inoperable. The only robots that survived the long centuries of dormancy were the handful that you saw and—thanks to you—now on-

ly six remain active. We'll need a weapons master to help us fashion a new and better robot army—someone who also possesses the fighting skills necessary to help program and train the robots. Someone who understands tactics and strategy, who has a grasp of the present military situation on Rigel IV." She looked pointedly at him.

The door to the balcony opened again, and Lord Vantor emerged, looking alert but unsteady on his feet. The gnome-like man was dressed in a loose-fitting gray robe tied at the waist, and his hair was still damp from the stasis chamber. Vantor cast a hateful glance at Fletcher, then turned his venom to the woman. "What is this outsider doing here? This man who wears the garb of a southland sellsword? He's an intruder who should be slain out of hand!"

Radea raised her voice in anger. "Henceforth I will command here, not you. You were once a great alchemist, but you no longer have the strength to lead, to give orders. It has been over one thousand years since we went into stasis—not the eighty you promised! And most of the fighting robots and techno-weapons you fashioned are useless. You have failed us, so it falls to me to salvage our plans. This man's name is Burke Fletcher. Yes, he is a sellsword, a skilled fighting man from the planet Earth who will serve as my consort and weapons master."

Fletcher was shocked and bewildered at her presumption. "Hold on, I didn't agree—"

"That is not what I planned when I built this wondrous tower," Vantor interrupted.

"I alone command here. And we do not need the help of this outworlder, this sword for hire."

"I will decide what we do or don't need from now on," she replied, looking at him with cold contempt. "You are old and frail, no longer fit for command. You may remain here if you wish and aid our conquests, but I shall rule here, not you."

The old man spat on the floor, then stormed out the balcony door.

Fletcher turned on Radea. "Why did you say that? I haven't agreed to be your weapons master or even to stay here." He was desperate to get back to Llana and help her somehow. This woman was crazy. She had no right to include him in her mad schemes.

Radea replied, "With our surveillance monitors, I watched how you conducted yourself against our mechanical roc and our warrior robots. I was impressed—you are clearly a skilled fighting man. We have need of such as yourself. Give us the Alchemist Stone that you possess and remain here as my consort. Help us design and rebuild our army of warrior robots. Together we will be unstoppable. We shall conquer an empire!"

"I can't remain here with you. My wife is out there. She's injured and requires medical attention, thanks to that damned gunship of yours."

"If you agree to join us, I will activate a medic program to enable one of our robots to go treat your wife and take her by hovercraft to the nearest town. But I will do so only if you swear to forsake her and remain here to aid in our conquests. Our robots will stop you from leaving in any event. But if you do not commit to this, your wife will needlessly be left alone to die."

Fletcher grit his teeth in frustration and emotional turmoil. His beloved wife was badly injured and alone, without any means of transport. Stripped of his raygun and sword, he had little chance of stealing a hovercraft and escaping from Radea and her squad of robots.

Fletcher hated to agree to Radea's terms, but there was really no choice. If she kept her word, at least Llana would survive. Otherwise, there was no hope for her. And perhaps, if he bided his time, he would find a way to escape from this lunatic warmonger and make his way back to his wife and the outside world. He would also find a way to warn Baron Amalrik and the other nearby rulers of this threat. Fletcher bore no love for Amalrik, but it was these people, not Amalrik, who posed an existential threat to the social order of his adopted world.

Lord Vantor burst back onto the balcony armed with a heavy gauge disrupter rifle, his eyes boring hatred into Radea. He raised the weapon and aimed for the center of Fletcher's chest, shouting, "I will take care of this outworlder and deal with you later, Radea!"

As Vantor pulled the trigger, the mercenary's battlefield-conditioned muscles reacted instantly. He dropped to the floor and rolled.

Fletcher felt heat as the red flame of death flashed past where his chest had been just moments before. He went to one knee and grabbed for the throwing knife in his boot.

Radea faced Vantor and yelled, "Stop, fool!"

She dashed between Vantor and Fletcher, just as the master alchemist's finger closed on the trigger for a second time. There was a flash of red energy, and Radea went down, a hole burned between her breasts.

"Radea!" Vantor screamed in horror at what he had done.

In a single motion, Fletcher hurled his throwing knife at Lord Vantor. The blade flew straight and true, catching the master alchemist in the throat. He collapsed to the floor, blood spurting from his wound.

Fletcher ran over to see if anything could be done for Radea. Kneeling down, he cradled her head in his arms. Her flesh was cold to the touch. Examining the gaping wound in her chest, where Fletcher had expected to see blood and organs, he was shocked to find, instead, exposed wires and a broken endoskeleton. Radea was not a person—she was a lifelike android, and, moreover, she apparently didn't know it.

"Please, Burke Fletcher," came the raspy, weak voice. "I know I am dying. Kiss me, and let me share my last moments with you."

Fletcher leaned his face in and granted her wish. Her lips felt like cool steel, but he put that aside and kissed her with as much passion as he could muster. He experienced a brief twinge of guilt as their lips met, but how could his beloved wife be jealous of an android—especially one that would be dead and lifeless in moments?

Radea smiled weakly and said, "There's a hovercraft stored in the chamber below. But you must beware the roc robot—with us gone, it will seek revenge for what you have done. It..." The mechanical voice trailed off. Fletcher had further questions, but Radea now lay still and lifeless.

Fletcher stood and looked over at the six robots. They hadn't taken sides in the conflict between their two masters, and now, lacking direction from either one, they simply remained frozen in place. Fletcher went over to where Lord Vantor lay, only to discover that the aged master alchemist was quite human and quite dead. Apart from Vantor himself, the tower had been entirely populated by robots and techno-weapons. Fletcher retrieved his knife, wiping the blood off on the little alchemist's tunic, then returned the weapon to his boot. He picked up Vantor's disrupter rifle and slung it over his shoulder.

Fletcher made his way to the room Radea had indicated, where he found a compact open-top hovercraft. He opened a large bay door and sailed the hovercraft out of the tower, heading back to where he had left Llana. He was anxious to return to her, yet cautious lest he lose his way in the treacherous mountain pass winding through the dense fog and steep cliffs.

He thought of Radea. The fact that she had been an android, albeit a highly sophisticated one, explained her seemingly impulsive selection of Fletcher to be her consort and weapons master. It had been the result of rapid computer calculation—a far cry from the normal pace of human-emotion-laden decision-making. Still, her affection for him had been real in its way.

As Fletcher approached the plateau where the wrecked flyer lay, he heard the beating of wings and looked around to see the mechanical roc pursuing him from behind. He pushed the hovercraft faster, but it was no use; he couldn't outdistance the swift creature. The tiny hovercraft began to rock in the wake of the roc's flapping wings as the fierce beast closed in from above.

Fletcher grabbed the disrupter rifle he had taken from Lord Vantor. Aiming up from the open cockpit, he looked into the menacing eyes of the roc. At this range, he could hardly miss. He took a moment to brace himself and aim the rifle dead center between the monster's eyes, then he fired. But the effect was no better than when he had shot his blaster at the beast earlier. The roc absorbed the blast with no ill effect. It only roared and closed in on the hovercraft.

"Burke, get down, give me a clear shot at that thing!" It was Llana's voice, shouting.

Fletcher's battle-hardened instincts engaged. He shoved the joystick forward to bring the hovercraft hard to ground. As he skidded to a halt, Fletcher watched his wife ahead, the Alchemist Stone extended high in her right hand, her gaze fully fixed on the approaching roc. Suddenly, a blast of blue flame shot out from the sapphire stone. Fletcher saw the mechanized bird blow apart into gears and metal shards. Then Llana collapsed to the ground.

Fletcher leapt out of the hovercraft and ran to her. "Llana!" he cried out, kneeling over her.

She lay there dazed for a few moments, then raised herself up on her elbows. "I'm exhausted, love, but I'll be all right. An Alchemist Stone has the power to instruct a mage on the means of its use, and I have learned some useful things while you were away. The magic of alchemy has its price, and it took much strength for me to destroy that creature, but I'm young and strong. I should fully recover in a few days." She looked at the hovercraft. "I see you brought something for us."

"Are you well enough to travel?"

"I think so. Help me in."

Fletcher gently lifted Llana and set her down in the hovercraft, then he took his place behind the controls. The young alchemist was a bit wobbly in her seat, but she looked like she would be all right.

"What happened to you?" Llana asked in a rasping whisper.

"It's a long tale. I'll entertain you with it as we journey home."

"Look forward to hearing it. Then I'll entertain you with what I've learned of the powers of our Alchemist Stone!"

Richard L. Rubin's science fiction tales appear in various magazines including Cirsova, Broadswords and Blasters, and The Weird and Whatnot. In a previous life he worked as an appellate lawyer, defending several clients facing the death penalty in California. He lives in the San Francisco Bay Area. Richard's website is www.richardlrubin.com.

To the Sound of a Silent Harp

By WILLIAM HUGGINS

Harp, a deadly and addictive vidliq, will possess you forever—much like Cavan, the magnate who built his fortune on it! Ciaon, Cavan's errand boy, finds himself caught in a deadly web of deception—can he escape, or is he, too, a man possessed?!

The pigeon sat at the roof's edge, pecking avidly at something Ciaon couldn't see. Ciaon spat. He hated the ugly birds—hated them with the same intensity as the godmen who dressed like them, sooty blacks and grays. So many birds extinct, yet pigeons held on. *Survivors, like me.* They so rarely landed on rooftops anymore, but today Mellen needed to relieve himself—too much kaf—and this was the closest empty place.

"Step it up, old man!"

"Moment!" cried a voice on the far side of an electrical box, behind a row of solar panels.

"Tell it to Cavan! We're behind already!" *Twenty minutes, and counting.* If that didn't move the old fool, nothing would. Cavan had more patience for pigeons than tardiness.

Mellen dashed into view, tying his trousers as he ran. He fumbled at the car, leapt inside. The passenger door popped open.

"Moment." Ciaon opened his coat, pulsed his left arm. The straydart fired, and the pigeon disappeared in a sudden burst of feathers and blood, without even a cry. Ciaon dropped into his seat and slammed the door, a satisfied grin on his face. "One less parasite."

They set down on an empty street, and Ciaon looked both ways as he stepped from the car, straydart at the ready. The sidewalk empty, he took three quick steps and entered Bakeburg's, a world of garish contrasts. Ciaon always imagined the casino's designer worked high on the latest vidliq. Cool aquamarine slid smoothly from mid-ceiling's frothy grey-white, navy by the time it met the floor. The sharp reds of the pew-like booths, maroon and light cherry, circled the dull brown tables and chairs in a crimson halo. In the back left corner, a neon riot of color swirled around the slot machines. Chandeliers and stained glass lamps cast low silver light around the periphery. The whole place reminded Ciaon of popular Lunar Vegas vids. Not for him, but Bakeburg's clientele seemed to enjoy it.

Bakeburg, slightly less old than Mellen but more rotund, had run the small casino since his and Ciaon's acquaintance—a little more than two years now. But Bakeburg had been there far longer, as much a fixture as the furniture and odd regulars clustered at the bar's end, looking away from the streetlights' glare whenever the doors opened.

"Afternoon, kid," Bakeburg said, gold incisor highlighting his smile. "Late."

"Delays."

Bakeburg grunted. "Always. Moment." He picked up a tray of colored sculpted glassware, carried it to the far end of the bar. He returned, wiping his hands on a towel. "Drink?"

"Would that I could, Bakeburg."

"You're not channeling for the godmen, now, are you?" They shared a laugh. Ciaon was semi-famous for dropping a godman at the entrance to Bakeburg's nearly a year ago. The thin wraith had leapt in Ciaon's path, screeching the sin of drinking and gambling and drugs. Ciaon had hesitated a moment, considering, then pulsed the straydart. Later, showering at Darla's, he'd found a chunk of tissue attached to a tooth in his hair. He wondered if you needed teeth in the godmen's paradise. Bakeburg took Ciaon much more seriously after that—possibly because his entryway stood unobstructed since the incident.

Cavan found the whole event incredibly amusing.

"And the Man?"

"Never better," Ciaon lied. "He sends greetings."

"Return them." Bakeburg's eyes drifted around the club, taking in the entire place in one smooth glance. Few people at midday: a couple shared a drink in the darkness of the lounge, the few odd regulars perched like crows at the bar's far end, gazes glassy, drinks clutched protectively close, and one lost soul hammered a slot machine, seeking and simultaneously losing a fortune. *Fool.* Bakeburg dropped behind the bar and rose with a palm-sized steel box. He flipped the lid open and held it out for Ciaon to inspect.

Seven green capsules. The Harp.

Cold-hearted orbs. Seeing them always struck Ciaon like a punch to the gut. He despised addicts as much as godmen. He'd seen too many in his time as a streetboy, devoured by religion or vidliqs. *The Harp, so much worse.* Threllian in origin, part of Cavan's legend, the foundation of his fame and empire. Ciaon knew the story too well: Cavan stowed away on a starflyer to Threll, stayed long enough to steal the chemform for their indigenous vidliqs, evaded Threll's legendary Inspectors, returned to Earth with a brief stop at Peren. Cavan came home and conquered two markets, Peren's artisanal artwork providing cover for Threll's narcotics.

No one could resist the Harp—once you took it, you belonged to it forever.

Cavan deliberately stayed away from the market he had created, hiding behind the scenes, though he still dealt in low-impact Terran vidliqs and consistent if not always legal imports. But the Harp was the foundation of his fortune. *Legend.* The Harp, laced with dreams and madness, whose networks were complex and expensive to run. But Cavan loved a fortune as much as anything—as did Bakeburg, who profited handsomely.

Ciaon shook the thoughts off, looked up. "Nice. Today he wants a double."

"Cher," Bakeburg purred, "play serious." He closed the box, planted it firmly on the bar. "You know what it takes me to get *seven* for our weekly *tete-a-tete?*" A fat finger drew on the bartop. "To make this nice hidden circle for you? You…he has no idea. He wants a double, he needs to let me know sooner."

"Oh, he knows, Bakeburg." Ciaon let his voice turn solicitous. Everyone took side action. *Life.* "Reach down again. He wants a double."

Sweat appeared on Bakeburg's brow, quickly wiped away. Ciaon could imagine who the other boxes might be for: police, judges, councilors, senators, captains of industry, fools who lost enough in his rigged slot machines, children of powers with the resources to ride the Harp—idleness and wealth bred its own luxury.

Bakeburg dithered. "You ever wonder what he wants these for?"

"Who set up the system that's making you rich? Who never asks for an accounting?" Bakeburg's face colored. "A double," Ciaon said firmly.

"Seven's one a day as it is, cher. You know what that means."

"You having conscience troubles, Bakeburg?"

The large man's face went red. "To hell with you, kid. I deal with the Man. I

don't—"

"No, *you* don't understand." Ciaon stepped back, letting his coat fall open just enough for Bakeburg to see the straydart peeking at his chest, its many-sided sharpness glinting in the dim casino light. "Mr. Cavan asks politely. I don't. A double order."

"To hell with you." Bakeburg glanced once at the straydart. A thick hand passed over his forehead again. Ciaon could see him working the balance and knew greed would win the day. Bakeburg had too much to lose. He reached under the bar and dropped another box before Ciaon.

Ciaon tapped the nearest paypad with his credigit, scooping both boxes as he did, almost like playing jacks when he was a streetboy. He knew the scene would be forgotten when he came again. Bakeburg had what he wanted—as did Cavan.

Business.

"'Til next week," Ciaon said.

Mellen popped the door, charitable as always. His face twisted in a mixture of curiosity and concern. "All well?"

"Right enough." Ciaon slammed the door down. Hard. *Bakeburg.* He would enjoy killing him. Cavan hadn't let him taste that particular pleasure in… a long time. *Too long.* The safety belt glided over its rollers, pressed against his chest. He let his head fall back, eyes closing.

"Tough buy?"

"You never need a break, Mellen?"

"Had one."

Ciaon barked a laugh. "Hell, Mellen, half

your day is a break. Waiting for me."

The old man chuckled. "I fly."

Far as Ciaon knew, shuttling him from place to place was Mellen's only function in Cavan's empire. The old man knew the town better than the car's guidewheel. Probably pushing seventy now, but he spent his time in Cavan's fitness room, and it showed: striking features, oval, handsome face, dark green eyes, hair that passed grey entirely, moving right on to white—old, but the body was firm and fit, more than a little bit intimidating.

Only one of us with any brains, Ciaon thought often. *He flies.* Easy job for a man who didn't tolerate failure.

Ciaon ran a finger across his readboard. Bakeburg's name vanished. "All right, next, Della—"

"We go back," Mellen said.

"Mel. We've got three more stops." Ciaon looked uneasy. "I had plans with Darla tonight."

"No. Back now."

"We bumped Della yesterday. We have to stop."

Mellen shook his head. "He called while you were inside."

Ciaon groaned. "Let me call him."

Mellen's look was hard.

Ciaon's hand strayed to the readboard, even scrolled to Cavan's name, but Mellen's wisdom got the better of him. *Damn.* But Cavan never did anything without a reason.

Ciaon craned his neck until it popped. Tomorrow he would have to deal with two very unhappy customers—not to mention Darla. *Damn.* "All right, go. I'll make my calls—" slapping the readboard—"on our way."

Calls through, rough as two of them were, earlier stops and other trivial data of the day logged and processed, Ciaon reclined his seat, relaxing. Darla: coupled for over a decade, both of them kids of the streets—she always understood delays. Working for Cavan meant the inconveniences were acceptable. They had a stash box of credits hidden at her place that Ciaon filled every week when they met, his promise to her, to get them away somewhere.

And they were close to where they needed to be. *So close. Maybe another year.*

The city passed some thousand meters below, an electric glacier, sprawling. Lights, people, buildings, other cars and transports passing at all angles, like a dance—even to a streetboy, it was a vibrant kaleidoscope, alive. What seemed beautiful and colorful above belied the darkness below. Ciaon knew too well, now, how the kaleidoscope really worked.

The sun, near setting, threw long shadows. Mellen made a sharp turn, and they passed over Cavan's outer guard wall, compound lights, copses of trees and playcourts and small buildings. Then the pyramid rose before them, dominating their field of vision—in shadow, foreboding. Clouds gathered to the east. In the sun's ebbing, the pyramid gleamed a dull red, all the windowseals down. Ciaon noticed the solar collectors on the southwestern edge were shielded, too.

"Storm," Mellen said.

"Maybe." A few streaks of lightning crossed in the east, small and distant. The sky grew darker, not only from the setting sun. "Probably as well we came back."

Mellen focused on the target door, a thin horizontal bar of light just below the apex. The car spun, and Mellen killed the engines. Restraining nets caught them. Ciaon opened his door, slid from his seat into the coolness of the bay.

The lift doors opened at his approach. He tapped his code, and the box rose.

Tension grew as the floors passed. His hand played nervously with the boxes in his pocket. In the beginning, working for Cavan had been the sweetest job in the city, a job some would have killed for—some did, or tried. Ciaon killed his predecessor in a disagreement over a streetgame, not knowing who he was. Since then, two tried to best him. Best work he'd ever had.

Until...*damn.*

He feared the Man showed signs of slipping. Cavan, once so involved in the day-to-day, active and focused. Now...the Man seemed distant, distracted. Ciaon loosed the boxes from his grip, ran his hands through his hair.

The lift came to rest with a slight bump. The doors opened, revealing a room with windowseals down, the only source of light a pair of fluorescents dangling from the ceiling. A dispenser sat like an irresistible temptation at the room's center. Ciaon walked straight to it. "Whiskey, ice." Instantly the drink slid from the machine's top in a thin tumbler, liquor caressing a sin-gle large cube. He took a sip, letting the sweet, fiery taste play over his tongue before he swallowed.

"A drink, Ciaon? So early?"

Cavan sat behind his desk, eyes bright and alert, cigarette in his hand almost gone. Against the dark backdrop of the seals, his pale form dominated: blond hair falling over shoulders, sharp, elven features, whipcord-thin frame. He took another drag from his cigarette and blew the smoke out before him, creating a haze that took a moment to clear. He crushed the remains. With his free hand, he indicated the chair closest him. Ciaon took it, stretching the tension from his legs as he settled.

"Success at Bakeburg's?"

Ciaon nodded.

"No trouble with the double order?"

"Why should there be?"

"Is that an answer?"

Ciaon rubbed his free hand across his face, shrugged. "A little trouble. He came through."

"Well done."

"He acts like he's concerned about you. He know what the Harp does? He on it?"

Cavan chuckled, smiled. "I think not."

Ciaon sipped again from his drink. He reached inside his pocket, liberated the boxes. He leaned forward, setting them on the desk. Cavan took them, opened the latches, and raised the lids. They touched with gentle taps on the desktop. He looked at them, then turned his gaze on Ciaon, eyes happy.

"Beautiful." One of his hands took a capsule, held it delicately between two fingers. "Tell me, Ciaon, have you ever—"

"No."

"Perhaps you aren't ready."

"I'll never be ready. That's for addicts, fools. It would impair my ability to be effective for you." He took a drag on the whiskey.

"Yes," Cavan said, nodding. "The unknown contains danger. But also beauty, Ciaon, and joy."

"Maybe for you, Mr. Cavan. I make my own decisions, and I choose not to experience *that* unknown."

Cavan's eyes weighed Ciaon, slid across his face, probing. Cavan scared him lately, but he knew his boss despised weakness. Ciaon stared back. After a time, Cavan smiled and a low chuckle escaped him. "I'll leave the decisions of your life to you, then. For now."

"Thank you." Ciaon set his empty glass on the floor. "Mr. Cavan, we need to talk."

Cavan's eyebrows rose.

"About business."

"Problems?"

"Not yet. Potentially. A few of our...customers aren't too happy about being forced to wait for merchandise. Della especially. She sounded frantic when I told her we wouldn't be over until tomorrow."

The hint of a smile emerged. "Tell her to learn patience."

"Delineu, either. It just doesn't seem like...like a wise way to treat people, Mr. Cavan."

"No? Are you telling me my business, Ciaon?" Cavan's tone was casual, almost bantering—his eyes not.

"Absolutely not." Ciaon tried to sound conciliatory. "But I'm out there, and you're here, sir. My opinion might be valuable. I deal with these people."

"I value you, Ciaon, very highly. Most highly. Do as I say. All will work out for the best, rest assured. We aren't losing anyone." Cavan smirked. "Certainly not those two."

Ciaon rose and strode to the dispenser, called another drink. After a sip, he felt some anxiety slip away. *Legend.* He should trust what Cavan was about. The man survived and thrived. Yet something in the back of his mind ate away at him.... He shook the feeling off. He let out the breath he hadn't realized he'd been holding. "I suppose you're right."

He walked to one of the nearby couches, slid back the armrest, and tapped two keys. The windowseals retracted. The nighttime sky appeared in enlarging patches, the great city's lights dimmed by clouds and rain. Lightning danced over the cityscape and horizons.

Top of the world. Easy to think that here, a few hundred meters above the metropolis. The dull lights made Ciaon feel even higher, the city farther below him. *So far to fall.* He could feel the whiskey's effect in a rippling of energy across his skin.

A sudden smattering of raindrops pelted the glass. Moments later, a long tongue of lightning hung suspended across the sky, the coupling of two clouds, and when it vanished, the thunderclap it preceded broke with such force it shook the room. Closing his eyes, Ciaon could see the crystal afterimage of the thunderbolt. At his right he noticed Cavan resting on the sofa's far side.

The powerful man's eyes were wide, gaze fixed on the storm.

Ciaon sipped again. Neither man spoke. They sat quietly, watching the storm until Ciaon excused himself to sleep.

The next morning broke clean, purged by the storm. Water gathered in small pools across the compound, looking like a thousand clear eyes toward the heavens. Mellen brought the car out slowly until they passed over the outer guardwall, then increased thrust and swung toward the city. The metropolis glistened wetly in the sun's early rays. Ciaon knew by afternoon that beauty would evaporate like the water that preceded it.

Mellen broke into his reverie: "First?"

"Della." Ciaon reluctantly turned his mind to business. "Not a happy woman."

Mellen said nothing, set course northeast.

Della lived in midtown, or what had been midtown, a name that meant something before the great city swallowed everything in its mad growth. What had once been individual municipalities now formed a massive urban corridor nearly 2,500 kilometers long. After half an hour, Mellen brought them in on a slow glide to street level, letting the AI do most of the work avoiding traffic. Tires emerged, and the car slid smoothly onto the road, making two quick turns before stopping at the main entrance to Della's building, one of the old centuries' models, rebuilt time and again, pushing the limits of the original structure.

Ciaon took Della's bundle from the back seat, a meter-wide box light enough for him to carry on one arm, flashed an ID at the door guard. The elevator opened for him, and he rode to the 111th floor, stepping out onto soft carpet and the rich smell of hyacinth.

All the excuses he planned for missing yesterday's appointment faded when Della opened the door. He tried to keep the shock from his face. Della looked half a decade older than the last time he'd seen her, eight days past. *Hell and damn.* Her shoulder-length raven hair showed nothing of its natural beauty, hanging in ratted wisps about her head. Her eyes sunk deep within their sockets as if hiding, dark half-moons hovering below. Della, always dressed with dignity, today wore only a bathrobe, held closed by a sash knotted to one side, her feet bare.

"Oh, Ciaon," she said, putting a hand to the doorframe, unable to keep the relief from her face. She stumbled forward and wrapped him in an embrace. She drew back as quickly, with a haggard smile, looking slightly embarrassed. She ushered him into the living room. Ciaon set his package down on the sofa, slid out of his coat, placed it over the sofa's back.

"Drink?"

"Too early." He laughed. "Can't stay. Fell too far behind yesterday."

"I understand." Della crossed the room and surprised him by pouring a healthy shot of brandy from a crystal decanter. The room, clean and immaculate as always, belied the state of its owner. Della's beloved figurines—ornate, alien carvings from the odd orange and ruby stone blends from

Peren, a world Cavan allegedly visited on his raid of Threll—lined the walls and shelves of the apartment, gleaming in the low lights she'd arranged. She nodded to the package. "All there?"

"Truly, Della, you question me?"

A smile broke through her weakened features. With it came a flame that flickered warmly a moment, highlighting all that made her so beautiful. She was his favorite visit in all his transits. Her eyes shyly sought out his. "Sorry about the hug. I'm just…relieved."

Ciaon waved a hand. "Sorry I'm late. Please don't apologize. I haven't had a hug in too long." Which made him think of Darla and other plans delayed.

Della laughed, a strange, tense bark. His eyes kept moving to the box. Ciaon let his gaze drift around the figures. *Such a collection.* There had to be nigh two hundred. Della and Cavan's association went back a decade or more. Ciaon's eyes caught something on the far side of the room not there on his last visit: a vase of a dozen roses, each a different color, wilting and faded.

He looked a question at Della, but she lost the smile and looked sadly at him. She sipped from her glass. "How is he?"

"The Man?" She nodded. "Well. Hasn't been out in weeks, but nothing new there."

She ran a finger through a wisp of hair. "Does he…ask about me, ever?"

Ciaon deliberated over the value of a lie. He knew there had been something between her and Cavan, though Cavan told him since day one never to mix business and pleasure. Still….she looked so tired and frail. *What could cripple her so fast?* He decided on truth, said, "No."

She nodded, raised her glass in a toast, and downed what remained. "To your honesty." A wistful smile spread itself over her lips. "I know he thinks of me. He won't forget, Ciaon. Ever." She reached out and touched the box. "Go now. I want to be alone."

"Problem?" Mellen asked, seeing Ciaon's face.

"No." Ciaon sighed, tapped the readboard. "Now Delineu, then—"

"Tomorrow," Mellen said, indicating the phone. "Delineu tomorrow. What's next on the list?"

"You can't be serious, Mellen. We've already delayed him one day."

Mellen turned the car into the street, fired the engines. The AI swung them wide to avoid a passing truck. Thrust engaged, and they rose at a steep angle. Mellen raised his hands. "I fly, Ciaon." His look firm. "Delineu tomorrow. Next stop?"

*D*amn long day. Delineu screamed through the readboard until Ciaon killed the line. Darla was understanding but unhappy. When the elevator doors opened, he went straight to the dispenser, shot the whiskey down, cube cold against his upper lip, then coded another. Cavan stood with his back to him against the windows, the cityscape bright beyond him.

"Ciaon. I trust everything went smoothly."

Orders. He channeled Mellen. "Yes." He

took a small sip of whiskey to calm his nerves. He and Mellen accomplished a lot in the city by skipping Delineu, truth to admit. A godman had pulled a knife on him outside a restaurant, and Ciaon took his arm with the straydart, leaving him on the sidewalk screaming.

But he'd hoped to be with Darla tonight. *Orders.*

"And Della?"

Ciaon hoped his surprise didn't show. Cavan never asked about Della—not once in two years. "Tired, sir. Run down. Morning, and she was drinking."

Cavan's hands clasped at the base of his spine, unmoving—until the mention of her drinking. He dropped his head, tapped his foot once, twice. "Well, that isn't good."

"No, sir."

He turned on Ciaon, eyes intent. "You find it odd, Ciaon, that I ask about her."

It wasn't a question. "Yes."

Cavan smiled, his eyes tightening a fraction. "You want to ask if there was something between Della and me, yes?"

"People talk." Ciaon waved the subject away. "Not my business, sir."

"True." Cavan stepped to his desk, sat, lit a cigarette. He indicated the chair before the desk. "I feel like telling a story tonight. The storm inspired me."

"Mr. Cavan—"

Cavan's upturned hand, palm forward, forestalled any comment. Cavan rested the cigarette on the ashtray's edge, steepled his hands, and Ciaon sat.

"You may find this amusing, Ciaon, for I know I do, but I was once in love." Cavan took a drag on the cigarette and blew a cloud carelessly away. "Not as most men love, though, for I am not most men. I was not content to follow in the wake of the undistinguished with poetry, flowers, fine dining, traveling the globe or even the stars, all in order to impress my lady—though I did those things. No long walks along the impressive seawall at sunset, dinners on a high patio, the symphony, theater—though I did those things, too." Cavan snickered with disgust. "Mine was an unconventional love, as unconventional as my life."

Ciaon took a sip of whiskey. "And you tell me this, sir, because—"

"I know you have a lady friend, yes."

Ciaon nodded.

"And you do not get enough time with her?"

Ciaon let his mouth curl into half a grin. "Not as much as I would like, no."

"But the time you have is dinner, the act of love, the usual."

Ciaon shrugged. "I have little time for her. But yes, we do what we can with the time."

Cavan rose and walked to the windows. "I've seen so much, Ciaon. So, so much." *Tell me*, Ciaon thought. *Those are the stories I wish to hear, not...whatever this odd confession is.* "I suppose she loved me unconventionally in her way—she being Della, of course. She seemed happy just being together. We engaged in some of those petty things I already mentioned, though I found them so boring."

Ciaon shook his head. To be a woman in a relationship with a man like Cavan...he couldn't imagine.

Cavan ground out his cigarette. "Well, I won't lie. I wanted more. I've always wanted more. I make no apologies. The world is a dull place, Ciaon. And while most people want the same things, those simple desires do bring benefits." Cavan indicated the room with a smile. "So it is with love. Nothing lasts. I became insensate—bored, to tell the truth. And it hurt her." To his credit, Cavan looked unsettled at this admission. "So I took steps to correct this… unhappiness."

Cavan leaned against one of the window supports behind him. "What to do when love goes away, Ciaon? Sacrifice yourself for the happiness of another?" Cavan shook his head. "Never. Only fools in stories do that. And she would not have been happy with anyone else. Not truly." Cavan sighed. "And yet I could not let her go, either. Odd, that. In all my life, I never felt that."

Ciaon leaned forward, about to speak, but Cavan waved his comments away. "Inspiration came, as it always does. I did the only thing I could."

Cavan stopped speaking. Silence swooped in like a bird of prey. Ciaon felt uneasy, afraid of what had been said and equally afraid that more was on the way. The words and the look on Cavan's face had the tinge of madness. He was already worried enough.

Cavan raised a hand, two fingers and thumb together, and waved a pattern through the air. "Music, Ciaon. Music. I gave and continue to give her what she could never have gotten from me. Bliss."

Ciaon cleared his throat. "Mr. Cavan, I have no idea what you're talking about."

Cavan shrugged. "No matter. I remain true to my convictions."

"You mean the statuettes, sir?"

Cavan snorted. "Don't be daft. She pays for those, like any other customer. No, I give her something much more unconventional." Cavan's face seized on a thought, and he looked at Ciaon directly. "Which reminds me: is Delineu's package ready?"

"Yes, sir. For two days now."

"Good. Good. Get it to him at first light, then. And apologies for the delay. It should not happen again."

"I hope not, sir. Delineu was raging. I cut the line."

"Pay no attention to Delineu's moods, Ciaon." Cavan opened the drawer of his desk, pulled out the case, and lifted a capsule from it. "If you're stressed…"

"I don't need that, sir." He finished his whiskey, stepped to the dispenser for another. "I need some sense of stability. Two years with you, and I feel like things are coming apart, and I don't know why. Della and Delineu are two of our best customers, high-end artifacts, solid on my route since I started for you. I don't see how treating—"

"I don't need lessons in business from you, Ciaon. Visit me tomorrow after Delineu." Cavan lifted a capsule before his eyes and stared lovingly at it. Ciaon carried his whiskey to the elevator and stepped in as soon as the doors opened. He had more to say but it could wait until tomorrow. He rubbed his eyes. There were many forms of madness, and he knew he was surely facing one now.

Mellen keyed the systems to life as Ciaon climbed into the car, shivering. The bay was cool in the early dawn, high and uninsulated. Ciaon rubbed his shoulders.

"Have you seen my coat?"

"No."

"Damn." He couldn't remember where he could have left it. "Give us some heat, then."

The sun barely above the horizon line, Mellen turned the car and flew east. The city seemed pure around and below them, half asleep in the dawn, little movement on the streets or in the air. They rarely went up this early, but the flight to Delineu's took three hours.

Orders.

In Ciaon's estimation, Cavan returned from Threll perhaps two decades ago. He glanced at Mellen behind the wheel. *How long with Cavan? Since his return? Since before, waiting?* Two years flying together and Ciaon felt maybe he could ask a question or two, even though they rarely spoke about more than their duties and destinations.

"You've been with Mr. Cavan a long time, Mellen, yes?"

Mellen tapped a key, took his hands off the wheel, and faced Ciaon.

"Since Threll?" No answer. "Since before?" Mellen's head may have inclined a bit at that, Ciaon couldn't tell. He let the silence between them linger.

Finally, Mellen scratched his cheek absently. He took a breath. "I like you, Ciaon.

The others before you, not so much. You, I like." Mellen blinked, once. "I fly. You—do what you do."

"Mellen, if you've been with him half as long as I think you have, you have to...you have to know, see—dammit, he's changing."

Mellen hit the key again, put his hands to the guidewheel. "I fly."

Their course took them out over the great wall that held the rising ocean at bay, the slick gray barrier hammered by titanic waves. The wall ran as far as the city it protected, curving and weaving along what remained of the coastline, so much of it gone, great wind turbines stretching out as far as the eye could see. From time to time, the odd cliff stood out uniquely as natural color against the blankness of the wall and the rumpled blue of open water.

They flew in silence until Mellen banked the car right. Gradually, they descended toward a patch of green, a vast home sitting at its center. Mellen landed, opened his door, and walked toward a small rise where he could see the sea. Ciaon took the package from the car's back and held it in one hand as he ascended toward the house. He usually went up the stairs and into the foyer to conduct business. Today, two heavily armed men stepped through the doors. One raised a hand. The other tightened his grip on his weapon—a carbine, military-grade.

Ciaon wished again for his coat and straydart. *Fool to leave it.* They'd made so many stops yesterday.

To the left and right of the stairs spread

Delineu's gardens. Ciaon's visits lasted minutes, dropping a package and rarely seeing the old man. Standing at the foot of the stairs, he saw the garden around him as if for the first time. Rows of flowers in brilliant colors ran to both sides, some low groundcover, others the height of an average man. Ciaon recognized sunflowers, hyacinths, others that he knew from memory or experience. He thought Darla would find all this beautiful. To the right, he noticed a patch of roses in ten or fifteen different colors, the red ones bright like beating hearts, oddly familiar.

Delineu's house rose like a crenellated castle, complete with ramparts and towers at the corners. Delineu, rich in his own right—a fortune in plant hybrids, from what Ciaon understood. Ciaon looked up the staircase made of dark inlaid granite and saw a servant coming down the steps with Delineu.

He nearly gasped. Delineu, well into his second century, tapped ReGen every fifty years as the wealthy could. Usually the image of a vibrant athlete, today only the strong hands of the man beside him kept him erect. Delineu shook as if with palsy, his limbs thin and frail.

Ciaon bowed. "Mr. Delineu, I extend Mr. Cavan's apologies—"

"Quiet, fool," Delineu hissed, in a voice made of paper. "I have little time and no wish to waste it on you."

Ciaon extended the package before him.

Delineu waved a wrinkled hand. "Take it back to him. Nothing, no apology could—you tell him—" Delineu doubled over, his body rocking with coughs. The servant held him. When he recovered his composure, he looked fiercely at Ciaon. "You tell him he can play his games with me but not with her. Not with her!" The old man shook with emotion.

"Sir?"

Delineu's eyes unfocused, and he shut them a moment. He put a hand to the servant's shoulder and steadied himself. A small smile crept over his features, and when his eyes opened again, he looked mockingly at Ciaon. "He never told you, did he?"

"Never told me what, sir?"

Delineu laughed dryly. "Of course. Just like the ones before you. Little errand boy." Delineu waved a hand dismissively. "Begone. Go, fool. Tell him it's a hollow victory."

Ciaon moved forward, but the two large men closed the gap as the one behind lifted Delineu in his arms. He carried the old man up the stairs. The other two followed, rifles at the ready, taking one backward step at a time.

Ciaon stood, unsure what to do, finally turning back to the car. On the way, he realized with a start where he had seen Delineu's roses before: Della's apartment.

Cavan waited for him in the dim light—again before the windows, hands clenched behind his lower back. Ciaon passed the dispenser, walked straight to the desk. Cavan turned and took his seat, in shadow.

"He wouldn't take the shipment."

Cavan nodded, looked away, called the

lights up a fraction. Ciaon spoke into his silence. "That's not all." Cavan looked up. "He said you can't do that to her."

"Anything else?"

"That it's a hollow victory. Whatever that means." He waited in the growing silence then spoke again: "Mr. Cavan?"

"Ciaon, it is unfortunate that you became entangled at this time."

"Sir—"

"You see, Ciaon, complications. Life." He sighed. "Delineu was Della's lover before me."

Ciaon concealed his surprise badly, sat on the chair's arm. "I had no idea."

Cavan laughed. "Of course not." He hit a fist on the desk, hard, causing Ciaon to flinch. "Complications! They make life exciting. Delineu—he clung to his passion, Ciaon, poetry and flowers in the face of *this*." Cavan looked thoughtful. "But it was Delineu who inspired me, the genesis of my perfect expression of love."

"Sir?"

"You see, Ciaon, I gave Delineu my hatred. And when I saw it work, I knew it could also work with love. Two sides of the same coin."

"I don't understand, sir. You speak in riddles. Are you deliberately trying to confuse me? I deliver the artifacts for you. What does that have to do with hatred or love?"

Cavan held him in a long stare.

A feeling crept up Ciaon's spine. "That is all I deliver, sir, yes?"

"Ciaon—"

"What have you had me doing, sir?"

"Ciaon, relax." His voice soothed, his look seemed genuine in its concern. "Difficult work, this. Calm yourself."

"Answer my question, sir."

"No. The contents of what you deliver are not your concern."

"Is it the Harp?" Cavan's head snapped up. "That does this to you? You aren't the same, Mr. Cavan."

Cavan laughed. "You truly think that?"

"I think Bakeburg does. I... maybe."

Cavan's laugh mocked, and Ciaon cringed beneath its insult. Cavan pulled the metal case from his desk. "You think I would taint myself with *this*? I did not go to Threll and back to become an addict."

Addict. The way Della looked two days after the scheduled delivery, the way Delineu looked after three—those deliveries weekly and routine as anything he did. "Bastard."

"Perhaps you are wise, Ciaon. Bravo."

"You're out of your mind."

"No, I have been giving her my love. The purest kind of love." Cavan made a fist. "Then Delineu and Della met with someone they should not have and...well, I had to make an example."

"You know what the Harp does. To force that on someone and then take it away..."

Cavan raised a finger. "The problem, Ciaon, is that you think too conventionally."

Without thinking, Ciaon leapt at the desk, but Cavan was ready and moved swiftly to the side. Ciaon slid across and came up running, chasing Cavan to the room's center. Cavan waited and threw a fist, unexpectedly quick, that knocked Ciaon to the floor, ears ringing. Ciaon lunged, but strong hands grabbed him, pulling both arms behind him. One hand took his wrists, the other rose to his throat, half choking him. He heard Cavan move to the desk and open it.

"Do not judge me, Ciaon. You have not had my experiences. But I can rid you of your conventions."

A pop sounded, then a cool liquid spilled into his mouth, crisp and cold and tasteless. The hand moved from his neck to cover his mouth, and he swallowed unwillingly. The effect of the Harp was instantaneous: a sound that was not a sound erupted around him, and an interior aurora—bright bands of colors across the spectrum—spread around him as he slipped from consciousness.

His eyes felt the pain first—light, insistently bright, piercing them. He turned, fleeing the glare, jamming his face into the pillow. Moving sent a fiery pain through his entire body.

Senses began to return, slowly. He lay on a bed, though its softness did nothing to ease the pain coursing through him. The warm weight of a blanket covered his lower body. He pulled it over his head to block the light. Waves of agony rose like phantoms from parts of his body he rarely acknowledged.

He heard the click of a button, then a voice: "He's awake."

Mellen.

A softer voice answered, muffled—no doubt who that was. Ciaon pulled his face from the pillow. He remembered his bedroom, all the furniture colored red-brown, the light cinnamon mist he used to clean the air.

"Ciaon?"

"Don't speak to me," he said, coughing up the words. His throat so dry speech felt like acid poured over a fresh wound. Mellen moved and held Ciaon's head while he let him drink from a cup. Ciaon lay back. "Is this what he did to them?"

Mellen nodded.

Pain conquered him. He let tears seep from his eyes. And he must have slept for a time, because when he woke Mellen was again across the room.

"How long?"

"Two days."

Ciaon sat up and drank from the cup again, shaking. He knew he would need another dose soon. Though he would fight it…he wasn't sure he would win.

Mellen threw fresh clothes beside him. "Shower. Dress. The Man wants you above."

"He can go to hell."

Mellen reached into a pocket and drew out one of the capsules. "Another day without, and you die, Ciaon. You do what the Man asks."

Painfully, Ciaon pulled himself up and moved to the bathroom.

Mellen walked him into the bay, helped him into the backseat. The chill intense as the floodlights, leaving Ciaon wishing again for his jacket.

"You look well." Cavan sat to Ciaon's left, dressed in a fine black suit and tie, dark green trenchcoat draped over his knees. A pink carnation hung from his lapel.

The cold numbed Ciaon. His body throbbed with a deep, dull ache. His head went dizzy. He fell back against the seat. He heard Mellen's door close and felt the car begin to spin.

"Where are we going?"

"We? Nowhere. You are delivering a message, and I am going out to dine."

"Dine?"

"Yes. I haven't been getting out enough, don't you agree?" The car accelerated. "I have a dinner engagement with a lady." Cavan grunted. "Not very unconventional, no. Not yet. But all things must be rightly prepared, Ciaon." Cavan chuckled. "Met her at the symphony. She sat in Delineu's box. Ironic. A relative of his or something."

It all makes sense. Ciaon saw Delineu's outrage clearly now. And Della's hurt. They must have met with the girl and tried to warn her.

I'm a fool.

He opened his eyes halfway and watched the cityscape pass below, familiar, landmarks he recognized like a personal map. He knew where they headed. "What message am I to deliver, sir?"

Cavan's face curved in a smile, the corners of his mouth spiked like horns. "Yourself."

Della stood anxiously in the doorway, spectral and thin, though not as haggard as two days before. Her eyes passed over him and erupted in tears. Neither of them could be easy to look at. Her eyes still haunted in their retreats.

"Ciaon." She reached for him with a trembling hand. He touched her shoulder and felt its frailty, could sense the sharp edges of her bones, the paucity of muscle. "He sent you."

He nodded, following her inside.

She pointed to the phone. "I got a call. Delineu died today."

Ciaon looked down.

"It's over." She went to the shelf and filled two glasses with brandy, brought them back, and toasted him. "To Cavan," she said, and began to weep.

"Della—"

And suddenly she was in motion, flinging her glass across the room where it broke in small crystal shards. The tight, controlled Della he knew replaced by a wind of passionate rage. She grabbed her Peren figurines and threw them, too, some breaking in large chunks, some too strong to break. Ciaon finally caught her hands and brought her down to the floor.

"Della, Della, stop." She sagged in front of him. "There must be something we can do, go to Bakeburg, or—"

"You think we didn't try?" she shouted, looking up with dark, teary eyes. "If Delineu couldn't free us, no one could. You know how the Harp works." Futilely, she hit the floor. "Dammit, Ciaon, all I ever did was love the man."

Ciaon shook his head, looking around at the mess. She was right—once the Harp had you, it never let you go, you had a lifetime of it waiting for your next dose...or death. The Threllian vidliq coded itself into your DNA. *No escape. None.* He rose and grabbed his drink. As he sipped, he noticed something on the sofa.

His jacket.

His resolve returned. "I have to go. He's waiting. Goodbye, Della."

He took his coat as he crossed the room and left.

Cavan smoked, reclining comfortably, tossing the ember out the open window as Ciaon entered. The window rose with the car, acceleration pushing Ciaon back into his seat.

Mist hovered low over the dark buildings. They passed between two highrises, their tops shrouded in cloud, lights dim through the haze. Another car passed below them. The drone of its engines reminded Ciaon of the dull throb of pain through him, diluted somewhat now by a sense of purpose. He wiped a hand over his brow, tried to keep the shivers in his body down.

"Feeling it now, yes?" Cavan said.

"What happens to me?"

"Mellen will take care of you after you drop me off."

"You've no use for an addict."

"No. This could have gone differently, Ciaon. I had high hopes for you."

"Me, too." He thought of Darla and the place he wanted for her, like Della's—a place for them both. *Gone now.* At least she had the credits.

Cavan's face cocked in a cynical grin—his gaze regarded Ciaon like an insect. Ciaon felt this was an endgame Cavan had played many times, maybe even on Threll—the game he played with Della and Delineu, with him and others before him, now again with Delineu's niece.

No.

"I suppose we all have our faults, sir."

"Faults can be overcome, Ciaon. Just like conventions."

Ciaon nodded as if in agreement. He settled back against the seat. "Perhaps I can help rid you of the last of yours, then, sir." He let the flap of his coat fall open. He twitched his left arm, and the straydart fired deafeningly in the small space, shattering Mellen's head and passing on through the windscreen. A freezing wind filled the car, its voice a sinister howl. The look on Cavan's face gave Ciaon all the satisfaction he needed.

Darla, even legends die.

They plunged like a shrill note through the city's nighttime lights, a harp string broken and falling.

William Huggins lives, writes, works, and explores the desert southwest with his wife, daughter, son, and four rescue dogs. His passion for science fiction began in high school and hasn't wavered yet. His short fiction and essays have appeared in many digital and print media. He is the author of two books, Ghosts, a novella, and Regenesis, a finalist for the Prism Prize, from Owl House Books. He is almost done with his third novel.

Queen of the House

By J. MANFRED WEICHSEL

A door-to-door salesman promises a fantastic cleaning device that can get rid of anything and everything! But what can get rid of a salesman who won't give up?!

I was sitting on the soft leather divan in front of the coffee table, reading a videozine on housekeeping, when I heard the hum of a space car landing on the house pad. I got up, opened the curtain a bit to peek out through the window monitor, and saw on the screen a man exit a small VW Spacebug™ as its wings retracted and walk across the plastiGrass towards the front hatch. His features were silhouetted by the blue sky I'd recently had installed because, call me a town girl, but I just can't stand the sight of outer space.

He rang the doorbell. I pushed the button to turn on the outside speakers and said, "I'm sorry. I am not interested in learning about the outer-world saints."

The man replied, speaking through a radio inside his spacesuit in a nervous, stuttering voice, "Pardon the interruption, ma'am, but I happen to have an invention in this bag I am carrying that will make your life one hundred percent easier. No, one thousand percent! It is called the quantum vacuum cleaner."

Intrigued, I asked, "What is a quantum vacuum cleaner?"

"It is a revolutionary new way to remove any kind of mess, from dust to grease to grime. It will clean up any spill, no matter what substance is spilled or how stainable a material the substance is spilled upon."

Our Miss RoboMaid™ was dormant in the corner of the living room, waiting to go to the shop to be repaired for the second time this month because her artificial intelligence chip had been acting up again. There certainly was a lot of cleaning to do, so I pressed the button to let the stranger in.

I watched through my window monitor as the outer hatch slid upwards and then back down behind the man as he entered the hatchway. Then, the inner hatch opened, and he stepped into my humble home.

The man removed his space helmet and hung it on the helmet rack by the door. He unpacked and assembled his doohickey as he explained that there would be no more disposing of bags full of spacedust, as the marvelous invention he held in his hands was powered by a miniature black hole that sends dust, grease, and grime to a parallel universe.

I had no intention of purchasing such a silly gimcrack, but my house was a complete mess after my Robomaid™'s latest malfunction, so I decided to let the salesman test his whim-wham out, just in order to get a free cleaning.

The salesman screwed a metal rod into a plastic piece. At the other end of the rod was a clear, hollow, crystal globe, and floating in the center of the globe was a black void of nothingness.

The salesman let me hold the plastic end by its two handles and, with his voice full of wonder, marveled to me about how lightweight it was. I agreed that the thingamajig was very light and handed it back to him. Taking it from me, he asked what needed cleaning so he could begin his demonstration.

I pointed to the carpet. I have two young boys who track spacedust all over it after playing outside and a spacehound that sheds, and without a functioning Miss Robomaid™, the carpet had become a complete disaster.

The salesman held his gizmo by the two handles at the plastic end, placed the crystal globe directly above the carpet about four feet from the ground, and flipped a switch. There was a whirring noise, and the black void in the center of the crystal began to swirl around as the dust on the carpet took on a purple glow, lifted into the air, and floated towards the globe. When the dust reached the crystal, there was a zapping noise, like bugs flying into a bug zapper, and then the dust vanished. The man explained to me that the zapping noise was the sound of the dust being sent into the parallel universe.

I looked the carpet over. It was now so clean that it looked as if it had just been laid there that morning. "That was a very convincing demonstration," I said, pleased with myself for having gotten a free carpet cleaning out of the man, "but the carpet wasn't really all that bad. I want to see what your gadget can do with a real mess. Come with me to the kitchen. The oven is just dreadful."

I was understating the condition of the oven and doubted that the man could do much with it, no matter how wonderful his hoobajoob was. Since Miss Robomaid™ had gone on the fritz, I had used it to cook roasts, turkey, duck, goose, and ham, and without my Robomaid™ to clean it, it had gotten to the point where I was contemplating buying a new one. But at least, I thought, the man could help with the surface grease and maybe get me a few more months out of the oven.

The salesman bent over, stuck his head in the oven, and rubbed his chin, deep in thought. "This is a very dirty oven," he said.

I put my hands on my hips. "Well," I said, "If you feel that way, I would be remiss not to remind you that you are an uninvited guest in my house and can leave any time you wish."

The man apologized profusely and assured me that his miraculous invention was capable of performing a deep clean on an oven five times as dirty as mine. He flipped the switch on the plastic handle and stuck the crystal globe into the oven. Just as before, the black void of nothingness began to swirl, and the grease on the sides of the oven glowed purple.

This time, however, the apparatus shook in the salesman's hands, and perspiration formed on his brow, which was furrowed in concentration, as he planted his feet and flexed his arms in order to hold the contraption steady as the swirling black void became a tempest inside the crystal. The grease trembled as it struggled to remove itself from the oven walls, and floated shakily to the globe, where it was sent to the parallel universe with a much louder zapping sound than before.

When the man had finished, the oven sparkled as if it were brand new. The man, however, was covered in sweat and panting for breath. He removed his jacket and discarded it on the back of a table chair. His toy looked worse for the wear, as well. Smoke was rising from the top of the crystal and there was a dark discoloration where the crystal was attached to the metal rod, as if the rod had overheated.

"That was a very impressive demonstration," I said, "but I am not quite sold. My bathtub is just a horrible mess, and I want to see what you can do with it before I decide to buy your little appliance."

The salesman lost his cool. He turned to me and shouted, "What do you want from me? Did you see the job I did on your oven? Look at my poor invention."

"Well, if your piece of bric-a-brac isn't up to the task of cleaning my house, I don't know why I should purchase it."

"Of course my quantum vacuum cleaner is up to cleaning your house. This is just a display model. It has had a lot of wear and tear. The model you will purchase, that is, if you decide to purchase one from me, would be a factory model."

"Well, I want to see this one in action first. Come with me."

I led the man to the bathroom and opened the door. He stood there and stared at the tub, and I could see beads of sweat forming on his forehead. You see, I just love taking baths, and I always use a lot of product. Without Miss Robomaid™ to clean up after me, the tub had become quite a problem.

The salesman bent over and inspected the ring of grime on the tub closely, stood up, and turned to me. "I implore you, ma'am, this gravitational cleaner has seen enough use for today. Perhaps I could come back with a new one tomorrow and demonstrate it on your tub."

I crossed my arms and said, "It is really too bad. I was considering buying one of your conversation pieces, but now that I see that it is unable to pick up a little bit of grime..."

"A little bit of grime? You call this a little bit of grime? Ma'am, I have never seen a ring around a tub like the ring around this one. Ha! A little bit of grime."

I stood there glaring at him and said, "If your little novelty item can't remove the ring from my bathtub, then this demonstration is over. I am going to have to ask you to leave."

His face turned white. He ran a finger beneath his collar, swallowed hard, and said, "Ma'am, although I am the inventor of the quantum vacuum cleaner, I am not the manufacturer. I get credit for making these sales, I have a quota I need to hit, and I have spent a lot of time here and... Oh, for the love of! I will remove the ring from your tub."

The man stood there sweating as he lifted his doodad and turned it on. The black void became a tempest even worse than before. The purple-glowing grime shook as it loosened itself from the tub, and some grime lifted off the tub and floated towards the crystal globe where it was sent to the parallel universe with zaps that sounded almost like tiny bursts of thunder. But much more grime remained on the tub than lifted off, shaking more furiously and glowing more brightly as it struggled against the side of the tub. The crystal ball shook, and the tempest inside of it became like a hurricane of nothingness, as if the thingy was working beyond capacity trying to lift the grime from the tub. The man was drenched in sweat, and his hair was matted to his forehead as he struggled to hold the apparatus steady. His teeth began to chatter, and he let out a yell that sounded like a sheep's bah because of the way he was shaking so much.

His body glowed purple and stretched towards the crystal ball as if it had become unfettered from time and space. He yelled, "Call the manufacturer! The number is in my case. They will be able to retrieve me from the parallel..." but before he could finish his thought, his stretched-out body touched the crystal globe, and he vanished with a zap.

The odd invention fell to the floor when the man holding it disappeared and then turned off on its own. I picked the device up, and I heard a thin voice coming from inside it yell, "Call the manufacturer," as the voice faded away to nothing.

Of course, I am a very busy person, and I had no intention of calling the number and being put on hold for an hour while I waited for the AI to get around to taking my call, so I went downstairs and dropped the device in the trash bin in the kitchen and went back to reading my videozine.

I had forgotten all about the incident with the man and his crazy invention when I heard a rumbling coming from the kitchen. I put my videozine down and went to see what it could be, and I was startled to see the trash bin shaking as it sent up plumes of black smoke into my kitchen.

Then the sound of tiny explosions came from inside the twenty-two-gallon trash bin, and two arms reached out of it, grabbed onto its sides, and the man hoisted himself up from it into the kitchen. He was covered from head to foot in dirt and grime. He stood there, panting heavily, and said to me through gritted teeth, "One thousand years..."

"What?" I answered.

"I have been in the parallel universe for one thousand years!"

"Well, I really don't see how that is possible."

"Because time moves along a different plane there. You didn't call the manufacturer. I told you to call the manufacturer." The man had clearly gone insane. I could tell because he looked at me with crazy-person eyes. "But during that time," he continued, "I grew in power and in stature in the parallel universe. And now I am the King of Filth. Come, Filthy Minions. Come and get my revenge!"

The trash bin shook again, and three menacing little goblin-like creatures, one made out of dust, one made out of grease, and one made out of grime, climbed out of the trash bin and left nasty trails behind them as they ran around the kitchen floor in all different directions. They bounced off the cupboards and the walls, leaving large spots on whatever façade they touched, and slid across the countertops, leaving streaks in their wake. The two made out of dust and grime ran through the kitchen door, and the one made out of grease dove into the oven and rubbed itself all over the oven's interior.

I retreated to the living room where the creature made out of dust was dancing on the carpet, leaving dust everywhere. I wondered what I should do when my eyes landed on my Miss Robomaid™.

Without hesitating, I clapped my hands twice and said, "Miss Robomaid™, turn on."

My Robomaid™'s eyes lit up, and she turned to me on her conveyor belt platform and said, "How can I be of service?"

"Quick. Clean up the filth monsters that have invaded my home!"

"Am I Queen of the House?"

As I said before, my Miss Robomaid™'s artificial intelligence chip had been malfunctioning. She would not perform any of her duties unless I acknowledged that she was Queen of the House. This was extreme-

ly unfair because I was Queen of the House and I saw no reason why I should abdicate my title to my Miss Robomaid™. I was about to turn my Miss Robomaid™ off again when the grease monster burst through the kitchen door and skidded across the carpet, leaving a trail of grease in its wake. Grease??? On the carpet??? This was too much!

The grease and dust monsters waltzed with each other all around the living room, rubbing themselves on all the furniture they came by, as the King of Filth laughed maniacally.

In a panic I said, "Yes, Miss Robomaid™, you are Queen of the House!"

My Miss Robomaid™ pivoted, stuck out her vacuum cleaner appendage, ran after the dust monster, and sucked it up. She then stuck out her scrubber appendage. The grease monster backed away in horror. Miss Robomaid™ rushed after it and wiped it with her scrubber until it washed away into nothing.

There was only one monster left, the grime monster. I could hear its maniacal laughter coming from upstairs.

"To the bathroom!" I cried.

Miss Robomaid™ slowly climbed the stairs as I followed behind her. She rolled across the hallway and opened the bathroom door. Inside the bathroom was the laughing grime monster, sliding around and around the inside of the tub, leaving a ring of grime in its wake.

I recoiled at the sight of it, but Miss Robomaid™ bravely stepped forward with her mop appendage outstretched. The grime monster screamed and recoiled as Miss Robomaid™ bent over the tub and mopped it away to nothing.

That left The King of Filth hopping up and down in the stairwell in anger as he shouted at us, "What are you doing up there? You think you can be done with my Filthy Minions that easily? I have more just like them in the Land of Filth. I'll get my revenge. You'll see!!!"

Miss Robomaid™ turned, rushed out the bathroom door, and rolled halfway down the stairs where she grabbed the King of Filth, lifted him off the stairs, and stuffed him into her garbage disposal unit. A mechanical whirring noise and horrible screaming came from inside Miss Robomaid™ as the King of Filth was chopped up into little pieces.

And that is why in this home we call our Miss Robomaid™ Queen of the House.

Queen of the House is J. Manfred Weichsel's fourth appearance in Cirsova Magazine. He is the author of the jungle adventure novels Jungle Jitters and Ebu Gogo, and the Gothic horror sex farce Five Maidens on the Pentagram.

The Creation of Science Fiction

By MICHAEL TIERNEY

Ask the name most responsible for making the *Science Fiction* genre into what we know today, and some fans might cite Hugo Gernsback, editor of *Amazing Stories*, the first magazine to be devoted exclusively to the genre he coined *Scientifiction*, an unwieldy term that was later changed to *Science Fiction*.

But Gernsback would never have had the fertile genre of speculative fiction to mine had it not been for the work of another editor. A couple of decades earlier, one writer was so worried his first novel might considered the product of an unbalanced mind, that he submitted it under the alias of Normal Bean, implying that he was indeed 'normal in the head.' When the typesetters unintentionally changed his credit to Norman Bean, the intent was lost and he abandoned the alias, subsequently revealing his name to be Edgar Rice Burroughs. The editor who claimed the discovery of Burroughs was Robert Davis, known to most as Bob.

Bob Davis seemingly had printer's ink for blood. He started in the publishing industry as a composer of lead type for his brother's newspaper, the *Carson City Daily Appeal*. Back then the type was assembled and framed by hand into blocks of wood, hence the term of a *block of type*. But this job was trickier than it sounds, since the type had to be assembled in reverse for the process of letterpress printing, where a roller put ink on the reversed letters, which were then pressed against the paper, creating the printed sheet. This was the same process used in the creation the Gutenberg Bible—when the printing process was invented during the mid-Fifteenth Century.

By the time Bob Davis was working as a composer for the San Francisco *Examiner* newspaper, his profession that had existed for nearly half a millennia was suddenly rendered obsolete by the invention of Linotype machines, which were keyboard operated. What seemed like cosmically bad timing caused Davis to try his hand at writing a baseball news story. He won the editor's prize for best story of the week and his career as a newspaper reporter was launched. Soon he was the lead reporter for a trio of San Francisco newspapers, and then took his talents to New York, where he exposed the deplorable conditions being suffered by enlisted men being fed rancid meat by the military. Davis ascended to become the editor for the *New York News*, part of the *Munsey* empire of publications, but his timing seemed to once again be late as the print industry had become over-saturated and the *News* folded. But publisher Frank Munsey saw something special in Davis, and to keep him busy until another newspaper editor's position opened up, put him to work sifting through the piles of unsolicited fiction manuscripts submitted to his line of magazines.

In the early Twentieth Century, pulp magazines filled the racks of newsstands and were the dominant form of entertainment. With many titles competing on both a weekly and a monthly basis, several hundred thousand words of new prose were being published every month.

Davis found material worthy to fill those pages in the piles of unsolicited manuscripts, and was soon established as the fiction editor for the whole Munsey line.

In a memoir about Bob Davis, written by William C. Lengel for the January 24, 1920 issue of *Advertising and Selling*, Davis was described as someone who "...defies Time and Fate, a personality that is too vivid for a typed portrayal." About the job of being an editor, he quoted Davis as saying "Editing is no job for a sick man; it is the most exhausting game there is," and attributed his success to having "A cast-iron stomach, the digestion of a horse."

One area that Davis had a special knack for developing was what he called *pseudoscience* fiction. Stories of fantastic fiction that were published by Munsey before Davis' editorial tenure are mercifully forgotten to-day—they were *that* bad. After Davis became fiction editor, established authors like Max Brand (Fredrick Faust), O. Henry, and Erle Stanley Gardner took cracks at the new genre, as did the prolific Julian Hawthorne with his *Cosmic Courtship*. But it was Davis' knack for finding new talent that made him special. It was under his guidance that writers like the aforementioned Burroughs, Victor Rousseau, Charles Stilson, J. U. Giesy, Ray Cummings, Austin Hall, A. Merritt, and many others were cultivated to feed the public's growing taste for well-written fiction with fantastic themes.

When Thomas Newell Metcalf, the managing editor of *All-Story Magazine*, lost one of Davis' discoveries, Edgar Rice Burroughs, to the competing *New Story Magazine* because of repeated demands for unnecessary rewrites, Davis immediately took charge. He not only took on the additional duties of Metcalf's job, he also paid Burroughs to travel to New York where they negotiated a number of future deals that would solidify their relationship for years to come. While Davis was known to often refer to the creator of *Tarzan of the Apes* as "Battling Burroughs" because of their constant disagreements over word counts and pay, Davis consistently paid Burroughs a rate several times that of his contemporaries.

When Davis decided to quit the fiction business in the early 1920s and became a literary agent, he already had 43 first books dedicated to him by all different authors who credited Davis with their discovery.

While work as an agent was financially rewarding, Davis found it to be unsatisfying, and decided to return to his "old chair" and the editorial game. But his time away may have dulled his intuition. Not long after his return Davis, rejected *Triplanetary* from "Doc" E. E. Smith because he found the story to be "too wild." Hugo Gernsback and *Amazing Stories* did not make the same mistake, and the space opera of the Lensmen was born.

Not long after this, Davis retired a final time and left the fertile genre of *pseudoscience* to be shepherded by a new generation of editors.

Davis returned to journalism, and his 1926 Rome interview with Benito Mussolini earned him an honorary lifelong membership with *The Associated Press*. He also focused his energies on photography, and toured from city to city with a gallery of portraits he had taken of famous people. While many of the faces from his exhibit are long forgotten today, the legacy of the authors he discovered while an editor still remain.

But, had not been for the Linotype machine that eliminated his job as a composer, Bob Davis might never have started down the literary road that put him in a position to cultivate *pseudoscience fiction*. This means that the creation of *Science Fiction* might really be the result of a mechanical invention.

Michael Tierney's credits include myriad Wild Stars titles, Tarzan and the Mysterious She, the weekly online strip Beyond the Farthest Star, and Edgar Rice Burroughs 100 Year Art Chronology. His Robert E. Howard Art Chronology is coming soon. He has also collaborated with Cirsova publishing to restore the near-lost All-Story Weekly works of Julian Hawthorne.

Notes From the Nest

What to put here, but endless, inarticulate screaming? It's tempting, but we have a lot of news.

It's been a rough year, and I've been busy beyond my wildest imagination. I think that a lot of good things have come of this year, even if it has put a lot of things I'd meant to get to on the backburner.

2022 will be different. I'm sure I'll be just as busy, but we'll be refocused. The magazine is going to be bigger and better than ever before. We've got a bunch of illustrations lined up from DarkFilly AND Jesse White. Should we change the volume number and subtitle to Cirsova Illustrated? I don't know if I'm ready for that level of commitment, and it would further complicate our number [who do I think I am, Charlton Comics?!]

In spring, we launch the serialization of Wild Stars VI: Orphan of the Shadowy Moons. This. Story. Is. Awesome. So awesome, we've got Jesse White [*Deus Vult]* to illustrate all four installments.

We're beginning to head down the home stretch of Mongoose and Meerkat. Volume 2 will be collected next year, but things are coming to a head for our dynamic duo.

In Summer, we'll begin serialization of D.M. Ritzlin's sword and sorcery novel, Vran the Chaos-Warped.

Did you like our cover story from Mark Pellegrini? I sure hope so! Because we've got another story from Mark, who we're dubbing "The King of Gen Y Horror," in our next issue.

We have a lot of returning favorites next year, and I'm sure you'll have a chance to hear us gush about them in some venue, but I'm running out of space here!

If all went according to plan, we've fired one of our printers. They've treated us awfully ever since we started using them. Unfortunately, this also means that you probably weren't able to pre-order the print version of this issue. But if you're reading this, you bought it anyway, so we cannot thank you enough for your continued support over all these years!

The Strange Recollections of Martha Klemm should be coming out in either all or some of its myriad forms sooner or later, so please check that out. Julian Hawthorne ate up all my free time in 2021 and the only consolation is that his stories are fantastic.

The collected edition of Michael Tierney's Wild Stars V: The Artomique Paradigm should be coming out in late Spring/early Summer.

Did you check out Jim Breyfogle's The Paths of Cormanor? A lot of people slept on that one when we did the Kickstarter, but folks who've read it are saying it was even better than M&M Vol 1. So, check it out, and all of Misha Burnett's stuff! Duel Visions goes out of print in like 2 weeks, so order it ASAP!

P. Alexander, Ed.